Sin & Surrender

Also by K.F. Breene

DEMIGODS OF SAN FRANCISCO
Sin & Chocolate
Sin & Magic
Sin & Salvation
Sin & Spirit
Sin & Lightning
Sin & Surrender

DEMON DAYS VAMPIRE NIGHTS WORLD
Born in Fire
Raised in Fire
Fused in Fire
Natural Witch
Natural Mage
Natural Dual-Mage
Warrior Fae Trapped
Warrior Fae Princess

FINDING PARADISE SERIES
Fate of Perfection
Fate of Devotion

Sin & Surrender

By K.F. Breene

Contact info:
www.kfbreene.com
books@kfbreene.com

Chapter 1

Alexis

HUGE, BARE INDUSTRIAL bulbs hung down from a high ceiling crisscrossed with pipes, exposed electrical wire, and other odds and ends most people would consider the guts of a building. Strategically placed space heaters blasted warm air into the hollow, mostly empty space but couldn't quite banish the chill. Even in San Francisco, winter clung to February like a child does its safety blanket at bedtime.

"What do you think?" Aubri, my fashion consultant and stylist, swung her perfectly manicured hand through the air, indicating the row of carefully placed and accessorized dresses glittering in the harsh, barren bulbs overhead.

"I can't believe you rented an entire warehouse just to show me the wardrobe for the Magical Summit," I grumbled, seated in a plush white recliner. Thankfully it was leather, or I would've worried I'd dirty it. A small round table sat on my right, there for the sole purpose of supporting a glass of bubbling champagne. The silver stand holding the ice bucket and bottle waited on my left. Staff stood behind me, ready to leap should I need anything. Literally leap. They were the type who'd throat-punch an old woman standing in their way if they thought I needed a napkin.

Maybe it was the whole almost-losing-me thing, but Kieran had come back from Demigod Lydia's mansion determined to pamper me. When I'd argued that I didn't want any useful stalkers, he'd suggested that I needed to know how to act with service staff.

Which was true. The Magical Summit was only a month away, and I *did* need to know how to act with service staff. I needed to know how to politely tell them to get lost. I needed to hide how uncomfortable I was when they fawned all over me. Having them around all the time was like etiquette boot camp.

"Maybe your Demigod is finally branching out and spending what you're worth," Harding said, standing beside me, surveying the dresses. He waved a hand through the air. "Nah, that can't be it. He'll be cheap until the day he dies. He's one of Poseidon's line, after all. It's in his blood."

I rolled my eyes. "Real useful, thanks," I muttered. Harding had been hanging around more often of late, training me and helping me prepare for the Summit. Given that when he'd been alive, his Spirit Walker magic had been used as a weapon for assassinations by someone not even magical, and he'd thus been hidden away, he didn't have practical knowledge of what I was about to face. He also didn't have great things to say about Zander, who'd ultimately been the one to kill him. His support was welcomed, though, and training invaluable.

Daisy started forward, dressed in plain black from top to bottom, ready for action. Zorn had been relentlessly training her, trying to ready her for the Magical Summit. She'd be the only non-magical person there, and while she'd be afforded some protection as my ward, Zorn was preparing for the worst, and preparing hard.

"It's too flashy for Lexi," Daisy said, looking over the outfits.

Bria and Red stood back by a long table loaded with enough food for a ball. The caterer had gone too far. So had Aubri, considering the least fancy dress in the bunch was still encrusted with jewels. So had the guy who'd stepped up to wipe my mouth when I'd accidentally dribbled champagne down my chin.

Daisy was right: this whole situation was so not me.

Donovan, Thane, and Jerry stood somewhat removed from the proceedings, standing in the open space with arms crossed over their chests, watching us with bored expressions. They'd come along in case something bad happened. We were close to the territory line separating magical and non-magical San Francisco. People from the two sides tolerated each other at best. Zorn had insisted we have protection against a possible attack, even though I had tried to explain it was a non-issue. We had magic…they did not. End of story.

Or it would usually have been end of story. Zorn wasn't feeling reasonable. He didn't show stress often, but it was clear this Summit had him anxious. Kieran needed to manipulate his way to a solid placement within the leadership hierarchy (a big ask, considering the other Demigods were all older, more experienced, and more manipulative than him), all while defending his right to rule magical San Francisco. It was a lot to ask, but the safety of our crew depended on it.

"No, no…" Aubri waved her finger at Red, who was loading shrimp onto her little white plate. "That's not for the hired help. The hired help aren't supposed to eat at the same table as the premier guests, of which Lexi is one by association. You need to act within your position so you can practice." Aubri lowered her voice, as though suddenly unsure. "Demigod Kieran said so."

"What? That's all supposed to be for me?" I asked, even as Red took a bite of shrimp.

"Right, well." Aubri dusted off her hands, as if wiping them clean of Red. "He won't be happy, but I guess you don't care."

Bria grinned and grabbed a brownie. "Lexi is one by

association," she murmured. "This is going to go *so* badly. So, *so* badly. I can't wait."

Donovan snorted, and I tried not to sink into myself.

I had a feeling she might be right. Only two things could save me from being challenged at the Summit: an official sanctioning of Kieran's mark or a certificate of marriage. Demigods were supposed to get approval before they marked someone. The other magical leaders didn't like that Kieran hadn't asked (which he couldn't have, since the first time was accidental), and rumors abounded that he'd done it to claim me, not out of love. The mark would be authorized after the fact (or not) by a special judgment committee at the Summit. As for hurrying to the altar—call me a diva, but I would not rush a huge and important moment of my life because a bunch of age-old turds wanted paper proof that I loved Kieran. If I gave in, they'd probably just find another reason to make my life hell. I'd get married when and how I pleased.

"She shouldn't try to be one of them, she should be herself, unapologetically." Daisy stopped in front of one of the dresses, a long, flowing affair liable to trip me. "This is last season."

Aubri's mouth dropped open and her cheeks flamed. "It was released between seasons. It was a special release!"

"It's old and it was made for the masses." Daisy waved it away and kept walking down the line. "Kieran is a Demigod. Custom should be all I see. If you don't have the top designers' info, I can forward it to you. I'm friendly with most of them. If she shows well at the Summit, I'll have them all." It sounded like she was collecting trading cards. She gave Aubri a frosty stare. "I shouldn't need to be telling you this."

Daisy was only newly fifteen, but lately she sounded thirty. If surviving were an art, my younger ward would be van Gogh, except the lost ear would belong to her enemy.

Aubri sputtered, at a complete loss. In fairness, Daisy was probably right about the gowns. My ward had a knack for style. She'd always been a dreamer, poring over magazines and wishing she could be as glamorous as the people in them, but with Kieran's bottomless credit card, she'd made those dreams come true. What he lacked for clout in the magical world, he could make up for in funds. He could buy his way in. Which meant we could, too.

"I've always said it..." Bria paused to grab a chocolate-covered strawberry with her bare fingers, ignoring both the servant trying to do it for her and the tongs resting right next to the dish. "Lexi rocks the wild, natural look. Demigod Lydia is traditionally beautiful, but next to Lexi, she looked ridiculous. Too much sparkle and shine—like she was compensating for something."

"Alexis has the natural gift of being the most striking person in the room, regardless of what she wears or how she acts," Jerry said. "Like her father."

A chill ran through me. I still hadn't heard from Magnus, not even in spirit. He'd faded into the background after his intervention at Lydia's mansion. Given I'd see him again in no time, I knew he wasn't gone for good. This absence was planned, I just had no idea what the plan was, only that I was somehow going to be part of it.

Daisy snapped her fingers. "Yes!" She pointed at Jerry. "Good work, giant. Yes!" She spread her arms. "Did you notice what he wore? Black on black with a tiny pop of gray. Excellently tailored and the finest quality, but no flash. No bling. Not an eye in the room would have missed him."

"Because he was saving our asses," Red said. "What else were we going to focus on?"

"There's a reason no one likes you," Bria said to Red.

"Good," Red replied.

"That guy is used to having eyes on him," Daisy said. "He is used to commanding a room, you could tell. He doesn't need any flash or bravado to get attention, and the same is true of Lexi. This is all too flashy. Lately she looks more like a socialite than a magical misfit. It's not *her*. No, she needs to take a lesson from dear old Dad." Daisy turned toward me. "None of this is going to work. We need a new direction."

"That's ridiculous. This—" Aubri started.

"No." Daisy waved it all away and gestured me up out of the chair. "We're leaving. I'll be styling her from now on, and I'll be doing it without all these people standing around, eager to wait on Lexi. It makes her uncomfortable, and it shows. That's not what we're going for."

She said it so resolutely that I had to wonder if this had been her plan all along.

"That's absurd." Aubri braced her hands on her hips and an indignant expression crossed her face. "Alexis hasn't been called out for looking silly since I started dressing her. I've kept her consistently on the best-dressed lists. Because of me, articles *praise* her for her fashion."

"Ew, all you need to impress those people is to wear something released this year." Daisy rolled her eyes, her attitude starting to grow back. She was a teenager—it was never far away. "Anyone shopping in the high-end stores could do that. You've helped Lexi blend in with all the other clowns in the circus, when really she should be standing out."

"Oh yeah?" Aubri popped a hip in annoyance.

"What do you know?"

"How to survive," Daisy said, and motioned me up again.

"She just won that argument," Bria murmured to Red.

"The kid is spot-on about Magnus and Lexi. That's what won the argument," Red replied.

"There is literally no talking to you," Bria said, exasperated.

"Good," Red replied.

I rolled my eyes at their antics, but I was already getting to my feet. Daisy had won me over, and not just because she'd offered me an out from this sparkling, servant-crowded nightmare. She was a survivor, more so than anyone I knew. Who better to equip me for the challenges ahead? Flash and sparkle had always made me feel awkward and unnatural. If Daisy had another strategy, I was inclined to trust her. Hopefully this would also give her some control and more confidence going into such a dangerous situation.

"Sorry, Aubri." I gave her an apologetic smile. "She does have a point. But I'll still need someone to do hair and makeup."

I followed Daisy toward the door, and the others filed in behind me, although Bria made a grab for another brownie first.

"Wait...*what*?" Aubri's voice rose in pitch. "Are you

kidding me?"

"We'll need someone new for hair and makeup after this," Red said as we stepped out of the warehouse, the bright sunlight raining down on us. Kieran controlled the weather in magical San Francisco, and he'd kept it chilly but sunny. His anxiety of what was to come was getting the better of him, and the sunshine helped cheer him up.

"Oh, totally." Bria nodded as we walked toward the waiting stretch limo. I didn't get to drive anymore. If I didn't have such an awesome car, I wouldn't have cared. Given I did—well, this restriction was going into the "nope" pile after the Summit. "She's going to be made of sugar and spite and everything terrible after this."

"Clever," Red said sarcastically.

"She has a select sort of clientele, and she works great for that clientele." Daisy grabbed the door handle as the driver walked toward her. He hurried to intercept, but she was already ducking into the interior. "Her specialty is in leading the small-minded fashion sheep. Right now, her inspiration is the Demigod fashion sheep, but if Lexi tried to run around the Summit looking like Lydia, she'd be a laughingstock. She'd never pull it off. Lexi needs to do her own thing."

"And you know what that thing should be?" Bria ushered me into the limo in front of her. I slid along the bench seat next to Daisy, followed by Harding, who kinda hovered in the middle of the space.

"No." Daisy clasped her hands and stared out the window in front of her. "I need to think about it. Talk to Zorn and Amber."

"Wait, whoa." I gave her a stop motion as Red and Donovan got in. The others would follow in the Town Car behind us. Jerry took up the space of two people, and Boman was a brick of muscle. Not even a stretch limo could hold everyone comfortably. "Amber has the sexy, lethal thing down, I'll give her that, and Zorn can rock a tailored suit like no one's business, but they aren't fashion gurus. They aren't the right people to dress me."

"No sh—crap, Lexi." She huffed, and I scowled, knowing this no-swearing thing was only in effect when I was within earshot. It really defeated the purpose of having the rule. "Obviously I know they aren't the people to pick out your actual wardrobe." She rolled her eyes. "But they can walk us through what we should be conveying with your image."

The others had given me some training about etiquette, but Bria had suggested it would be best if I didn't know everything. My mother's chaos magic had helped us before, and it did best in uncertain situations. I said as much to Daisy.

"Yeah, well, you should look like you're too important"—she squinted in thought—"or maybe too scary?" She shook her head. "You need to look like you're too *something* to remember those details."

"Does Kieran have all his stuff picked out?" Bria asked, looking through the stocked refreshments on ice. She was digging all this extra treatment.

"He had a bunch of new suits and tuxes tailored." I tucked a lock of hair behind my ear. "Guys have it easy. They have less options. Less wondering about how much or little to reveal, less worrying about how this cut looks on this portion of the body…" I sighed, pushing away my nervousness. "I'm glad I don't have to deal with all the politics, though. He's really studying up. He'll probably know his top opponents and hopefully allies better than they know themselves."

"Pay attention, because as co-ruler you're going to have to know all that stuff, too. *While* worrying about fashion and not tripping in heels." Bria settled back with an apple juice. "As soon as you get married, you'll officially have a place by his side. He's been pretty clear about that. Maybe he's just doing it because he knows his dad will roll over in his grave, but whatever, it's a rare opportunity. Run with it."

"Have you broken it to the others that they can't be by your side?" Harding asked, studying me. He meant the collection of ghosts that hung around, including Jack, who was loath to be left behind. We couldn't risk one of the other Demigods or their Necromancers snatching them up and using them, though. Demigod Lydia had already messed with my people; I didn't want a repeat.

I nodded, looking out the window.

"I'll have to be entirely absent, too, remember," he said, and a weight settled in my middle. "My dear old dad will be at that thing, as will the guy who killed me. They'll lose their minds if they catch me hanging around, for opposite reasons. You'll be *entirely* on your own this time. I can't be there to save you."

He'd never saved me a first time, preferring instead to watch the show, but his presence had always been comforting all the same. If I had questions, or needed help with something, it would've been nice to think he'd be around. Not this time, though. He was right—that Summit was no place for him.

Fear washed through my middle, followed by butterflies and a flipping stomach. My phone rang a moment later.

"What's wrong?" Kieran asked after I answered. He'd felt my turmoil through our soul link.

The limo rolled down the highway beside the beach where we'd battled his father. We'd gone into that fight not knowing if we'd see another dawn. And yet the prospect of becoming Kieran's co-ruler frightened me more than facing down the former Demigod of magical San Francisco. Doing so without the lifeline of the guy who was an expert in my magic…

"We're not in danger," I said, swallowing down the lump in my throat. "I was just thinking about the future."

"Everything is going to be fine." His deep voice trickled through my anxiety, soothing me. "Not as many people die at the Summit as everyone seems to think. It's really just the weak who get picked off. We don't have any of those. There is nothing to worry about."

Another wave of fear washed through me. As a teen who lacked magic, Daisy would surely be targeted as one of the weak ones. It would be clear to everyone that she was an outcast, and more, that she didn't belong.

"Maybe we should leave Daisy behind," I murmured, turning away from her.

"I'm going," Daisy said.

"She doesn't belong there. She doesn't have the tools to properly defend herself," I continued.

"I'm going," she repeated. "I have the paperwork and enough money to get myself there if you try to leave me behind. I'm part of this family too. I—"

"If we leave her behind, she won't be acknowledged as one of my house," Kieran said. We pulled up in front of our house, completely renovated since Valens had lived there. "She needs to be officially recognized as a special case and allowed in the magical areas, and for that, she has to show up in person. I know it's hard to accept, but our hands are tied on this one."

We'd had this conversation a few times already. I'd spoken about it with Zorn and Amber too, and with Daisy many, many times. I *knew* they were all right, but damned if I didn't want to find a way around it.

"It'll be okay," Kieran said softly as I climbed out of the limo, and I knew he was reacting to my emotions again. "We've planned for this. We're preparing her. Zorn says she is exceptional for her age, magical or not, and passable competition for an adult magical fighting person. She can handle her own already, *but she won't have to*, okay? One of my people will be with her at all times."

I nodded as Bria pushed open the front door and stood back. The two enormous cats, which had thankfully stopped growing, met me at the door. They were as big as Great Danes, their heads to my waist, and just as sturdy. Also somehow magical. Harding, the (dead) Spirit Walker who was training me, pleaded ignorance as to how they'd gotten some spirit-type powers, but I knew he must've done something. These snow-white devils were in no way the offspring of two normal, non-magical cats.

Chaos, the male cat, with his luminous green eyes, rubbed against my leg in greeting. I staggered to the side. He hadn't yet figured out his own strength. Havoc, the female, purred softly, sitting in the middle of the entryway so I'd have no choice but to greet her or go around. She slowly blinked her bronze eyes, burning brightly with intelligence.

No, they were not ordinary cats. Not by a long shot. They'd helped us battle Demigod Lydia, who, last I heard, still had nasty scars from Chaos's claws.

"Okay," I said into the phone as I dropped my hand to rub Havoc's head. Only then did she move out of the way.

Kieran stepped into the hallway as I approached the living room overlooking the ocean. I dropped the phone from my ear, my chest tightening. He always did this to me. It didn't matter if I hadn't seen him for a day or an hour, when we reconnected, my heart surged.

He stood framed by the hallway, his shoulders broad and body corded with muscle, cinching down into trim hips. A plain white T-shirt hugged his defined chest and faded blue jeans adorned his powerful legs. Shiny black dress shoes looked out of place, and I knew he must've just finished a fitting. His stormy blue eyes regarded me, supportive and understanding, from his incredibly handsome face.

I focused on his full, shapely lips, and when I neared him, I slipped my phone into my pocket and hooked my arms around his neck.

"Hi," I said, my voice breathy, pushing my body

against his.

"Hey." He brushed my lips with his. "I will protect you and the kids, Alexis. I've been planning for it. I won't let anything happen to you. My job is just that—a job. You are my family. I will always choose you first."

I tasted his sweet lips and soaked in his heat. "I just spend a lot of time worrying these days, that's all."

"I know," he whispered. "We all have our doubts. Sometimes the scariest thing is the unknown." He kissed me again, languid and sensual, before stepping back and taking my hand. He walked me to the living room. "How'd the fitting go? Did you like what she came up with?"

I grimaced. "Daisy fired her."

A grin pulled at Kieran's lips. "Oh?"

I narrowed my eyes. "Aubri already called you, didn't she?"

His grin turned into a gleaming smile. "She called my assistant, yes. I haven't returned her call yet, but I got the gist of the problem."

I tried to step toward the couch and ran into Chaos, who always seemed to be in the way. He was much slower than his sister, who tended to pick a position that would give her a good view of the entire room. If Chaos was the brawn of the operation, Havoc was clearly the brains.

"Move." I shoved him with my knee, and he jumped

into the air, not unlike a normal cat. With a *mewrr* sound, he darted toward the far doorway and into the next room. His tail *thwapped* a vase on the way. Porcelain clicked on the glass tabletop as it rocked, threatening to fall over. "He's a *menace*," I said, sinking onto the couch. "Two kids, and now two cats? This house is turning into a zoo!"

"So what happened?" Kieran must've had a million things to do, but he sat down beside me, his fingers still entwined with mine. "The dresses were too flashy?"

I glanced at the doorway, wondering if Daisy would come in to defend her case, but no one had followed us. They were giving us some alone time, something we didn't get enough of as we prepared for the Summit.

"If I'm being honest, they looked like a cheaper rendition of something Lydia would wear," I said. I dropped my head onto his hard shoulder. "They were really nice on their own, and I'd probably look the part, but Daisy thinks I need to look more natural. A *less is more* kind of situation." I ran my lip over my teeth. "Like Magnus."

Kieran tensed for a moment, his uncertainty filtering through the links we shared. "What about Magnus?"

I went over what Daisy and the others had said, and outlined Daisy's plan for me. At the end, Kieran was nodding, his eyes far away. "She's exactly right about Magnus. That's an interesting take."

"Jerry helped make her case."

"Jerry?" Kieran was back to smiling. "Hidden talents, *Jerry*," he said softly, mimicking the accusatory tone the guys used when they picked on him.

Harding popped up outside the window, hovering in midair. My spirit-repellent magic kept him from getting too close to the glass. He could have found a new cat to host his spirit, which was, in a roundabout way, how we'd ended up with Chaos and Havoc, but instead he'd resorted to this kind of behavior.

"I think Daisy has the right approach," Kieran said, noticing Harding. "You're gorgeous in anything you put on, or nothing at all"—he turned his head my way, and desire pooled in my core—"but if I were forced to choose, I'd pick your natural beauty. I'd choose you just how you are, sweet and sensual and fierce and powerful. You don't need glitter or gold to stand out. You just need to show up."

I laid my free hand against his strong jaw and pulled his face closer so I could kiss him again, letting my desire flower and grow. Letting heat sizzle across my skin.

"We can't right now," he said against my lips, his breathing uneven. "You need Harding's training. But the second he leaves…"

I smiled, stealing another kiss. "I'll dress down to my birthday suit and climb you like a tree."

"Yes, please." He chuckled. "I love you. Everything is going to be okay next month, you'll see. We'll be ready."

I stood from him and headed out to Harding, who wore a firm mask of uncharacteristic seriousness. He looked this way more and more when we trained. I had a feeling Kieran wasn't going to be as ready as he thought.

I didn't think any of us were prepared for what was coming.

Chapter 2

ALEXIS

OUR TRAIN OF limos wound along the gorgeous coastline of the remote tropical island that housed the Magical Summit. The small landing strip that played host to the various officials' private jets lay behind us. Each jet was allowed a certain amount of time to land, unload its cargo, and leave again. With no boats in the harbor, we were, in essence, trapped here with the most metaphysically powerful people in the world.

"No one told me about the island situation," I murmured, seeing something emerge from the sparkling blue waters. A tentacle? It slapped down, spraying water into the air before the swell of a wave covered it.

"This location has been used for hundreds of years." Kieran sipped his whiskey. The kids sat at the other end of the limo, dressed nicely, as befitted people of their status within Kieran's company. The rest of the team, including the cats, followed in the other limos. It seemed wasteful, but I knew it was the first of many shows of strength. "It is large enough for all the gathered leaders and most if not all of their magical crew, it has access to all the elements, and there's ample space for any visiting magical beasts to roam, which matters in the offseason when they have the magical beast convention."

"There's also no way in or out."

"Thus ensuring our privacy."

"Thus ensuring our vulnerability. If this situation goes tits up, we've got nowhere to go."

Kieran took my hand, entwining our fingers. "Don't think that hasn't been brought up multiple times, especially by the non-Demigod leaders. We're all in the same boat, though. *No one* can easily come and go. Greed and alliances keep people safe here. Everyone watches everyone else to make sure no one steps over the line. The art is in walking the line, and my father was one of those who did it exceedingly well."

I chewed my lip, seeing another tentacle splash down—clearly someone was watching the coastline—and prevented myself from pointing out the obvious: Kieran didn't have any alliances, and he was short on greed. While everyone had to start somewhere, most people came to the Summit for the first time with tiny territories and budding teams. Not Kieran. He had a prosperous territory that he'd taken by force, a Spirit Walker by his side, and a team with some serious power players. We would stand out, and we had no one to guard our backs.

"It'll be okay," Kieran said softly, and squeezed my hand. The kids looked my way, and I could see the uncertainty on their faces. Zorn and the guys had trained them well—they knew the challenges that lay ahead as well as I did. "I'm sure I can get Dara. A handful of others have been watching me—they want to see if I'm as good as they hear. They'll see that I am better. By the time we walk out of here, we'll be in good shape."

"Just like you thought Lydia would be an ally?" Daisy murmured.

"I'm not one to ignore my mistakes," Kieran replied, a note of gruff disapproval in his voice.

"Doesn't matter," Mordecai said, his body tense and his hands clasped in his lap. "We have all week as the new kids on the block. We'll take a beating. The other teams will want a go at us."

"Today we'll set up the lodge and take a stroll as a unit." Kieran checked his watch. "It's standard protocol. The crew will be with you the whole time. All of them."

The crew was what we'd taken to calling the Six (minus Jack, who'd stayed home, like Harding) and Bria, plus the new additions who hung around as family. Jerry and Dylan had become part of our unit, eating with us, helping to cook and clean up, and training the kids. Amber hung around, too, but there was a certain awkwardness to her involvement. She kept silent more often than not. At first we'd tried to weave her in more, but everyone had accepted her as a living ghost around the house, there to help Daisy and soak in the community but not quite comfortable enough to blend in. Unbeknownst to her, she was usually close to Jack, who also hung out on the outskirts of the party.

"I'll take the new people you guys don't know very well," Kieran went on, stroking my hand with his thumb. It wasn't just for my benefit—I could feel the turmoil rolling through him like a brewing storm.

"If you don't take any of the crew, you'll look as green as you are," Daisy said. "The other Demigods might send most of their best people off to challenge the other crews, but you can be sure they keep a few for themselves."

"I want to alert people to who I think is most important—not me, but my future wife and her children."

"Significant others don't usually get that sort of high-level treatment." Daisy crossed her arms over her chest. "They'll think she's the most important because you want to protect your assets. You have what everyone else wants, and you've affixed your mark to it. Na-na-na-*na*-na. That sort of thing."

Kieran's eyebrows shot up. "Zorn said you'd soaked up all his and Amber's teachings like a sponge. He was right." He sighed. "That is partially true, yes. Only partially because other Demigod's partners aren't in danger. They have protection…which Lexi won't have until the judgment committee approves my mark on her. They could call that meeting tomorrow, or they could wait until the end of the week, I can't say.

"In the meantime, I intend to keep the best together to combat the assault that is sure to come. Everyone at this Summit knows my name. What I bring to the table, out of the gate, is unprecedented. I have two rare magics on my crew, neither of them from Poseidon's lineage, which give us representation from the three most powerful gods. I've battled and beaten two established Demigods. My team brought the giant down from the mountain, something many others tried and failed to do, and found a Lightning Rod the world had presumed dead. We travel with two magical cats with strange though extremely potent abilities. Most importantly, I found a Soul Stealer off the street and sizzled my mark across her body. I've turned heads without officially establishing myself, and everyone will want to see what my staff can do. Mordecai's right—they *will* come at you."

"Finally! The truth." Daisy threw up her hands. "How long have I been asking questions to get you to admit all that, and you've been all 'Oh, I'm Demigod Kieran the Magnificent, everything will be fine, I've got everything covered, want to shake hands with my colossal ego?'"

"Everything *will* be fine," he said, a smile wrestling with his lips, "everything *is* covered, thanks for the new nickname, and don't bother getting up—my ego can reach you from here."

Mordecai huffed out a laugh that melted away quickly as he looked out the window. The landscape was changing, from white, sandy beaches pounded by sparkling surf to rocky ground and a few small, shedlike structures.

"This isn't anything like I thought it'd be," he said.

"Because they decided to keep the details from Lexi and everyone knows you have a big mouth," Daisy said with a smirk.

Fair point.

We passed the first large building, a structure similar to a warehouse. Soon we were winding through more of them, some alive with activity—suitcases being emptied from other limos and staff rushing into the large front entrances. "At least if the shit hits the fan, we know where to find a few limos," I said. "How many people can say they've been in a limo chase?"

"I bet Bria has." Daisy bent over her phone.

"It'll be okay, Lexi," Mordecai said, and I could hear the urgency in his voice. "We always come out ahead when we stick together. Always."

His eyes implored me to see the truth in that statement. To be at ease so he could be at ease. He didn't have Daisy's iron resolve, her instinct for individual survival. He worried more about his family—his pack. He felt everyone's distress as though it were his own, and he worked to make everyone comfortable. He'd be an excellent leader someday, especially if he followed Kieran's example.

"It'll be fine," I mumbled to myself as the limo slowed and turned into a small driveway.

"Yup, I figured." Daisy lowered her phone as she peered out the window. "She's been in a limo chase. She said there are different rules for limo chases than regular car chases. It is essential to be drinking champagne through the danger, apparently. Maybe a little cheese and crackers or caviar, depending on who has stocked the refreshment area."

"Sure, yeah, only logical," I mumbled. "We'll remember that."

"We're in closer than I expected." Kieran pulled up a map on his phone. "I should have zero status going into this Summit. I have no established political ties. We should have been relegated to the outskirts of the living area, with the smallest, least luxurious accommodations. This is…"

From the few specifics I'd been told, the living area was a collection of individual buildings (clearly huge warehouses) that surrounded the hub of the Magical Summit in a crescent. The Summit itself was held in a large business park pressed up against a wide beach, with conference rooms, lounges, nooks and crannies for small gatherings, restaurants and eateries, and places for servants to gather supplies.

The challenges between the teams took place in three areas, ranked from easiest to hardest—the wooded paths outside the Summit, a few inner courtyards designed for public challenges, and a maze of halls for private duels. A team's success, or lack thereof, reflected on their leader.

I had two goals in this place—give Kieran a leg up and protect my kids. If I needed to meander through those halls, yanking out some souls, so be it.

Come at me, bro.

"What'd you just say?" Kieran and the kids were all looking at me funny, and I suspected I'd said that last bit out loud. My face heated, and thankfully, the limo stopped and the driver came around to open the door.

"Nothing."

Bria and the cats met us as we were climbing out of the limo. The guys were still exiting behind her.

"So this is interesting," she said, and lifted her hand to indicate the large warehouse-looking structure with two wings off the back and Lord knew what else. Bria turned and pointed the way we'd come. "We should be *way* back there."

"I know." Kieran walked toward the front entrance confidently, but I could sense his unease. We'd just shown up and already things weren't going as expected.

I straightened my formfitting beige suit jacket and smoothed my gray slacks. It didn't make sense—when I chose plain beige items, I was told I looked frumpy or unfashionable. When Daisy chose them, they looked perfect on me and "accentuated my natural wild beauty." I honestly didn't see the difference, though I had to admit, the ensemble she'd put together made me more comfortable than anything I'd worn under Aubri's guidance. Other than the quality, which was beyond fine, it reminded me of something I might have worn in the dual-society zone. That life had been a constant struggle, but it had made me *me*.

"It might be because Magnus put Alexis under his protection," Amber said as she walked up behind us, Henry at her side.

"Or it might be because of the highly desirable staff members you possess." Henry looked out at the street as though expecting an enemy any moment. "If they'd positioned us at the periphery of the living area, without any nosy neighbors, someone might have tried to make a grab. We have a reputation for fighting back and winning—no one wants the Summit to devolve into a war."

We entered the front doors into a plush environment I wasn't expecting but probably should've, given the nature of Demigods. A foyer led off into two rooms and a hall down the way, one room a grand entertaining area decorated with an appalling amount of gold and silver, the other a cozier setting without the bling and bells and whistles. The furniture was just as fine and clearly well made, but it was upholstered in earth tones and looked like it might actually be comfortable.

"That room is typically reserved for the Demigod's significant other to entertain his or her friends and allies." Kieran slid his hand along my lower back and hooked his arm around my waist. "The residences at the edges of the living quarters don't have these spaces. They hardly even have private space for the resident leader." He must've seen the look of horror on my face. He leaned in a little closer, a smile ghosting his lips. "Don't worry, you won't be expected to use it until I achieve status."

I couldn't help the sigh of relief. Given I still wasn't comfortable with service staff, I couldn't think of anything that would go worse than putting on a high society party for a bunch of important people.

The "warehouse" offered everything a person could hope for in a permanent residence. A state-of the-art kitchen held all the little machines and appliances that made life easy. The bathrooms had trendy sinks and furniture, and the entertainment room had all the recent tech and game systems my kids still hadn't gotten into.

My mouth fell open when I saw the hot tub in the bathroom of the enormous master suite.

"What are our plans, sir?" Amber asked. Henry wasn't standing next to her this time—it was Zorn.

"Get everything unpacked and put away. Find out where the other teams are located. I want an up-to-date map when we head out for our stroll at dusk."

"Which of your people would you like to take for the walk?" she asked.

"Just the kids and the crew. Dress for the purpose, not for any surprise attacks. We must show everyone we're not concerned others might break custom and come at us."

"Yes, sir." Amber turned and slipped by Zorn, leaving the master suite.

"Daisy will need to be checked in immediately," Zorn said. "Today is better than tomorrow. How do you want to handle that?"

"Lexi and I will take her right after…we get settled." Kieran pulled me against him and slid his hand down over the swell of my hip. "A limo is still standing by, correct?"

"Yes, sir, as per your request."

"We'll take it to the registration office. I want her on

the books before we walk the grounds. What about Mordecai? It's not necessary, since solo shifter registration only applies when shifters are of age, but people might wonder why he doesn't have a pack. It's pretty unusual for their kind, obviously. If they even halfheartedly look him up, they'll find out about his past sickness. That might make him a target if there are any other shifters on premises. I don't want them trying to pick him off as a weakling who has history of being kicked out of a pack."

"They won't think he's weak when they see him fight," Zorn said. "He has the knowledge and ferocity to fight for placement in a pack right now. If he were eighteen, he'd be able to take over a lesser pack."

"Without a clue how to lead it," Kieran replied. "He knows nothing of pack life or true leadership. We need to start incorporating that into his training."

My heart clattered against my ribs. "But he's not of age—it's illegal for anyone to challenge him so young."

"It is illegal for them to challenge him, but not for them to answer a challenge from him. They'll know how to goad him into action, Lexi. You need to harden yourself to the brutality of the magical world. We're in the big leagues now. We're with people who spend their lives manipulating others. Mordecai is ready for this, and he's smart enough to handle it. It's time to let him."

I took a step back and stared Kieran directly in the

eyes, fear eating away my rationality. "Do not tell me how to parent my kids. I will take what you say under advisement, but I want us both on the same page—he's still my kid, and he's under my protection. *My* protection. Ultimately, I am responsible for him. I will not let him walk straight into slaughter, whether or not you think he's ready for it. Do I make myself clear?"

They both wrestled with grins. Zorn took a step back. "You're wrong, sir. Mordecai has knowledge of pack life, just not the traditional kind. We've all got a ways to go before we challenge mother bear."

I narrowed my eyes at Zorn. "If you are mocking me, you won't like what happens next."

He lifted his hands in surrender and his eyes twinkled with delighted malice. "We'll do just fine here. All of us." He closed the door behind him.

"What's with him? He's acting strange," I said, still staring at the door.

"We're all keyed up." Kieran turned toward me and wrapped his arms around my middle. "We're going to be okay. We will get attacked, and they'll throw a lot of stuff at us, but we'll make it through. We've been battling for placement in the magical world ever since we met. Everything we've been through has prepared us for this moment. We just have to make it through the next week."

"I hate to be Negative Netty, but you were also optimistic about the Demigod Lydia fiasco."

He sighed and kissed my forehead. "Will I never live that down? One mistake that almost changed our lives forever, and no one can let it go."

I laughed and leaned against his body, taking comfort in his strength and warmth.

"Let's take a moment to unwind, and then we'll confront the next thing," he whispered, then slipped his large hands down to cup my butt cheeks.

"A moment to unwind?" I angled my face up to him as my fingers danced along his belt line. "What did you have in mind?"

He covered my lips with his, and suddenly we were ripping at each other's clothes, desperate to feel skin on skin. Desperate to lose ourselves in each other's bodies for a few moments before we plunged into danger.

I freed his large erection from his pants and slid my palm along its smooth skin. He sucked in a breath as he tossed my shirt to the side. I sank to my knees, using my free hand to pull down his pants.

He stepped out of them as I licked his tip and then encased his head in my mouth. His breath hitched, and I worked my hand and mouth in tandem, starting a rhythm.

He grabbed my upper arms, and suddenly I was cradled against him and he was hurrying me to the bed. He ripped the covers to the side and laid me down gently before bending down between my thighs. I groaned as he licked up my center and his lips took in my nub. He swirled me in his mouth, and any worries clinging to my mind fell away.

"Hmm, Kieran," I breathed, clutching the sheets.

He kissed and licked his way up my fevered skin, his fingers taking over for his mouth, working me higher. I gripped his shoulders in eager anticipation. His hot mouth encased a nipple, sending sparks of pleasure through me. My eyes nearly rolled to the back of my head as he took in the other.

"Kieran, please," I said, running my legs along his sides, desperate for him to enter me. To move inside of me. "*Please!*"

He kissed up my neck and dragged his tip along my core. His weight settled on me, pushing me into the mattress. His cock lay against me and he moved his hips slowly—too slowly!—letting his cock trail through my wetness.

I wiggled under him, trying to angle up. Trying to find purchase.

He sucked in my bottom lip and pushed forward again, skimming me maddeningly. We breathed the same harried breath, his control about to give out, his teasing undoing him as much as it was me.

Unable to help it, I reached between us and took his base in my hand. I directed him where I needed it and gripped him with my thighs.

"Fuck me," I commanded, desperate. Drowning in desire.

He met my gaze, fire and love smoldering within his eyes, and shoved forward, filling me to bursting. Color exploded behind my eyes, pleasure within my body.

I groaned and held on as he pulled back before crashing into me again, the sensations almost unbearably good. I rocked up to meet his thrusts, mindless, mad with passion. My body wound tighter and tighter. I dug my fingertips into his solid muscle, holding on for dear life as my body moved of its own accord, control utterly lost. The sound of skin meeting skin filled the room as we strove harder, headed for release. Relishing in each other.

"Oh!" An orgasm tore through me, blindingly good, and pleasure vibrated through every inch of my body.

"Hmm, Lexi," Kieran exalted, shaking over me.

Fire sizzled across my skin and passion exploded in our kiss as we climaxed together.

Afterward, my body melted into the mattress. Kieran made no move to get off me. The stress of what was to come throbbed just out of reach, but in this moment, I felt utterly relaxed.

"I love you," I said softly, feeling his ring encircling my finger. Feeling the promise of our life to come.

"You are my forever," he said against my lips, as

though he'd heard my thoughts.

I let my eyes droop. I'd relish these quiet minutes with him. I'd take these moments for the godsend they were. And then, when we entered the magical battlefield beyond these doors, I'd turn on Beast Mode.

It was time to show the magical world what I was capable of.

Chapter 3

ALEXIS

"JUST LIKE WE practiced," Zorn said to Daisy as the limo came to a stop in front of a walkway leading up to a nondescript door in the absolutely enormous Magical Summit building that reached five stories into the sky and sprawled across the land. Plenty of room for the inner courtyards, plus the lethal maze of hallways lined with rooms people could use to hide or lie in wait so they could pop out like a deranged jack-in-the-box when their chosen prey happened by.

"Waste of resources, all of this," I murmured as we waited for the driver to come around and open the door. "It's like a nightmare fun house, full of serial killers on the loose. Why can't people just talk things out, like non-magical people?"

"When non-magical people don't get their way, they engage in expensive, destructive wars that kill thousands." Kieran held my hand as Zorn left the car. "At least here innocents don't get hurt."

"Stop making sense."

Daisy stepped out beside Zorn, followed by me and then Kieran. Mordecai got out last, this party small and intended to be as nondescript as the door we were about to enter.

"Has a non-magical person ever attended the Summit?" Mordecai asked quietly.

"Not in recorded memory." Kieran dropped to the back of the group. "Some magical people have non-magical pets, but they leave those at home."

I scrunched up my face as Zorn reached the door. He opened it, pausing for a moment as Daisy and Mordecai lined up at his back. They entered together.

"Pets? Is this the part where you adopt the gross lingo other Demigods use?" I asked, lowering my voice so the strangers waiting inside—three souls clustered in close proximity—didn't hear.

"Yup." Kieran held the door for me and then followed me in. It was like the guys expected us to be attacked at any moment.

A woman as old as the hills waited behind the counter across from us, seated in a tall chair. Half-moon glasses clung to the edge of her nose, and a non-living helper stood at her side, a man in his mid-forties with an annoyed expression. I couldn't tell if the woman knew she had company or not. A brown door closed off what had to be another office, holding the third soul I'd felt when approaching.

Not one piece of paper existed in the whole office. A printer sat against the wall, but there was no evidence anything had ever been printed. Instead, there were two tablets on the counter, one in front of us and another at the empty station next to us. Other machines sat near or next to the computers, including what looked like a thumbprint scanner.

The woman looked over from her computer, peering down her slightly raised nose through her glasses.

"Yes?" the woman asked, gruff and uninterested.

"Demigod Kieran, unofficial leader of magical San Francisco, here to check in two minors." Kieran stepped up next to Daisy, and Zorn filed in behind him, blocking us off from anyone who might walk in the door.

The woman turned back to her computer. Her fingers flew across the keys.

"That's that Chester we were told about," the nonliving man said with a sneer. "What has the world come to that they are allowing Chesters into a strictly magically sanctioned area, the filthy animals—"

"That's enough," I said, unable to help it.

The woman's fingers paused and she slowly turned her head to me, her dull eyes showing no reaction to my interruption.

"Sorry." I held up my hand, then pointed at the snarling man to her right. "I was talking to the guy hovering around you. He's a spirit. I can see spirits."

"Me?" the guy said, peering harder at my face. "But you're not a Demigod."

"You know about my ward, but you don't know who brought her?" I asked the man. "You don't do a good job picking up information."

He started before turning around and looking behind him.

I sighed. "Yes, I can see you." I gave the woman a smile. "I apologize. He was saying some…rude things. I'm a Spirit Walker."

The woman stared at me for a moment longer. "Yes, I gathered."

The guy sucked in a breath. "No one mentioned a Spirit Walker. A Spirit Walker bringing a Chester?" His eyes narrowed. "What sort of trick is that? What games are you playing, girl?"

"Do you know the man?" I asked as the woman's fingernails clacked against the keys. "Would you miss him if his presence left the office?"

"I'm pretty sure I know who it is, and I haven't noticed his presence since he died a few years ago in a mysterious accident," she drawled, talking and typing at the same time. "No one knows what happened."

"I know what happened!" the man said indignantly. "You killed me with a sledgehammer, that's what happened!"

She paused and pointed at the tablet on the counter,

which suddenly glowed to life. I suppressed a smile as Daisy looked down at her photo.

"Is that you?" the woman asked.

"Yes," Daisy answered in a steady tone. If she was nervous, she didn't let it show.

The woman nodded and went back to her computer screen.

"You snuck up on me when we were doing the year-end filing and clubbed me in the head," the man went on, shouting at her now. To me he said, "One minute I was double-checking her report, and the next I was looking down at my collapsed body. What a mess she'd made, too! All over the clean floor. She didn't even do a good job cleaning it up—there's still a stain. And the old shoe they got to replace me! Well—"

"I can get rid of him if you want," I said to the woman. "He seems like a negative presence."

"No, that's quite all right." The woman reached under the counter and came back with what looked like an identity card. Daisy's picture showed at the top in a little square, her name and affiliation printed beneath it. Emblazoned in the corner was a red crest. "He used to get such joy out of micromanaging me and telling me what a bad job I was doing. Now, he can yell to his heart's content, and when he realizes I can't hear him, he'll be in his own little hell. The office has been downright pleasant since he was mysteriously killed."

"As soon as someone gets around to investigating, they'll have *you* killed," the man yelled. "You put as little effort into covering up the crime as you do your day-to-day work. Mark my words, your days are numbered."

The woman focused on Daisy. "Keep that with you at all times. You have been granted access to all public areas of this island. Your presence here is official. Next?"

Mordecai stepped up, and they went through the same drill, the spirit grumbling all the while. After Mordecai received the same pass, we were sent on our way.

"I thought I'd get shade from the staff here," Daisy said as we filed back into the limo.

I had a feeling the woman had intentionally acted nonchalant in order to upset her spirit boss, hovering over her in frustration.

Daisy's knuckles turned white as she clutched the ID tightly. "That woman didn't even show surprise," she said.

"She seems like she has a tedious job," Mordecai responded, and tucked his ID into his wallet. He wouldn't need it like Daisy would. "She's probably numb with boredom."

"Or still pleased with herself for killing her old boss and getting away with it." I looked out the window as another limo pulled up behind us. "Is that how things go here? Even if the staff is murdered, no one cares?"

Before the occupant of the limo stepped out, we were back on the small road leading to our quarters.

"Depends on the person who died and their value," Kieran answered. "Clearly her boss wasn't valuable enough to worry about. Given he was probably not well liked or respected, and couldn't have had any family since no one raised a fuss..." He shrugged. "He's out of her hair."

"This magical world doesn't seem so bad." Daisy finally tucked away her ID.

"One trip to a seldom-used office should not color your view of the establishment," Zorn growled. "You haven't seen anything yet."

"WHY ARE WE leaving Red behind?" I asked as everyone readied for our first public stroll.

Kieran was showing off the best of his wares, me included. He'd parade us around, letting the other leaders size him up while their staffs sized us up. Daisy and Mordecai would be going as my wards. Kieran wanted to show we were a family.

"She doesn't have a blood oath," Bria said as she checked the contents of her backpack. "She doesn't belong."

The guys in the crew waited outside by the small

fleet of golf carts and four-wheelers, our chief mode of transportation now that the last limo had been sent back. There went our chance for a limo chase, not that I'd been looking forward to it.

"Yeah, but...*you* don't have a blood oath," I replied as Daisy opened the side door of the warehouse-residence and waited for us.

Bria straightened up and slung her backpack over her shoulders. "Necromancers are kind of magical cowboys. We're common enough that Demigods won't go to war for a level five, and we typically go where we please. The best of us can definitely get placement in an inner circle, but it doesn't weird people out if we don't. We're just the add-ons standing in the back. People try their best to ignore us. I mean, walking dead people around is hardly a glamorous profession. Red's fighting magic is used for protection. Given her lack of a blood oath, if she came with us, it would look like she was brought along to protect you. That's not the message Kieran wants to send."

Everything had multiple layers of meaning in the magical world, something I doubted I'd ever understand. I wasn't sure I wanted to.

I walked through the door and onto the stone walkway leading into a nice garden setup. A wooden gazebo sat off to the side, its sides covered in prickly vines dotted with little flowers. The chairs within it held bright yellow cushions with cute white buttons to match the flowers. A flamboyant tree lived up to its name, the bright red-orange flowers providing a spray of color. Horseshoe pits had been set up by a round patch of perfectly tended green grass. Multiple seating setups dotted the way along the path, with benches or chairs overlooking the ocean a hundred yards from our back door. They'd put the Demigod of Poseidon near the water, which was a nice touch.

The whole place was a nice touch, actually, spacious and welcoming, with everything we could want and an abundance of subtle luxuries. Only Kieran's entertaining area was gaudy, if I was being honest. The rest seemed to flow more with the times and our tastes.

I suddenly wondered if he'd made sure that was the case, although that didn't explain the hideousness of the front room.

The cats slunk out of the door before I could shut it.

"No, no, back in, you two." I motioned at Havoc as Kieran strolled out past me, looking decadent in a crisp blue suit tailored to fit his perfect body. His black shoes gleamed in the dying light and a cream waistcoat and pocket square gave him a debonair look. He wore his hair in a stylish, messy do, short on the sides and long on top. He paused to wait for me, his stance easy and powerful and confident, as if nothing in the world could ruin his day or his carefully laid plans for world domination. He was the height of trendiness and all things sexy.

In contrast, I wore a loose, flowing number in plain gray that hid all my curves. The new stylist we'd brought, who hummed beautifully and didn't talk much, had given me a messy, loose curl that made me look half crazy, a smoky eye, and one piece of jewelry—a sort of crystal that looked like it had come from a flea market. My team had gushed about my *look*, and I'd stood with a confused grin, waiting for the punch line.

Apparently the punch line was me, especially standing next to Kieran.

"The cats are coming," Kieran said, holding out his hand for me.

The expression from earlier returned to my face, I knew it. Was this the joke? Were they intentionally dressing me up as a crazy cat lady?

"They don't have leashes. I doubt animals are supposed to come." I gestured Havoc back into the house. She was the leader—her brother did whatever she did.

"We need to set the precedent that those cats go where you go. They are protection as well as…very interesting. They'll add to your profile. The cats need to come."

"But…" I looked down at myself.

"You look beautiful and those cats are cool, baby. I promise, they'll make you look more badass, not like a pajama-wearing…whatever Harding always calls you."

"Pajama-wearing cat lady, and I call myself that, not him." I deflated, knowing a lost cause when I saw one. "And if you think that's bad, you should hear what he calls you."

Kieran handed me into the front seat of a white golf cart with a bench seat across the back. He sat in the driver's seat and Thane climbed onto the back. The kids got in with Zorn and Dylan, and I had no idea who took the cats. Everyone else took their rides and off we went.

Watch out, magical world. Here comes the pajama-wearing Soul Stealer with her overgrown white cats.

Chapter 4

KIERAN

KIERAN STEPPED OUT of the golf cart as the rest of his people parked, the spacious lot already half-full and alive with activity. The people who'd shown up early would be on the lower half of the status scale. This walk wasn't mandatory, after all, and its main purpose was to allow leaders to gauge worth in the eyes of those around them. Those of high status already knew their worth, and many of them didn't bother with the first night's walk within the gardens reserved solely for this. Or so Kieran had heard.

This was all part of the game. Every movement and action had a purpose. Every slight or smile hinted at what was to come.

Kieran would glean a great deal from tonight, and not just from the way he was received. This was also Lexi's debut. She was a loose cannon, clueless about many of the protocols of the magical world. They had ensured it was so—preparing her only for certain aspects of the Summit. The people here lived by rules, and the unpredictable threw them off. *She* would throw them off.

Her greatest defense wasn't her magic. It was people's fear of the unknown.

He was walking a fine line with this approach. Magnus's not-so-subtle hint that Kieran should educate Lexi in the ways of the magical world had not failed to make an impression. But he'd decided this was the safer strategy for her—walking the fine line between knowing and not knowing.

A team of over two dozen congregated on the sidewalk at the edge of the garden promenade, and though Kieran couldn't see who led the group, he assumed it was a someone with little power or status. Only someone who lacked confidence would bring such a large group to this event. It showed weakness. That, or they were new and hadn't done their homework, which also indicated weakness.

Another group half the size gathered at the other end of the sidewalk, much more organized and streamlined. A woman in a sparkling dress stood at the front, her head held high, her people businesslike and purposeful. Given the distance, Kieran couldn't make out who it was, but she was clearly not a novice.

Other teams were still assembling in the parking lot, some teams finding their places quickly, like his, others less organized.

The breeze ruffled Lexi's hair as she took her place by his side. His mark glowed on her soft skin, amplifying her natural beauty. Her dress moved and shifted as she did, pressing against her breast one moment, and against the swell of her hip the next. It was like a peep show, alluding to delights hidden between the folds of fabric. In the same breath, the viewer couldn't help but remember that her magic held hidden horrors bubbling beneath the surface. The dichotomy was electrifying. Daisy had her own hidden talents.

He entwined his fingers with Lexi's.

Her eyes widened a little as she looked up at him. "I thought only married leaders were supposed to hold hands with their partners?"

"Fuck 'em." He grinned, feeling light as a feather. They were likely going to break a great many rules this week, so why not blatantly start now?

"Ready, sir," Zorn said.

Without a word, Kieran led the way, cutting through the parked golf carts to the sidewalk, where the large group still struggled to organize. Why getting in a line was so difficult, Kieran couldn't say, but their disorderliness no doubt spoke to how their territory was run.

"Any news?" Kieran asked as the breeze picked up, flaring Lexi's skirt around her legs. He struggled to take his eyes off her.

"No important sightings yet," Amber said from directly behind Kieran. Zorn walked next to her, taking Lexi's back. The kids would be right behind them.

They took the path between the hedges, only wide enough for two or three people, depending on size. Palm trees lined the way, flanked by hedges, until they reached a curved walkway within an extravagant garden. Flowers bloomed every which way, flares of color. Trees and bushes not native to a tropical paradise reached over the path or wept beside it. To the left of the path, a willow's leaves arched over an outcropping of seats. Demigod Arnold—mortal and showing it—sat there with his people fanned out around him, analyzing everyone who passed.

The moment the older Demigod noticed Kieran's team, his eyes widened. His limbs shook, as though he intended to expend the effort and get up.

Kieran let his gaze slide by. Arnold was of low status and not someone to engage. Kieran had bigger fish to hook on this walk, and limited time. Only the desperate stayed out here all night.

Lexi tensed and then rolled her shoulders. "Do you feel that?" she asked quietly.

"What?" he asked.

She peered beyond him, then to her other side. "I don't know. It feels like…pressure, kind of. Like we're being watched."

He clued in, putting all his senses on high, but only his nervousness for what was to come registered. "Do you feel any souls?"

"Not that I can see." She shrugged and moved her hair across her shoulder. "I'm just keyed up."

"We're all keyed up." He squeezed her hand.

As they reached the main promenade, a wide path set into the various flora, Kieran paused to let a team of twelve saunter past. He couldn't see who led the group, but his or her team was made up solely of high level fives. One of those, a woman with deathly pale skin, hair so blonde it looked white, and eyes the palest of blues, glanced their way. Her gaze lingered on Kieran for a moment before sliding to Lexi. Her eyes widened and her step hitched, her gaze zipping back to Kieran again before her mouth moved subtly.

Another team member looked back, a man with fire-red hair and eyes so dark they looked like the night sky. His gaze moved from Kieran to Lexi to the rest of the crew.

"Yeah, keep staring, jackass," Lexi mumbled, and Kieran barely suppressed a laugh. She likely didn't realize she'd just said that out loud—she often reacted aggressively to unsolicited attention, the effect of trying to stay invisible all her life, he wagered.

"Left," Amber said softly. She knew most of the inner circles in this place, having come here with Valens for years and years. Given she was walking away from the group that had taken notice of them, their leader wasn't on her short list of potential allies.

The next team they came across was an overly large group led by a high level five. As Kieran walked by, avoiding the man's searching gaze, his father's voice thundered through his head: *A level five as a territory leader? I'll never understand the point.*

He shook it off, continuing on, but when they passed another group—a Demigod with a disorganized, ramshackle crew—it happened again.

She should be ashamed of herself. What a waste. If only there were a way to strip people of their magic.

After that came Demigod Helga, her expression just as severe as her name, and her people perfectly in line.

"Pause if you can," Amber murmured softly behind him.

He let his gaze travel toward Helga. She was a strong, immortal Demigod with a currently middling territory that had been flourishing a few centuries back. Word was that she'd put the brakes on a declining territory, found her ambition again, and was eager to make a comeback. If she could restore herself to her former glory, she'd be a useful ally.

That damned woman was a thorn in my side at the best of times. Thank mighty Poseidon she's finally dwindling away.

Kieran flinched. He felt haunted, ill at ease. He didn't even know when he'd heard his father say such things. But they'd clung to him, clogging up his thinking, polluting his views. Information was always handy, but the last thing he wanted to do was travel down the path of arrogant superiority paved by his elitist father. Kieran would not end up there. He *would not.*

He felt Lexi squeeze his hand, concern radiating through the soul link. In alarm, he slowed and looked down at her, wondering what was going on.

"Hi," she said softly, and squeezed his hand again. "We're good. I love you."

Love and support glittered in her soft brown eyes. Warmth bled through the soul link now, and it dawned on him that she'd sensed his melancholy and fear. Given how well she knew him, she likely knew the reason for it. And although she knew enough about magical etiquette to know she shouldn't steal his attention away from another Demigod, she was leading with her heart.

He did the same, smiling at her. "I love you too."

After a moment, her gaze slid past him to Helga, who'd been waiting patiently for him to take notice. She'd lifted her chin, but if she was angry, it didn't show.

He tried to contain his shock. He'd just accidentally slighted a Demigod of higher status. Helga should've moved on or called him down. Why the hell had she waited?

Wrapping his arrogant confidence around him like a cape, he finally met Helga's direct and forceful stare.

"Demigod Kieran, isn't it?" Helga's bearing was regal.

He offered her a nod, a little light for a greeting to someone of her status, but she'd put the ball in his court. "It is. Demigod Helga, I presume," he responded with a hint of boredom. He fell into strategy like it was second nature. And perhaps it was—he'd grown up watching his father command a room.

"It is, yes. Sorry to hear about the loss of your father. Regardless of the history, it can't be easy to bury a parent."

"It isn't, no. Thank you for your condolences." He turned toward Lexi, still holding her hand. "This is Alexis Price, my betrothed."

"The Soul Stealer who bears your mark, yes. I figured. And there's that handsome Lightning Bolt, I see, alive and well. What a shock. The legendary giant, your father's master spy… Quite the stable you have already. I expect big things from you. The only question is, what kind of things will those be? Will you go the way of your father, hunting for personal gain at the cost of others, or will you help us pursue the common good? Or maybe you'll roll over for those who've been at this much longer than you. It's no secret Magnus is trying to get his fingers in your pie." Her eyes narrowed. "You've entered the snake pit, boy, in a very flashy sort of way. You'll need your wits about you or you'll lose it all."

Insufferable woman. Has she no decency? She hasn't a delicate word in her mouth.

Kieran barely kept from flinching, shoving his father's voice to the back of his mind. Still, the voice of the past had been correct. Helga was going about this too dramatically, like a toothless tiger trying to find purchase on a jugular. She'd have a hard time making important friends this way.

His smile was slight, and he shifted his gaze ahead. "Morality can be hazy among Demigods, as my Thunderstroke will tell you. The *common good* isn't usually for common people. But my views will come at a cost, yes, and some will feel the burden. No one can say exactly who, yet, of course. This week should give all of us a better idea. If you'll excuse me."

He offered a slight nod, not looking at her, and continued on, showing his displeasure at the interaction. Two groups had watched them from the benches along the sides of the path. Everything here was for show. Every word and action was analyzed. It was how the game was played.

"Excellent," Amber murmured behind him, and he felt a note of pride at her approval.

"That's what we're going for, then?" Lexi asked quietly. "Being dicks to people?"

"Depending on status, yes, mostly," Amber replied. "Which you pulled off nicely, Alexis, capturing Kieran's attention for yourself and making Demigod Helga wait. You treated him like he was of higher status, and Helga followed your lead. Perfect."

"Oh. I…" Lexi trailed away as Demigod Jessup ambled along the path, proof that Demigods didn't automatically keep their shape.

Kieran ignored him completely. He'd been of little status for as long as Kieran could remember, and for good reason. His politics were messy, his allies were few, and he cheated and lied to keep his territory operating. He didn't deserve the mantle he possessed. It was time to demand more of Demigods, something Kieran would work for when he had some clout.

"Dara is up ahead," Amber said, and a surge of excitement rolled through the soul link. Dara had helped them take Valens down. She'd shown up in the nick of time in response to Daisy's summons, and at one point in the battle, she'd saved Daisy's life. Clearly Lexi had a soft spot for her.

Nervousness rolled through Kieran's middle as he passed a level-five ruler of no consequence, followed by a large but orderly crew. Dara was still a ways back, a crimson dress flowing around her legs and no one at her side. Behind her, her team stalked like predators, the best collection of elementals in the world, much smaller than usual for a non-Demigod. Dara was making a statement about her abilities. One she could back up.

He continued to move at the same pace, still holding Lexi's hand, but looked at Dara in a way that communicated he'd like to stop and chat. He was putting himself at her social mercy. It was the first risk of many.

The distance between them lessened. The woman behind Dara leaned forward a little, her mouth moving, giving advice or reminding Dara of their previously laid plans. In a moment, it became clear what her advisor had said.

Dara continued facing straight ahead. She would ignore Kieran's subtle desire to meet her on the path. She might've helped with Valens, but she was making it public that their connection ended there.

Fuck.

Frustration burned within him. He'd hoped for at least a nod—a small show of camaraderie to get him going. Careful not to sigh like a child who hadn't gotten his way, he swiveled his gaze forward, respecting her decision. The snub would make things harder, but it wouldn't sink him. Not yet.

"Wait, are you serious?"

Kieran jerked at Daisy's raised voice. He whipped his head back to look at her, unable to believe it.

She stepped out of the line with a hand held out in a stop motion. Her expression held disbelief, matching the way he felt.

"Don't you recognize me?" Daisy asked, her doll-like features and large eyes making her look delicate and vulnerable. Her pretty dress hung from her slim frame, her softness of face and slight curves shouting clearly that she was still a kid. Given the badge pinned to the light pink sash across her body, it would take but a moment for everyone to realize this was the Chester they'd probably heard about, crashing their magical party. Daisy was currently painting a huge "kick me" sign on her back.

"Lexi," Kieran hissed. "Stop this. She's putting herself in danger."

"You incinerated a guy who was about to slice my head off, remember?" Daisy put out her hands, very sassy. "We battled together against that nut-sack Valens. Thank heavens you and Demigod Kieran finally did something about that guy—he had to go. He was full of the wrong stuff."

Kieran's stomach clenched. While everyone knew how he'd come by his territory, Daisy—already remarkable for being a Chester among magical people—had just made a very bold, very public statement about someone who'd had a lot of allies. Kieran did not want to make enemies before he'd even made friends.

Mordecai stepped in before Lexi could drop Kieran's hand. "Daisy, leave her be," he said, putting a hand on her shoulder. "She's playing politics right now. This is for show."

"Do you know what's not for show? The important things—like guarding each other's backs during battle." She shrugged off Mordecai's hand. "And who cares? This is just a walk. The official thing starts tomorrow. Can't two groups with history shake hands and talk about the good times? There will be plenty of time to play politics."

Lexi was trying to make her way to Daisy, but Amber had stepped in the wrong direction and was standing directly in Lexi's path. Kieran fought to keep his composure.

"What do you know?" Mordecai pulled Daisy's arm, forcing her to take a step back.

"Sorry." Lexi had finally made it to her kids. Face flushed, her dress and hair billowing in a wind that touched no one else, she smiled at Dara and then at Dara's people, who stood stock-still behind her. The cats slunk through everyone, stopping at Lexi's sides. She didn't seem to notice, which made it seem entirely natural and, given their size and glowing eyes, probably nerve-racking. "I apologize. As I'm sure you remember, we didn't grow up in the magical world. I've clearly done a terrible job explaining the nature of this walk. This is my bad. Kieran was going by the book"—Kieran contained a flinch at the blunt acknowledgement of his actions—"but Daisy here was just reacting to a familiar face. I thought she had a better understanding of these things."

"I have a great understanding of human decency," Daisy said.

"Just no understanding of timing, that's all." Mordecai's smile and body language hinted at the ridiculousness of the situation.

Other groups veered to the sides, both in front and behind, watching the circus. Many faces held wide eyes, a Demigod Kieran couldn't place stared at the scene in clear disapproval, and a few snickered. This whole walk, the beginning of the Summit, was unraveling before Kieran's eyes.

Take matters into your hand and punish them! Show everyone that you are not weak. Show them that you rule with an iron fist and you will be respected!

Fear bubbled through Kieran. He'd seen his father "handle" his staff countless times. He'd routinely punished them in public, leaving them a bloody mess and walking on, not allowing anyone to help them. He'd even killed a few staff if the grievance was bad enough.

This grievance would've been deemed bad enough.

Daisy was embarrassing Kieran in front of his peers. She was hurting his chances of success. She was making him a laughingstock.

Kieran clenched his jaw and his fists, freezing. He dared not move a muscle. He was not like his father. Whatever this cost him in status, he would not lash out. He was better than that, stronger, securer. He could bounce back. He had allowed Daisy to come, and so he was ultimately at fault for her actions.

Lexi pulled her ward back a step, but then she hesitated. Into Dara's continued stare, she said, "Look, we're forever grateful to you, you know that. I think I gushed enough for a lifetime when you were in magical San Francisco. You saved our lives. Mordecai is right—this is a bad time—but just in case you and Kieran don't see eye to eye down the road..." Lexi brushed her hair away from her face, the wind no one else felt still blowing her clothes, reminding everyone what she was. "I stand by what I said way back then. If you need backup, call me. I owe you that and more. I might be rolling by myself, because no way would I let the kids endanger themselves again, but I'll do what I can."

Lexi nodded, seemed to notice her dress swirling around her legs, and suddenly the spirit wind stopped. She nodded again, and then marshaled Daisy and Mordecai back into place. She put her finger in Daisy's face. "Do something like that again, and you will rue the day, do you hear me? *Rue* the day. And you!"

She moved her finger in front of Mordecai, who now topped her height and breadth by quite a lot. It mattered not at all. Mordecai's back bent and his head lowered.

"What did I do? I was helping," he whined.

"Do you think I'm an idiot?" Her eyebrows settled low. "I will give you a thump you won't soon forget, do you understand me?"

"Yes, ma'am," Mordecai said glumly. Daisy stared in defiance.

Kieran could hardly control his anger when Lexi resumed her place by his side. He hardly knew where to look, or how quickly to start walking. His focus had been shattered, his hold on the situation lost. In any other place, he'd just call it a night and go home, but he couldn't do that here.

Reaching for the one thing that had always balanced him, he took Lexi's hand and slowly let out a breath.

"Demigod Kieran, might I have a word?"

It took him a moment to realize it was Dara who'd spoken to him.

She hadn't moved, blocking the path just as he was. Her eyes had warmed, and her body language had defrosted.

She gestured to the side, indicating they might find a couple of benches and have a chat.

He couldn't do much more than stare at her in confusion.

"She means you, dummy," Daisy said through clenched teeth.

He wasn't sure if he was awake. Had he slipped into some sort of strange dream turned nightmare?

Lexi stepped forward and all but dragged him along. He allowed her to lead him, their group stopping to wait for Dara's group to go first, giving way to those of higher status. Even Daisy and Mordecai hung back, a show that they weren't nearly as ignorant to the nature of this walk as they appeared to be.

"Just go with it," Lexi murmured, warmth flowing through the soul link. "Just go with the crazy. It'll work out. It always works out."

"Can we speak plainly?" Dara said once they were off the path and seated on a wide bench, in clear view of those passing by.

"Yes, of course." Kieran still struggled to regain focus. He was grateful Alexis sat beside him, grounding him.

"How you allowed Alexis to handle her ward just then reminded me why I stayed to help you keep magical San Francisco in order after Valens..." She let her voice trail away out of respect, he knew. Valens had been a tyrant, but he'd also been family. "It reminded me of why I didn't oppose you taking his territory. Hell, why we came to help in the first place. There is no way in Hades's underpants that Valens would've calmly stood by while one of his people stepped out of line. He would've painted the footpath red with them—I can think of a few examples."

"I know," he said, clenching his jaw.

"What I'm saying is, when you're with Alexis and her kids, I see a side of you that I feel I can trust. A side of you completely unlike the composed man who approached me on this path. Which man are you? I've paid attention to your activities after I left magical San Francisco, and I can't say I like what I've seen. You conquered the giant's mountain, you infiltrated a Chester town and stole a rare talent... Sure, you managed to actually acquire those talents, which speaks to your ability, but the act of trying, when neither of them wanted to be bothered, is an issue. I will not support someone like your father. I'm sure you can understand that."

Kieran clasped his hands together, hardly daring to breathe. This was a time for blunt honesty if ever there was one.

"We didn't conquer anything—Jerry could've killed us many times over. He didn't because Alexis was able to act as a middleman between him and his deceased fiancée. I wish I could say I convinced him to join us, but he came because of Alexis. Neither did we steal anything. Dylan, the Lightning Bolt, came *to us* after our battle with Demigod Flora. We'd left without him. You can check with the townspeople on that, since I doubt you'd believe Dylan."

"And Amber, Valens's right-hand snake?" Dara asked without lowering her voice.

"I had to allow logic to overrule emotion. Magnus sought to hire her, and Aaron attempted to kidnap her. I couldn't let either of those things happen. You must understand, Alexis puts me in a…sensitive position. My goal has been to gather the best team possible to help me defend her. I have not forced anyone into my employ, nor will I. Red, back at the homestead, does not have a blood oath. You are free to ask her questions if you doubt me. Please be aware, though, that I have excellent training, designed and governed by my father. I will use it to gain the status I need, just as I will use the other tools in my arsenal. I will even attempt to sway some of my father's old allies to my side. Some of them are uncommonly stupid, or so my father had always said. If those blind sheep want to follow me, I'm more than willing to lead."

"Even stupid gets a vote," Dara said softly, looking at the people strolling by, everyone playing the game. Everyone but Kieran and Dara, at present.

"My father always said that a crowd of stupid or ignorant people looking to be led is great for getting your desires achieved. If you are clever enough to manipulate them, you turn their vote into your own."

"A clever enough strategy…for a Demigod. My words can be as sweet as anyone's, but this place is full of elitists, and they look at me and see a level five."

"They look at me and see a child." Kieran shrugged, taking Lexi's hand again. "For now."

Silence fell between them, broken by Lexi.

"He won't turn into his father." She leaned around him to look at Dara. "You can trust Kieran. He's done great things for magical San Francisco. In just a short time, he's already made improvements for the people he governs. He can make a difference on a larger scale, too. If it makes you feel better, though, share a meal with Daisy. She'll tell you all you need to know about his faults."

A moment passed in silence. Dara's and his teams waited around them, silent and watchful. Patient.

The verdict was coming, Kieran knew. It was a chore to continue breathing evenly.

Finally, Dara stood. "I haven't taken a chance like this in a long time." She turned, waiting for Kieran to stand beside her. She put out her hand, her hard blue eyes rooting to his. "Let's see what you're made of. Maybe you can succeed where I have continually failed."

Kieran took her hand, hardly able to believe it. The

communication with her had been going so badly—nosediving into tragic, even. But Dara had just publicly done a one-eighty and stuck out her hand for all to see. She was creating an alliance with him before the Summit had even officially begun.

Fireworks exploded through his middle. An incredulous grin threatened to break free.

He shook her hand firmly and felt the power curling around them. She'd been his father's biggest roadblock, unraveling his plans when no one else had dared to try. She'd spoken up for those afraid to use their voices, giving them courage. She would be a hell of an ally. They could make headway together, he knew it.

Daisy hadn't unraveled his walk at all…she'd saved the day.

"Sir, we have word…" Amber stepped closer, facing the trees, a finger to her earpiece. "Aaron and Magnus have both entered the promenade on the west side, half a mile from here. Zander has left his homestead with his team, heading this way. The big dogs are coming out. They must be curious about some of the new people at the Summit."

"Nah." Dara grinned, her eyes sparkling. "They're curious about *you*. Everyone is. You've got people talking. Watch yourself—friends and enemies are often the same in this place."

Chapter 5

ALEXIS

As KIERAN WAITED for Dara and her people to head off, I grabbed Daisy and Mordecai by the arms and dragged them away from the others.

"What were you thinking?" I demanded, so mad I could spit nails. I knew for a fact Daisy was well versed in the protocol of this walk. She'd known exactly what she was doing. And she wasn't the only one in trouble. Mordecai had pretended to restrain her, but it had been all for show.

"Trying to help Kieran, obviously," Daisy said, full of indignation.

I barely stopped myself from stepping forward and shaking all the teenage angst right out of her.

"You took an incredible risk, and while it might have turned out okay for him—thank your lucky stars—now you have a big target painted across your back. Did you see all those people staring? All anyone will be talking about is the Chester that got out of line and stopped a leader."

"So what?" she said, putting her free hand to her hip. "We're a team. I had a way to help, and I did. I'll take what comes."

I clenched my fists, still struggling not to grab her and start shaking. "You didn't need to do it. Kieran would've been able to talk her around. He would've been able to recover."

"Kieran would've been publicly rejected by a level five," Mordecai said, sounding knowledgeable and therefore really annoying. "It would've been a bad start to the Summit, especially since they've fought together."

"Dara is of high standing—"

"She's a level five," Daisy interrupted. "You heard her: the elitists out there look down on her. They would look down on Kieran, too, if it got around that she'd snubbed him. At least now he has come out on top, creating an alliance without even discussing details or making concessions. That *is* a good look. That makes him look better than when he first got here."

"He knew the risk he was taking," I said.

"So did I. I'm a Chester"—she jerked her head at Mordecai—"and he's a wolf without a pack. We're a couple of teens Kieran allows to hang around in order to please his Soul Stealer. If Dara had turned away from me, we would've spread the rumor that you punished me severely. Since she didn't, Kieran gets a win without having to beg her to reconsider. Why do you think Zorn let me intercept her? If it had been Magnus, he would've stabbed me in the back to stop me. Why do you think Amber got in your way to give me more time? She saw what was happening."

For a moment I was struck mute. She sounded like an adult who'd been sitting in on strategy meetings. Her understanding of the situation was incredible.

But she was still my kid. A kid without magic and without the power to heal quickly.

"You just put a *target* on your back, Daisy. You need to realize that. You helped Kieran, yes, but to do it, you put yourself in incredible danger."

Daisy laughed without humor, acting far beyond her years. "I put myself in incredible danger just by showing up…and by being your ward. Wait a minute, let's go back further, shall we? Let's not forget I put myself in danger by trying to sell fake drugs for a little money before we met Kieran. By stealing medicine for Mordecai. By running away from a foster dad who beat me. By *not* running away from all those other homes. My life is danger, Lexi. For as long as I can remember, I've lived in constant danger. At least now I'm useful. At least now I have a group of people at my back that will help me through it. Kieran succeeding is the best thing for this family, and so I will do whatever it takes—I'll face whatever it takes—to help make that happen."

"Until he goes crazy and we have to kill him in his

sleep and then take off," Mordecai said.

"Yes, obviously." Daisy rolled her eyes.

I stared at the two of them and couldn't decide if I wanted to hug them or slap them. I settled for wiping away a tear and threatening them. "Do not do that again. Children are supposed to be seen and not heard. From now on, you stay silent, do you get me? If Kieran gets rejected, let him handle it politically."

Neither of them nodded.

"*Do you understand?*"

"Yes, ma'am," Mordecai mumbled.

"Fine," Daisy said.

"Alexis." Kieran was waiting to go back onto the promenade with the crew lined up behind him.

I took my place, trying to shrug off the anxiety coiling tightly within me as we started walking again. The beautiful surroundings should've helped me relax, but the calculating eyes of those we passed negated the effect.

"Pass him. Do not engage," Amber said, walking closely behind Kieran.

A man with a strange peacock robe passed us, his gaze rooted to Kieran. The look was not returned. The man's team followed him in a mostly straight line. The first couple looked beyond Kieran to his people, but the next few only had eyes for me. A glowing ball materialized in the palm of one, and another's eyes turned bright green, a warning of some kind. I had no idea what those magics might be.

"Do all Demigod's significant others get threatened?" I mumbled, anxious shivers racking my body. It was clear many of these magical people were bored with their positions. They were trained to battle, but instead of getting to use their talents, they were relegated to offices and lavish homes while their Demigods engaged in shady dealings and behind-the-scenes maneuvering. They were ready to stretch their magical wings, and they were clearly looking for the right opponents with which to do it. Like us.

It likely wouldn't happen tonight, but we *would* be fighting. I'd have to take my magic for a spin, and I would likely be standing in front of Mordecai and Daisy, protecting them, when it happened.

"Make eye contact, but do not stop," Amber said.

Kieran's head jerked down to me. "Who is threatening you?"

"Keep your focus," Amber hissed.

Kieran glanced at the passing woman, but his gaze returned to me too quickly. He was going to leave her hanging.

Trying to compensate, not thinking, I threw her a grin and a thumbs-up. The woman, regal and elegant, with a dress of purple satin and a perfect hourglass body, frowned in confusion before her face smoothed over, ageless.

Grimacing, because *what the hell was I thinking*, I ripped my thumb out of the air. I tried to affect an expression of boredom, but the facial gymnastics probably made me look crazy. My social reflexes had not been made around important people.

"Alexis, this is not a sports stadium," Amber said, pained.

"Sorry," I said, too loudly. The woman slowed, staring at me a little longer before finally going past. "God, I suck."

"You shouldn't be threatened here, no," Kieran said, slowing as he studied my face. "I haven't felt your concern. What sort of threats were they?"

"They weren't threats," Zorn said, "so much as previews of what's to come."

"Might I remind you that, as far as the Summit is concerned," Amber said, "she is not your significant other—she is your mistress with an unsanctioned mark."

"I understand that, but she is currently walking at the front of my people, by my side, holding my hand. She should be given the courtesy of her placement if not her standing," Kieran replied. "That someone would…offer her a preview, right under my nose, is crossing a line."

"Given that you didn't notice, it is merely walking

the line, sir," Amber said. "I would guess that they were looking for a reaction. Trying to get a clue as to her power and efficiency. You must remember that very few at this Summit have encountered a Spirit Walker in the flesh. Harding was an assassin with a perfect record, but Lexi is an unknown. They'll all want to be the first one to bring down a Spirit Walker."

"The first person that tries will get a horrible surprise," Zorn said, his deep, gruff voice full of uncharacteristic humor.

"I hope I am there to see it," Amber said.

"Me too," Zorn replied.

Kieran took a deep breath, his head held high. He made eye contact with the next woman to pass, and nodded a hello to the man who followed.

"We should've gotten married before the Summit," he murmured.

I felt a strange slice of spirit cut across my middle. I bristled, but souls were everywhere—some bright, some dark, some fluctuating—and I had no idea who'd just taken a shot at me.

"We would've had to do a quickie wedding." I scanned the faces at the side—the observers who were watching people pass. More than a few regarded me curiously, but none seemed hostile. A soul flickered through the trees and bushes, jogging by, quickly out of my range. "People would've just said you were marrying me to make the mark seem more legit."

"That is certainly true—" Amber's voice caught, and I felt another slash of spirit. Judging by Kieran's face, he didn't feel a thing. "We have a middle-grade attack here. Spirit. Given we've trained with Lexi, it's more annoying than anything."

"Who?" Kieran asked, his gaze staying straight ahead, though more than a few people were trying to catch his notice.

"Don't know," she answered. "As far as I know, we haven't passed anyone who can use spirit, either on the path or along the sides. There are new faces, though. I don't know everyone. Yet."

"Someone just ran through the trees behind that wall of flowery bushes." I felt for the soul again, straining to expand my range. "Gone now, though."

"Ah. There's your answer."

I glanced ahead to see what Amber had seen.

A short man in a silk fuchsia shirt that showed off all the wrong elements of his flabby upper body walked beside a slender woman with an upturned nose and sour mouth. His team stretched out behind him, as few in number as our crew, and all of their gazes were aimed our way. The man's watery stare landed on me and stuck like glue, his eyes hungry and his mouth set in a grim line.

"Demigod Aaron," Zorn hummed, and a shock ran

through me.

"Do not engage," Amber told Kieran. "Not here. Let him pass."

But I was already cutting across the path, unable to help myself. My blood boiled. Anger made me senseless. My cats bounded up with me, keeping pace.

"Alexis," Kieran said between his teeth, trying to pull me back.

I ripped out of his hold and made a direct line toward that miserable excuse for a man.

"Because of you, my wards almost died," I said, low and rough, as soon as he was within hearing. I didn't care about politics. This was personal.

His eyes narrowed and stayed rooted to mine. "Demigod Kieran, what is the meaning of this?"

"Demigod Kieran is my boyfriend and the holder of my mark, not my keeper, and you, sir, are a cowardly little bitch who needs his balls cut off."

"I will not be spoken to that way—"

I stopped in front of him. "Nice spirit shape, by the way. You know, the one you hid behind when you showed up in the dead of night with your army, trying to kill Kieran and kidnap me? Hilarious, that shape. Does everyone know you assume the shape of a huge being with a slim waist, broad shoulders, and huge muscles? There has never been a clearer example of a man compensating for his shortcomings, if you ask me.

Love that fuchsia top, by the way—your tailor clearly loves you as much as I do."

Someone seated to the side of the path snickered.

"Demigod Kieran—"

I leaned into his face and cut him off. "Kieran will not save you from me. *No one* will save you from me. You're a desperate little man clutching at straws. Just because Demigods don't get punished by their peers for breaking the rules doesn't mean they won't get what's coming to them. Maybe not today, maybe not ten years from now, but *one day* you will stand in judgment for what you have done to me and my family. Do you hear me?"

A smile showed his white teeth and his eyes glittered with malice. "I see your threat, and I'll give you one better. One day you will belong to me, and I will make sure you'll hate your existence until the end of time. What that Lightning Bolt went through will be nothing compared to your existence strapped to my bed. Do *you* hear *me*?"

"The better question is, does your wife hear you? Because it's some bullshit to say that right in front of her. Don't you have any respect? I won't even need to kill you—hopefully she'll suffocate you in the middle of the night with a pillow. You'd deserve it."

"Alexis," Kieran barked, and I could feel the worry threading through his middle. I'd pushed my hand as far as I could.

I straightened, beating my stare straight into Aaron's head. I'd meant every word—someday I *would* have my vengeance. This clown's clock was starting to wind down.

"You might want to control your woman," Aaron said to Kieran in a lofty tone as I walked back to my place. His wife stood beside him with a bland expression and a blank stare, clearly just enduring what had to be the latest distasteful conversation in her life. "She'll get you in trouble one day."

Kieran spread his hands. "I can't really blame her. Like she said, you attacked our family in the middle of the night and almost got her kids killed. She has a right to her anger. She hasn't harmed you, though. She has not broken the rules of this promenade, which is more than I can say for you. If your person in the trees attacks us one more time, I'll let Alexis tear them down, gain control of their body, and send them right back to you in a way you won't love. Consider yourself warned."

Dead silence filtered through the scene as Aaron's face turned red. He opened his mouth for a rebuttal of some kind, but Chaos dove for his feet, batting at the golden tassels. Aaron danced away like his feet were on fire, bumping into those behind him and tripping. Chaos bounded back with the grace of a cat a quarter of his size and darted through the trees. Havoc stretched out her paw and bent to lick it, not bothered.

"Your camp is a madhouse," Aaron hollered, tripping over someone else and staggering, nearly falling. "Despicable. You'll never amount to anything in this place, I will personally make sure of it!"

Kieran looked away, exuding bored arrogance. "You'll *personally* see to it, will you? Wonderful. I won't worry, then, given you haven't been able to follow through on anything else. Wave to Amber as you pass. Your ridiculous attempts to kidnap her were laughed about at our dinner table."

Kieran walked on, channeling every bit of the cool grace and infallible confidence I'd come to expect from him. His feelings through the soul link, for a wonder, matched. He wasn't the least bit intimidated by Aaron.

"Excellent," Amber murmured when we'd passed his collection of people and the gawking bystanders to either side. We'd held up the path for so long that we'd essentially gathered an audience. "I worried that Alexis had gone too far, but that played out perfectly. He will be your number one enemy, and extremely dangerous for all of us, but if you continue to make a mockery of him, you'll discredit his naysaying of your political ideas. People will think his gripes are personal and not professional. You'll make it harder for him to tear you down."

"Magnus wasn't lying about her Chaos magic,"

Zorn said as the male cat loped back toward us. "The cats just add to the effect."

"Hence their names, yeah," Bria said from the back.

As we continued on, the number of people standing or sitting along the sides increased, leaders taking a break to watch the crowds go by. I felt the heaviness of their stares—many calculating, some curious. As I passed, their looks slid to the rest of the group, probably landing on Dylan or Jerry next, maybe Thane, one of the stars of the YouTube videos released six months ago. Kieran made eye contact with a few, nodded very seldom, and only bowed once to an important-looking woman wearing designer labels from head to toe.

"Zander," Amber murmured as a man in a tailored suit ambled toward us. His style was impeccable, from the pocket square that perfectly matched his pale pink dress shirt to the accenting tie. His graying goatee and salt-and-pepper hair didn't match his smooth face, devoid of lines or wrinkles. A polished wooden cane swung lazily from his hand and tapped the ground every so often, clearly for show. His free hand held that of an elegant woman wearing a beautiful, flowing dress without any sort of bedazzling, her hair up in a French twist, her features embellished with a touch too much makeup. Her skin nearly glowed, enhancing her loveliness tenfold, and I knew that was Zander's mark burning brightly for all to see.

A flurry of nervousness bled through the soul link. Zander had a large, thriving territory and had been well regarded within the magical world for a long time. He would be a great ally for Kieran, but from what the others had said, he was slow to make new acquaintances and much slower to trust. He voted according to his personal set of morals and principles and only backed a couple of people.

I knew for a fact that Kieran hoped to someday be one of those people.

"Remember, Zander gave nothing more than a mutual nod of respect to Valens when they occasionally met on this walk," Amber murmured. "That's typically the most he gives anyone. You should openly look at him, but do not feel slighted when he ignores you. Alexis, keep your crazy to yourself with this one. Daisy, Mordecai, if you act up, I will literally peel the skin off your hide. With a very precise knife."

I swallowed down a sudden lump in my throat. It was clear she meant that threat.

Their procession drew closer. Chatter died down to a hum, then cut to silence as people watched from the sidelines, clearly wondering what Zander would do. I couldn't tear my eyes away from Zander's wife. The serene look on her face was that of a woman in love.

Though I was probably supposed to be all stoic and arrogant and bored, I couldn't help a budding smile.

They came closer still, only twenty feet away now, and her eyes flicked to me for a moment. Another two steps and her gaze returned, the pause longer this time. And again, even longer, until she was reading my face. She was probably just trying to interpret my smile, but maybe she saw what I did—that we both had a deep connection to our partners. From what I'd witnessed, it was a rarity in this world.

Unable to contain myself, I shrugged a shoulder and then nodded in hello. It was breaking custom, I knew, but screw it. Seeing the two of them together like that, enjoying this lovely walk without needing to worry about the stakes, resonated with me. I wanted that to be Kieran and me someday. I wouldn't be threatened, or a curiosity, and Kieran wouldn't be belittled for his youth and newness. We'd just *be*.

Dare to dream, probably.

She looked away again, but a small crease formed between her eyebrows as they continued to walk. I'd messed with her *chi*. Oops.

Zander, only five paces away from Kieran, looked over. Their eyes met, and Zander slowed for a moment.

Fireworks exploded through the soul link, followed by absolute shock. Kieran bowed deeply, his arrogance quickly stripped away. I stood there stupidly, wondering if I should bow as well. I hadn't done so with anyone else, but Zander seemed like a bigger deal.

A glance back to Amber and she shook her head then showed me her teeth, her signal that I had better turn back around or she'd probably try to kill me in my sleep.

When I faced front again, Zander's wife's gaze was on my dress. My subconscious had reacted to the pressurized situation by inviting in spirit, and it was caressing my skirt. I cut it out immediately.

My face flamed as Zander's gaze switched from Kieran to me. His gaze found my chest, and I knew he wasn't checking out my rack. His look traced the invisible line connecting my middle to Kieran's. He'd clearly heard about the soul link. He wouldn't be able to verify the rumors by sight.

Zander walked on, not speeding up. Looking back, braving Amber's stare of death, I saw why.

Dylan kept his eyes front, but his jaw was clenched. I wondered if his fists were clenched as well. He was being scrutinized by a Demigod of his magical line and not loving it.

"Should I—"

"Don't you do anything," Amber ground out through her teeth. "He is merely curious. All of Zeus's line will be curious. Gianna didn't show Dylan around much. You've heard why."

"Keep walking, baby," Kieran said softly, looking straight ahead. "Stay cool and keep walking."

It wasn't until we sauntered around the bend that a loud sigh escaped from Amber.

"We made it," she said, and her stress was clear.

"You need a strong drink, woman," Zorn told her as we continued on our way.

"Don't I know it," she replied. "It was never this nail-biting…the other times I was here. Things were always planned down to the last detail, and usually everything went off without a hitch. This whole evening has been a shit show, and I've been waiting for it to smear across our faces. Why it hasn't is beyond me. I'm simply amazed it has mostly worked out."

"The chaos isn't only Alexis's doing," Zorn said. "Demigod Kieran has always had a wild streak. He's not as orderly as he'd have you think."

"Telling all my secrets, Zorn?" Kieran asked in a light tone.

"Just helping her do her job," Zorn replied.

After a brief pause in which Kieran ignored someone trying to nod at him, he asked, "Why did Zander notice me?"

"I think he was giving himself leave to check out Dylan," Zorn said.

"I'd mostly agree with that," Amber said, "though he expressed interest in Alexis, as well."

"The soul link, I think." I turned a bit to look at her. "His gaze traced the connection between our—"

She shoved my shoulder to make me face front again. Kieran had gone rigid and nervousness bled through the link.

When I saw why, I stopped dead.

Chapter 6

ALEXIS

MAGNUS, MY FATHER, sat on a bench between the draping branches of a weeping willow. A small hole had been cut into the curtain to allow the observer to watch the goings-on in relative obscurity. His crew of people were pushed in behind him, standing stock-still within the branches, hardly visible.

Zorn bumped into me, and Mordecai crashed into him. Kieran tugged at me—he'd continued walking, not yet realizing I'd stopped. The cats bounded forward, Chaos launching himself at the leaves of the willow. That cat was clearly very good at identifying the source of my distress, and very bad at knowing how best to deal with it. He batted the leaves with his big paws, seemingly playing, his claws extended. Magnus didn't so much as twitch in discomfort.

Kieran glanced back, his gaze imploring me to get moving. I cleared my throat as Magnus stood, his three-piece suit black on black again, the only pop of color his deep blue tie. His intelligent brown eyes surveyed me, the exact same color as mine, ignoring Kieran completely. I remembered his face perfectly, his strong jaw defining his features, his thin lips and slightly too big nose doing nothing to detract from his striking appearance. His charisma almost seemed like a solid thing, oozing out around him. I had never been, even in my best moments, as cool as my father. That gene hadn't been passed down.

"Alexis," he said, taking one step forward. "Please, join me. Let those behind you pass."

On wooden feet, I walked toward him, a million emotions raging through me. I'd only seen him one other time, when he'd waltzed into Lydia's house and saved the day. To say the situation between myself and my father was colored in confusion was a gross understatement. He'd started watching me before the rest of the world had taken notice, and had saved my life a handful of times in the often baffling world of spirit. But he'd only bothered to intervene at the last possible moment in our showdown at Lydia's mansion, and he was as culpable as Demigod Aaron in Jack's death, Mordecai's near-fatal attack, and Daisy's abduction. I couldn't forget that.

And yet there was no denying part of me wanted to get to know my biological father. In a perfect world, I'd form some kind of a relationship with him, maybe share a meal on a holiday.

"Hi," I said, my face practically numb.

"Hello. How has your walk been so far? Fruitful?" He looked at Kieran now, his eyes flat and distant. He was greeting Kieran exactly how Zander had not long ago.

Kieran bowed, just as deeply as before. "Quite, yes," he said when he came back up. "Thank you for taking the time."

"Your party is inspiring a lot of interest. They will have a great many challenges tomorrow. As I'm sure you know, Alexis will be open for attack until your mark is sanctified. They will come at her from all angles, wondering what a Soul Stealer's magic feels like. What she can really do. I assume this curiosity will die down quickly, given her magic is not pleasant when used correctly. Still, the initial assaults will likely be hard and fast. I realize it is none of my business professionally, but personally, I'm sure you can understand my concern. Tell me, who are you sending out with my daughter tomorrow?"

Shivers coated me upon hearing him call me that so openly. Daughter. I snaked my arm around Kieran's, needing something solid to hold on to.

Kieran bent his arm to give me better purchase. "Those you see here," he said. "My best and most trusted."

Magnus looked over Kieran's people. "Yes, good. As

I'm sure you understand, the protection I pledged to provide is no good here. No one would attempt to force her into an oath, but it's not out of the realm of possibility someone might 'accidentally' kill her. Your Lightning Bolt, too. Sometimes it is seen as preferable to eliminate a potent, rare magic rather than to face said magic."

"Understood."

"I would not be pained to lose you, but I do not want to lose her."

"Understood."

Magnus nodded and reached out his hands. Confused, I just looked at them.

He huffed out a laugh. "I mean to take your hands, Alexis. There is no trick up my sleeves, I assure you. Just a father wanting to finally, properly meet his offspring. With all the pandemonium at Lydia's…living establishment, we didn't have the chance. Now that we are here together, I'd like to construct that bridge, if you will let me."

His hands remained in the air, reaching for me. People on the path slowed to watch us, their eyes wide, and stepped to the side for a better look.

I took his hands hesitantly, hope and fear warring. He was not one to be trusted, I had to remember that, no matter how much I wanted to believe otherwise.

"Will you dine with me sometime this week?" he

asked, his eyes direct but open, his touch light. It was genuinely a request, not a command. I could turn him down if I wanted to.

I didn't want to.

"Yes," I answered, my hands shaking a little.

His small, kind smile said he felt it, but I did not miss the cunning glitter in his eyes. He knew he affected me and was clearly wondering how he could use it to his benefit. I was starting to realize how Kieran had probably felt his whole life.

"I would ask you to join me tomorrow, but you will be tired from your day." He lowered our hands before he let go. "My people will be, too. Every year they are sought out by people who wonder if they're as good as they'd expect. They are, of course. I haven't lost anyone in…years. Decades. But the constant challenges take a toll, all the same."

"If I may ask…" Kieran let his words fade away.

Magnus took a moment to turn his head, and Kieran didn't continue until he did. Another game of status.

"Do you keep your people together for the most part, or do they break off into smaller groups? I've heard differing opinions."

Magnus made Kieran wait, as though considering if he would actually answer. A moment later, he angled his head slightly, and a short woman in bright clothes came forward. I recognized her from the confrontation at Lydia's house—she was the one who'd ruthlessly manhandled the Demigod's broken arm. Her pleasant disposition was not to be trusted.

"Those with experience and useful magic, like us, usually head straight to the halls. We find it easier to travel the tight space in smaller teams," the woman said, speaking directly to me. "We can change tactics on a dime, and it's easier to get away quickly, if need be." She paused for a moment. "With larger groups, an attack can quickly devolve into chaos. You seem to do very well in uncertain situations, Alexis, so it's a tough call. In the halls, though, without much room to maneuver…you and a large group would likely amount in a disaster of some kind."

"That would've suited her mother to a T." Sadness crossed Magnus's face so fast that I wondered if I'd imagined it. I wanted to ask him about it, but it wasn't the time. He gave a nod and the woman backed away.

Kieran bowed again. "Thank you. That lays my dilemma to rest."

"She'll do whatever the moment calls for, like she always has," Magnus said, and his tone spoke of history. Of knowledge about my life. "Alexis, expect a formal invitation to dine. You may bring your beau, if it pleases you, and your wards, of course."

Not Demigod Kieran, but my beau. This could not

be mistaken for a professional engagement.

I nodded and tried to tone down the pleased flush that I felt on my cheeks.

He is not a nice man. Do not be fooled by his civility. He's a kid killer!

"Well, until we meet again." He laid his hand on my shoulder for a moment before turning onto the path. His people fell in behind him immediately, organized and in sync, a well-oiled machine. Kieran and I stayed where we were, watching them go. It wasn't long before he turned off the promenade all together. He didn't plan on checking anyone else out.

The breath gushed out of Bria. "That was…unexpected."

"That guy is super suave. Lexi, how come you didn't get any of that in your genetic makeup?" Daisy asked.

"He's making a public connection to Lexi and humoring you in the process," Amber said to Kieran, looking in the direction Magnus had exited with narrowed eyes. "He's trying to call dibs on the Soul Stealer should anything happen to you, and he's doing it in the name of family. Smart. Too bad no one else gives a damn about family ties when it concerns a magic like hers. Expect others to try to establish a personal connection with her, too. I wouldn't have turned down Magnus, given he *is* her father, but anyone else should be scrutinized before she accepts their invitation. If the asker is a single male—"

"I already know her answer if it is a single male," Kieran growled, taking my hand and heading back to the promenade.

"Lemme guess." I smiled up at him. "It's yes, right? If a single male asks me to dine alone, you'll be all for it?"

He squeezed my hand and chose to ignore me, making me giggle. "Just a little longer, love, and we'll call it a night," he said a moment later. "We've gotten more than we bargained for. I don't want to press our luck."

In a rare occurrence for the Summit, nearly all of the big dogs had come out to sit or walk. By the end of the evening, Kieran had gotten looks or nods from a great many of the people he'd planned to seek out.

By the time we got back to the warehouse-home, my feet were aching from the shoes, and stress coiled tightly within my belly. After those couple of great meetings, I'd been so worried I'd mess something up that I'd spent the time clenched up tight, barely trying to breathe.

"I'd say that was a successful start to this Summit," Jerry said as we gathered around the kitchen island.

Bria shooed away all the service staff before rooting around in the cabinets for alcohol.

"Obviously that was a success, *Jerry*," Donovan said, emphasizing Jerry's name like an accusation as he grabbed items out of the refrigerator. The joy of mocking Jerry was still going strong, made hilarious when occasionally Jerry decided to volley an insult back.

"That went smashing, *Jerry*," Thane added.

"Smashing?" Boman gave Thane a funny look. "What are you, an Englishman from yesteryear?"

"Yeah. Got a crumpet in one of your pockets?" Thane clapped back.

"Considering how often he keeps reaching into them, he probably has his balls packed away in there," Henry supplied, taking a bottle of wine from Bria and opening drawers, looking for the wine opener.

"That was beyond a successful start to the Summit." Amber sat at the small, round kitchen table in the corner and pushed open her laptop. "We have something for everyone. We have a brand-new Demigod that stole a territory from his extremely capable father, a legendary magic as feared as it is coveted, a Lightning Bolt back from the dead, a giant who must now have a reputation for the longest enduring scowl during an outing"—the guys burst out laughing—"the first Chester to ever walk the promenade, a YouTube star Berserker, and a few other people no one noticed." She leaned back and rubbed her eyes before pinning me with a severe stare. "Tomorrow you will be the most sought-after group around. I hope you heard what Magnus's team leader said about being quick. She wasn't talking about running away from a fight. If you kill someone, get the hell out of there. Don't get caught standing by the body."

"I don't get it, though," I said. "Everyone knows people die here. Why would we need to get out of there? Besides, it's not like it'll be a mystery what happened unless we kill all the witnesses."

"Killing is technically against the rules," Amber said. "When it wasn't, bodies piled up. Demigods were losing a lot of their star players. They brought in the no-death rule to keep things a bit calmer. They need to hold the rule to keep things from devolving again. Now crews attack as hard as they possibly can without actually killing. That's the game. You maim *just* on this side of living. It's a show of dominance. A few times every year, someone goes too hard, and they kill or get killed because of it. Sometimes the kill is on purpose. Regardless, it's important to keep the illusion that it was an accident. If too many people start dying, an inquisition will happen, and those aren't any fun for anyone."

I took a deep breath and nodded. Magical people weren't known for being reasonable, but at least this was a nod to law and order. Still, the fact that people routinely got away with murder so long as they walked away made it pretty clear the no-murder rule was upheld by the honor system.

"How hard do you think they're going to go at us?" Donovan asked, his smile dripping off his face.

"Treat the halls and grounds like the Colosseum of Rome. With the Demigods away, their people will play. And we'll be the biggest prize around town."

Chapter 7

ALEXIS

I FLUTTERED MY eyes open when I felt the kiss on my forehead. The morning sun filtered through the windows and dappled the hard wooden floor. Kieran leaned over me, wearing a fresh suit and smelling scrumptious.

"Come back to bed," I said, letting my magic flower around him, knowing he loved the feel of it.

He sucked in a breath and closed his eyes for a moment, letting one of his hands wander across my chest and clutch my naked breast. "I wish I could." He ran his thumb over my taut nipple. "But I have to go to work. And so do you." His eyes opened again, sparkling with desire but serious enough that I knew he wouldn't get back into bed. "Be careful today, okay? Don't look for fashion in your clothes, look for ease of movement. As everyone keeps reminding me, you're still viewed as a normal Joe, so you don't need to look the part of a Demigod's wife today."

My belly fluttered and a smile pulled at my lips. I

would probably never get used to hearing that.

He bent and kissed me. "Remember what Amber said. People will want to try their might against you, and some of them will go harder than they should. Try not to kill anyone, but if you do, get out of there quickly."

I sat up. "I know, Kieran. We've talked about this. I know what I have to do."

"I will be stuck in meetings all day, so I won't be able to help. None of the leaders will." He paused, then said, "I know everyone has been talking about status and the pecking order, but I don't care about that right now, okay? Once we're married or the mark is validated, you'll be out of this. Then we can leave the others to show what they're made of. Until then, keep yourself safe, whatever you do, okay?"

"I will." The covers dropped away as I stood.

His gaze burned down my body, lingering on my chest before catching at the strip of hair leading to the fun zone. A muscle worked in his jaw and his hands found my hips. "Heavens help me, Alexis, you are so damn beautiful."

"Five minutes," I whispered, running my palm over his pounding hardness.

With what was obviously great regret, he pulled his hands from my hips, applied them to my shoulders, and gently held me while he stepped back. "I'm already late.

Tonight I'll massage you and pamper you and then make you scream my name, I promise. Just come back to me in one piece, okay?" Seriousness stole through him again. He shook me just a little to jog me out of my haze of lust. "*Okay?*"

Reality wrapped its bone-cold fingers around my spine.

I'd seen the way those people had watched me last night. The rest of the crew, too. They'd been sizing us up, in the way people did when they were planning to take someone on.

A lot of people planned to take us on.

"It's going to be okay." Kieran pulled me into a tight hug, forcing the air out of my lungs. He could feel the trepidation burning inside me. "It's going to be fine. You aren't as green as they think you are. You've been in some hairy battles already. You've taken on Demigods and won. You can do this." He looked down into my eyes. "Fight *your* way. You have better instincts than most people, and you have my crew. You've shown time and again that you don't need me there to claim your victory. This will be a walk in the park."

I felt the lie in his words. I knew he was just trying to build me up—to bolster my confidence. Logic wasn't letting it happen.

After a deep breath, I hugged him again, gave him a bruising kiss, and stepped away. "Last chance for a quickie."

His smile was short-lived. "I'll see you tonight."

It sounded like a command.

WE DISEMBARKED FROM our golf carts in the parking lot of the Summit building. Bria stood in front of a large flatbed hand trailer piled high with bodies. I couldn't help but wonder if the bodies had been provided to us or if they'd been on our private plane yesterday. No one had told me.

"Time to split into groups," Amber said, stepping in front of the group and turning to face us.

"No," I blurted. "You should go with Kieran."

I hadn't planned on saying that, but amazingly, the only person who seemed confused was Amber. "Kieran is safe. You're the one who needs backup."

Do it your way. Fight your *way.*

"All due respect, Amber, and it is monstrous respect, but I've never fought with you. I don't have experience with you. You were really stressed by the unpredictability of our walk last night. Well, this will be ten times crazier, trust me. I think it is best if you direct Kieran's guys. They're new and untested. You'd best watch their backs. They'll get beat on, too."

She studied me silently. No one contradicted me, which made me ten times more confident. These guys wouldn't hesitate to tell me if my ideas were terrible.

They'd done it often enough in our time together. If they were going along with my play, they thought I was exactly right.

Amber nodded. "Keep your wits about you, always. If you can get away with no deaths, that's the best outcome. If you have to, kill and run."

"I know. Kieran reminded me this morning."

"You have good instincts." Her gaze was intense. "Use them. Use everything you've got. This place takes some getting used to, and Demigod Kieran will have it harder than he realizes in the political arena. He'll need a win outside of politics. If you shine, it'll up his status."

Kieran had told me the exact opposite, but he was motivated by keeping me safe. I was inclined to believe her.

"Okay, we need to dominate. No problem." I rubbed my hands together for a little friction. My stomach rolled and churned with nervousness.

"We got this, Lexi," Thane said, stepping up to put a hand on my shoulder. "We pulled a lawless giant off a mountain. We can handle a few measly teams trying to poke us with sticks."

"Agreed," Jerry said, and he would know, given he was the giant. The rest murmured their agreement as well, and I felt the group's expectations rise. Just like when we'd gone to that mountain, we were championing Kieran.

"Fine, then. Here we go." I passed Amber, taking the lead. The monstrous Summit building mostly blocked out the view of the ocean, but I could just see a corner of white, sandy beach and the sparkling azure beyond it. "Where to first? The halls? The grounds?"

"The grounds," Bria said, pulling her cart of dead bodies. "Doesn't matter what Magnus's doll said. Let's start small, work out the kinks, and work our way up. The halls are the last place we should go. That's where the most people die." The cats bounded out in front of us, each taking a side. Daisy and Mordecai filed in behind me with the rest enclosing them in a protective bubble. They would be my main concern, obviously. I would make it incredibly clear to anyone who attacked us that if they aimed for my kids, they'd walk the line of death.

"Grounds it is. Let's get our feet wet." I paused. "Where are the grounds?"

"This way." Donovan pointed, looking down at the map on his phone. "This place is huge."

Bria fell back, needing more room for her pallet of dead bodies.

"Don't get too far back," Thane said. "We have a bet going to see how long it'll take Jerry to blow chunks."

"It's a disgusting type of magic," Jerry murmured.

"What are you going to use for ammunition, Jerry?" I asked as Donovan pointed me toward an intersecting path to the left. Another group clad in leather and thick boots walked up ahead, various weapons hanging off them. I made a point of noticing each of their souls. They were too far away for me to sense their magic, something I could do because of my soul connection to Kieran.

"There are decorative rocks all over the gardens," Jerry answered. "I'll roll some along with us when we head inside."

I nodded as the group in front of us noticed our presence.

"The thing about Amber is, she is familiar with a lot of people at this thing," Donovan muttered, watching them.

"She doesn't handle things the way we handle things," Bria said from the back. "She would confuse the situation with her logic and superior strategy."

"I don't have logic and superior strategy?" Henry asked, and I couldn't tell whether he was joking.

"There is nothing superior about you, *Henry*," Jerry said, and Donovan spat out laughter.

"Says the guy used to living with a pile of bones," Henry replied.

Once we made it around the building, a lovely garden scape greeted us, not unlike that of the promenade. Weeping trees dusted the ground beside quaint stone benches. Pockets of carefully tended flowers provided pops of color and fragrance. Purple tulips lined the path and tall sunflowers pointed at the sun.

The team in front of us, twenty strong, drifted to the right, but when we got there, they were gone, having clearly darted into the trees.

Shivers crawled across my skin. No one lingered on the benches or walked along the path. Everyone was playing an adult game of hide-and-seek. When we least expected it, they would emerge and attack.

"I changed my mind." I stopped dead, not able to will myself forward. "I want to take that *out* Kieran offered me a long time ago. You know the one—where my kids and I could escape the danger of the magical world and live in peace? Do you think that offer is still valid?"

"Don't be dramatic." Daisy patted the dagger at her side.

"Really? *I* shouldn't be dramatic?" I scowled at her. She scowled back, and hers had way more attitude.

"What's our strategy?" Donovan asked, putting his phone away. "Split you and Dylan up, or keep you together?"

"Together," Dylan said immediately. "Doesn't matter what Magnus's team leader told us. We're stronger together."

I nodded, watching the trees shiver in the breeze.

"We're all stronger together." Mordecai shed his

clothes and handed them to Bria. She stuffed them in a bag and tossed it onto the pile of dead. Jerry's face lost a little more color. "We eat together, we hang out together, we laugh together. We are a pack, and as a pack we excel. The total is greater than the sum of its parts."

"Frodo is right, though he got that cliché wrong," Daisy said, and it was a nice little trip down memory lane to hear her throw *Lord of the Rings* insults at Mordie. "We do everything together, including training. We aren't organized at all, but that seems to work for us. It always has in the past, anyway."

"Agreed," Jerry said.

"We stick together." Zorn adjusted the machete strapped to his back. I wasn't sure he'd gotten the memo that we *weren't* supposed to kill people.

I stared down the empty path. "Okay." Chaos stood in the middle of the walkway, stock-still, staring at something to the side. His tail twitched, and then he pounced, two front paws smashing into the bushes. Havoc sat behind him, watching. Nothing scurried away. "Do we take the walkway or go guerilla style through the trees?"

Silence greeted my answer. No one wanted to weigh in on that one.

"Fuck 'em. Let them come to us," I finally said, starting forward. "Let them think they're being sneaky and hiding. I'll feel them before they can see me."

"Beware the more open areas," Dylan said. "You don't have the farthest reach."

"I have a much farther reach, and there are plenty of rocks in this lackluster garden. We're good." Jerry's tone held both confidence and disgust, and I remembered his fiancée used to have plant magic. Apparently her gardens had far exceeded this one, which was hard for me to imagine.

"Speaking of a good reach, do you feel anyone?" I started forward, my heart beating faster than normal, pumping adrenaline through my body. I did better in the thick of things—this slow burn of anticipation was eating me alive.

"Yes. Many. They are mostly in clusters with ample space between them. The clusters are moving slowly, almost like they are scared to engage."

"They probably are. I'm scared to engage," I mumbled.

The second Mordecai shifted into his wolf form, the cats turned to stare, their glowing eyes eerie in this beautiful place. He trotted out to meet them, playing sentinel. I let him, since he was well within my range and I'd feel someone before they happened upon him.

A few minutes trickled by, then several more. Nothing happened as we walked. No one emerged or even moved in our direction. The clusters Jerry could feel continued to slowly move through the trees, avoiding conflict.

As we approached a bend, though, my senses went on high alert. A group of souls were lying wait in the trees and bushes ahead of us. They were completely hidden from view, and it would've been an excellent surprise attack if I hadn't felt their souls burning brightly.

Jerry must've sensed them, too, and slid a look my way, probably making sure I had.

"Up ahead," I whispered, trying not to move my mouth.

"What?" Donovan asked, leaning closer. Clearly I needed to work on the subtlety thing.

The cats slowed and Mordecai jogged back to us, his hazel eyes on me.

"Anyone speak shifter?" I asked, wishing Jack were here.

"He's alerting you that someone is in those trees," Daisy whispered, her voice as strong as iron. If she were in any way nervous, she did not show it.

"And the cats are alerting the people in those trees that we know about them," Zorn growled.

One of the souls shifted, the rustle giving them away. So they were better at hiding than stalking.

A little closer and I could tell they were mostly weak level fives and high level fours. Which meant they didn't belong to any high-status Demigods—or if they did, these were considered lackeys.

"I'll make us disappear." Boman pushed up through the group and took Donovan's position. His Light Bender magic wrapped around us like a curtain, hazing our view. The cats had been left out, still standing and looking at the hiding enemy.

They could defend themselves.

"What should we do, just walk along until they jump out?" The Line throbbed just off to my side. I could make them run, easily enough, but I wanted to keep my magic under wraps. People knew, broadly, what I could do, but some of my abilities would come as a surprise. I wanted to preserve that element of surprise for when the more advanced teams came at us.

"I can break a leg with a rock, if you want," Jerry whispered.

"I can break a branch off and take out a mouthful of teeth," Donovan murmured.

"I can go stick knives in all of them," offered Red, who'd remained silent up until now.

"Red, you go." I motioned her on. "Boman, cover her until she's out of sight."

In a flash, Red was running to the side, slipping into the trees under Boman's Light Bender magic. We walked along a little more, and another soul shifted position, edging closer to the path. I heard a scrape of a shoe.

"They're useless," Zorn said. "They shouldn't be in this place. They'll be killed in no time."

"Or maybe we shouldn't be in this garden with all the kindergartners," Daisy said, tapping her fingers against the throwing knives strapped to her left leg.

"That's probably more like it." Donovan cracked his neck, his eyes hard, preparing for battle.

I felt Red moving around the others, coming at them from behind. In a moment, she burst into their cluster.

The leaves and bushes shook. Screaming drifted out through the trees. Someone yelled for them to flee. Another asked where the onslaught was coming from. These people clearly had zero experience.

"Havoc, Chaos, Mordecai, help send them on their way," I shouted, walking faster now, my blood pumping in my ears like a battle drum. "Remember. No killing."

Havoc launched forward, and then the screams increased in pitch. Chaos bounded into the greenery with a deep growl that did not match his cute, fluffy exterior. Mordecai darted in at the side, taking the flank as the cats assaulted our would-be attackers head-on. Red whirled in the middle, barely visible in the thick foliage, looking like a tornado in the trees.

A man stumbled out of the melee and onto the walkway. The sun sparkled along the glistening blood running down his temple. He staggered and then his legs buckled, dumping him onto the concrete. A woman ran past, bleeding from three different locations. She didn't so much as look at her fallen teammate. The others scattered deeper into the garden, all different directions, no two people sticking together, until they were out of my range.

Red strolled out of the trees, wiping her blade on a black rag before tucking the dirty cloth into her belt. She stopped beside the man cowering on the ground. The cats and Mordecai slunk out from the greenery next, surrounding the man.

Boman pulled our cover away. Zorn shoved me forward so I was in the lead.

"Pl-please." The man looked around wildly, his eyes rounded. Havoc stopped near his feet and lowered her head, crimson splattered across her furry, snow-white face. He yanked his feet in tighter to his body. "Please do-don't hurt me."

Zorn shoved me forward again, and I took the hint, walking toward the man, no idea what I was supposed to do when I got there.

The man caught my movement, contorted so he could look my way, and started to shake. "Pl-please, I'm sor-sorry. Please don't hurt me."

"What in the ever-loving hell…" Jerry's confused muttering drifted away.

"He's begging," Boman said. "This dude does not

belong at this summit."

Taking a page out of Mick's book from the bar back home, I flung my hand like an old man trying to get kids or dogs off his lawn. "*Git!* Begone! I don't want to see you here again."

"Y-yes, ma'am. Thank you. Th-thank you, ma'am." The guy struggled to get up and groaned, clutching his side.

"This is hard to watch," Thane whispered. "It's a bit much."

Blood gushed from the man's side and ran over his hip. He doubled over, clearly in pain, and only managed two small steps before the strength went out of him again. He collapsed, whimpering, and curled up in a bleeding ball on the concrete.

"What's with the dramatics?" Daisy asked.

"Are we sure he has a blood oath and can heal?" I asked, worried we may have accidentally killed him.

Boman grimaced. The others shifted uncertainly.

I'd be damned if the very first battle ended in a death. "Havoc, Chaos, Mordecai—go round up one of his teammates. He needs to be taken to get medical attention. Zorn, go with them in gas form. If they can't corral someone, force them back, understood? We'll stay here and wait. Don't take long."

The cats wasted no time, able to understand me as well as Mordecai could, something I'd learned not to question. They bounded into the trees, Mordecai on their heels, and Zorn poofed into nothing.

"I mean…or we could just walk on. Nobody would blink about a guy bleeding out," Bria said, eyeing her hand trailer. "Everyone knows the risks when you bring someone without an oath."

"Don't you dare call *dibs* on him," Jerry ground out. Donovan and Boman snickered.

I rounded on her, incredulous. "Then why the hell are you here?"

She palmed her chest. "I'm a Necromancer. We play with spirits and cadavers. It's like I said, we're usually left alone. Red is probably fucked, though."

"I'm good." Red tucked away her cleaned knife. "This place is less dangerous than anything we've done as a group so far."

"True," Bria said as souls entered my radar again. "Though you had a helluva time healing after Lydia's thing."

Largely because she'd fought Thane in his Berserker state.

"I don't know how many times I can say sorry for that." He frowned. "I sent flowers. Chocolates. I gave massages, even. What else can I do?"

"Shut up about it, maybe," Red responded. "She wasn't talking to you."

Zorn emerged from the trees, dragging a couple of

terrified level fours, a man and a woman, by their upper arms. Mordie and the cats trailed behind him.

"The Soul Stealer is too sweet by half. She is sparing this waste of flesh." Zorn pushed the people at the cowering man. The injured man whimpered, his face ashen. "Get this sad sack some help. Looks like he's about to bleed out."

The guy's teammates stared at him for a moment, wide-eyed. Their gazes found me a moment later.

"Well?" I motioned at him. "You'd really run off and leave one of your own behind? Help him out, for God's sake! Hurry up."

The woman blinked slowly. She nudged the man beside her. "Thank you," she murmured, and grabbed the fallen guy roughly.

The other man bent to help, no gentler.

"Ow," the cowering man bleated, then followed it up with a long groan as the second man slung him over his wide shoulder.

"How deep did you stab that guy, Red?" Bria asked with a crooked grin.

She stared after them, disappearing into the trees. "I mean…pretty deep, but it wasn't worth all that agony. That guy is as green as they come. Or a pet of some sort. He shouldn't be out here."

"He doesn't have a choice." Zorn straightened his shirt over his broad chest. "If you are brought as part of a crew, you have no choice but to fight. That's how it goes. Those who cower in their living quarters will lower the status of their leader and pay the price for doing so. Come on, this garden is ridiculous. Let's check out the main building."

I didn't budge from my spot. "Upping the challenge is also upping the danger. Let's meet a couple of other groups first. We can cut through the trees and seek them out to get the show on the road."

"You're just putting off the inevitable, Lexi," Bria said.

"I agree," Boman said, his hands on his hips. "This isn't the right place for us. Now we know. We need to move up a level and reassess. It's inevitable we'll end up there anyway. Let's not drain our energy first."

I gave the trees a longing look and then heaved a sigh, knowing he was right.

"Fine. But just *one* step up. I'm not ready to face the halls yet."

Chapter 8

KIERAN

"AS EASY AS you thought it would be?" Dara grinned at Kieran as they broke for lunch. The meeting hall was decked out in finery, from the plush velvet seats to the glittering chandelier hanging down the middle. But he'd been too busy soaking everything in to notice the details of his surroundings. His empty coffee cup sat at the edge of his desk space beside his open laptop, already running low on battery. Five pages of single-spaced notes, haphazardly organized with slashes and bullet points, filled his screen.

He pushed the laptop closed and tucked it into his backpack. He'd need to plug it in when they reconvened for another grueling session.

"Just as, yeah." Kieran allowed himself a sigh and rolled his shoulders, something he knew he could get away with, given he'd seen Magnus and Zander both do it.

"You didn't say too much." She jerked her head to get him walking.

"I had nothing of value to add." He slung his cross-body satchel over his shoulder and affixed his suit button.

Kieran nodded to Demigod Flora, the Demigod he'd beaten to secure Dylan, and received a slight bow in return. He was too tired to care about how good that looked.

Demigod Lydia slipped by, her head down and her hair covering the scars still evident on her face. She wove between the other leaders without acknowledging anyone.

She is beat. She'll be useless within a decade.

Kieran let his father's voice slide right by. It had come much less frequently today than last night as Kieran got more acquainted with his role here.

He turned his head away to ignore Lydia. At the edge of his vision he glimpsed a somewhat glimmering, hazy area. It almost looked like Zorn's gaseous form.

Kieran squinted, trying to peer past the throng of leaders to get another glance. It wasn't Zorn, he knew, who was downstairs somewhere, clustered with Lexi and the others, but Kieran could've sworn it was the same magical look as his friend's gas form. Something rarely seen this side of the fae border. But when the throng of people opened up again, allowing him to see better, nothing was there. His mind was clearly playing tricks. Not surprising, given how mentally exhausted he was.

Lexi's momentary worry last night drifted into his mind. Frowning, he moved to see one last time. It was no use, though. Not to mention Lexi could still feel Zorn's soul in his gaseous form. The two issues couldn't be connected. Right?

He turned his attention back to Dara, somewhat surprised she was heading to lunch with him instead of her other friends. He was thankful, though. As far as status went, he knew where he should be—on the outskirts with almost zero pull—but that didn't fit the way he'd been acknowledged by the big players. He had the feeling no one knew what to do with him, and so he'd take his cues from Dara.

Take every advantage you can. Climb every stair offered, no matter how distasteful, until you make it to the top. Once you are powerful, you can avenge any wrongs dealt you during your rise.

His father had never put much stock in morals.

"It's a good sign…that you kept quiet when you didn't have anything to say. A lot of newbies aren't so wise." Dara glanced at him. "I may not like the parts of you that are so…heavily trained, but I trust this man beside me. I trust that I can speak to him about my concerns, and he will hear me. I trust the leader that garners such loyalty from his inner circle. Everything else is details. I think aligning with you will help me the most. I feel it in my gut."

"Ah. Now we come to the crux of the situation."

"Yep. You didn't think I was doing this for you, did you?"

He chuckled as she led the way into another room—a dining area set up for lunch. Dozens of single-occupant tables were arranged in tiers so as to give everyone a view of the open-air courtyard down below.

The courtyard was as fastidiously maintained as the gardens outside, and it had clearly been designed to provide ammunition for various magics, from the vines climbing the back wall to the deep pool of water in the corner, surrounded by rocks and metallic objects.

Red splotches marred the gray gravel path running through the space.

It was then he noticed the woman pulling herself along the floor, her right arm not working, her leg mangled. A thick line of crimson trailed in her wake.

No one reacted or moved to help her.

Kieran's stomach flipped over. The leaders would enjoy their lunches while watching various teams battle for dominance. There was very little chance anyone would die under their watchful eyes, but seeing that badly wounded woman pull herself along did something to him.

"You okay?" Dara sat at one of the tables, three rows from the lip of the balcony.

He hesitated next to the individual table beside her. He might've gotten a few nods and a couple of glances from the big dogs, but this was way, *way* above his position. Dara might be a level five, but she was respected. She had history here. No way should he be allowed to sit next to her. He'd said barely a dozen sentences all morning, choosing instead to try to take in all the incredible nuances of the problems being discussed. He certainly hadn't given anyone cause to believe in his political future. Nothing so far should've elevated him this high. Nothing.

Take the seat, his father's voice shouted.

"You're okay there," Dara said quietly, looking straight ahead.

Kieran's heart hammered, as though someone might forcefully remove him at any moment. "But..."

Magnus trod down the steps at the side of the room, heading toward the front row. He glanced up as he passed, taking in Kieran's hesitation. His nod was so slight that Kieran wasn't sure it was meant for him.

"Sit," Dara said through clenched teeth.

Not wanting to lose the opportunity, he lowered as quickly as he could, fighting the desire to wipe the nervous sweat from his brow.

"I shouldn't be here," he whispered as Demigod Larigold, as regal as they came, made her way to the front row.

"Honestly, Kieran, no one knows where you fit." Dara took a menu from the waiter who'd stopped in front of her. Kieran took one next. Demigod Phyllis sat at the table next to him, her jowls shaking as she got settled. She smiled in greeting at him and took her own menu. If she thought he didn't belong, she gave no sign of it.

Below, the woman in the courtyard still pulled herself along, the trail of blood seeming unnaturally bright.

Before Lexi, he would have barely noticed that woman. He wouldn't have had the urge to send someone to help her, or to lift her up and take her to get care. He would've only taken note that she'd lost her battle.

As a young playboy with no thought of a political future, he'd traveled the globe and visited many in the magical community. Battles like this, on a much smaller scale, were used for entertainment. Often the combatants were poor and unimportant, chosen for their desperation and for the fact that no one would miss them if they didn't make it out alive.

Now all he could think about was how unnecessary this was, leaving that woman to fend for herself. How brutal and twisted. Didn't her team want to help her? The woman was already beaten, so why demoralize her as well? It wouldn't make her better—it would only make her bitter, fearful of messing up, and more prone to snap. It would drag the team down as a whole.

He'd never realized the degree to which Lexi had changed him until this moment. He'd never been more thankful.

"Kieran?"

It took him a moment to realize Dara was still talking to him.

"Sorry, excuse me, what was that?" He leaned back, forcing himself to relax.

"I was saying, you've already earned your stripes and then some. You haven't even held your territory for a year and you've already improved it. Valens was known as one of the best businessmen around. For you to improve upon a thriving territory is pretty spectacular. That alone is blowing people away. You also turned a sticky situation with Magnus into…whatever is going on now. Did I hear right, he wants to have a father-daughter dinner? What happened to killing all his kids?" She shook her head when he didn't answer. "You're not following the norms, and you're not shy about using your power and might. It's exhilarating to watch, and so far it's worked for you, but I think everyone is kinda holding their breath for you to mess up, you know?"

"Basically, I am walking on a dagger's edge, and if I misstep, I'll cut my nuts off."

She laughed and leaned back so a younger guy with a tray of water could place a glass before her. "It won't be you doing the slicing, but yes, basically."

"What in the ever-loving fuck?"

It took Kieran a moment to recognize that voice. It took him another moment to clue into Lexi's proximity. His mind had been spinning from the overload of information this morning, and since he'd only felt mild anxiety through the link, he'd let her drift to the back of his mind.

Now, she came roaring back, front and center.

"What is she doing here?" he asked, sitting up as straight as he could so as to see down onto the battle-field floor.

"Apparently someone thought she'd be good enter-tainment for us today." Dara gave him a grim look. "She has a blood offering, right? She will heal?"

"Yes—"

"Who does this woman belong to?" Lexi strutted out into the center of the open space, stopping beside the woman dragging herself along. Her face showed all the disappointment and annoyance she usually reserved for Daisy and Mordecai when they were caught doing something wrong.

Zander, walking down the side of the room with Juri on his arm, flinched at the outburst. Magnus turned in his seat, just barely, and glanced back at Kieran. That look was clear—Kieran was doing a piss-poor job of teaching Lexi to color inside the lines.

Right then, Kieran was feeling the press of that dag-ger's edge beneath his feet.

Chapter 9

ALEXIS

"LEAVE HER BE," Zorn said in a low tone, standing off to the side with everyone else. The wounded woman was the only one on the battlefield, left there by her teammates.

I breathed slowly through my nose, trying to calm down.

So far, everything had seemed very organized inside the Summit building. A staff person had greeted us at the door and asked us to sign in so we could battle other teams in the few spacious courtyards. Upon learning who we were, he had looked us over, counted us up, and shepherded us off. The situation had seemed so mundane, so practiced, that I'd forgotten what sort of world I now lived in.

Three teams of people waited off to the side of the courtyard—our crew and our soon-to-be opponents, fresh and ready to do battle, plus this poor woman's team. The others were bleeding and broken, too, but none of them had suffered as much damage.

Not a soul seemed to give a damn about her. It was the scene in the garden all over again, only this time no one had run away in fear—this time, they were watching the show.

What was with these magical people? There they waited, strong enough to carry their teammate but hanging out off to the side so she could drag herself off the battlefield.

Fire rose through my middle. Why would they want to demoralize a teammate? What possible good could come of it? I couldn't imagine leaving Bria to drag herself away like this. Or Boman or Thane, or any of them. It was bullshit.

I rounded on her teammates. "Why don't you help her?"

A man with a face like the bottom of a shoe after it stepped in dog poop sneered at me. "What business is it of yours?"

"Don't you give a shit about her?" I demanded.

"She's learning what it's like to lose," the man said, lacking an ounce of sympathy.

"No, what she's learning is that she's on her own. Do you know what that means?" I paused for a moment, *this close* to gripping his soul and forcing him to his knees. When he stared at me silently, arrogantly, humoring me, I continued. "It means your team won't be a team at all—it'll be a collection of individuals.

When it comes to survival, each individual will only look out for number one. If that means another teammate goes down, well, at least it wasn't them, huh? At least *they* weren't the ones dragging their bleeding asses across the gravel." I pointed down at her. "*This* makes you weak. All of you. This is a stupid and despicable thing for a team leader to allow. Are you that team leader?"

He continued to stare, looking at me like I was nothing.

Anger turned my vision red. The cats came to sit by my side. Laughter bubbled up, the situation so absurd I was momentarily at a loss for words.

"You're a fool," I spat out. "She's not the only one who lost the practice fight. All of you did, you dumb shit. If we take care of our team today, they will take care of us tomorrow." I shook my head. "I'd offer to find you in the halls to teach you a lesson—make you drag *your* stupid ass around—but none of you are up to it, clearly. If you ever want someone to ring your bell, though"—I spread my hands wide—"I volunteer."

I sighed and looked down at the woman, her face incredibly pale. She'd lost a lot of blood.

"Jerry, help me," I said. "She's enormous."

The woman lifted her bleary eyes to me, but she didn't say anything. In her weakened state, it looked like it took everything she had not to pass out.

Jerry strutted out, all shoulder and brawn. When he met me beside the woman, his hard mask dissolved into one of sympathy. He helped me gently hoist her up, taking care not to touch her ripped-up limbs, and carried her to the side.

Absolute silence rang through the large area as I returned to the middle of the space, ready for battle. I was fired up now. I was ready to bust some heads. This place was ridiculous, the setup shameful, and now I wanted to let off some steam.

It took me a long moment to realize we had an audience. They'd been there the whole time, and I'd been so focused on all that blood, and all that pain, that I hadn't noticed.

It took me another moment to realize Kieran was in that crowd, looking down on me with pride swelling through the link. Magnus was there, too, his mouth a thin line of disapproval.

I stared at Magnus for a moment, not backing down. If he considered doing the right thing weak or out of character for a magical person, then we'd just have to agree to disagree. Or, hell, maybe we could get in a loud, drunken argument at a holiday dinner. That would make us family if nothing else could.

"Now that you're done making a show of yourself, can we get started?" Zorn asked as he stalked into what I now thought of as an arena.

I motioned for Daisy and Mordecai to get out of the space as Bria wheeled in her bodies and unstrung her backpack.

"They must participate," the man with the clipboard said as the opposing team spread out along the sides of the arena, one hunkering in a solitary bush.

"They are teenagers and one doesn't have a blood bond or any magic. They were not signed up. They will wait outside," I said.

The man looked at me steadily, almost bored. "They entered the room, and so they will participate."

"Door is still open. Daisy, Mordecai, get out of here!" I hollered.

The man turned, walked out the door, and shut it behind him before the kids had moved a muscle. The lock clicked over.

I started laughing, near tears. The Demigods looked down with flat faces, not an ounce of emotion between them, Zander's wife among them. Apparently, her love was just for her husband.

"Do none of you have children?" I demanded, looking up. "This seems legit to you?"

"It's fine, Lexi, we got this." Dylan took my arm. "Don't beseech the Demigods—they're as far removed from decency as a pack of people can get. We can handle this on our own. No one will touch the kids, I swear it." He turned me away, and I felt the turmoil within Kieran. Given he wasn't saying anything, I shoved our connection to the back of my mind. He was no help to me, clearly. "You can drop everyone to their knees, and I can fry them. Nothing to it."

"Mordecai has the blood offering so keep Daisy in the middle," Donovan said, jogging to her far side. Jerry stepped to her other side, and the ground beneath us rumbled. "Lexi, in back. You'll end it too quickly. Let's have a little sport. These very important people want a show."

"Do we want animated cadavers, or no?" Bria asked, kneeling beside her open backpack.

Rather than wait for Bria's magic, slower and clunkier than mine, I reached for the spirits I trusted, pulling Jack to me first, then John, Chad, and Mia. I stuffed them into bodies and started them out of the cart. Then I grabbed some of the other spirits who hung around our house, crazy ones driven mad by Valens's imprisonment, and gave them body suits. I even grabbed Frank, just because he could throw a wrench in anyone's plans. I wanted them all running around, causing a ruckus.

As my team fanned out around a very annoyed Daisy, who did *not* want to be protected, I walked to the side, in full view of the Demigods.

Nervous anticipation bubbled through my middle and set loose butterflies in my stomach, a feeling I always got before everything went haywire. Now was a great time for it. If these people wanted a show, I would damn sure give them one.

"We ready?" I asked my team as our opponents braced themselves, their eyes tracking the newly animated bodies. They'd clearly never seen a Necromancer get to work so quickly.

"Lexi, what's going on? Where am I?" Jack said, jerking and rocking, trying to get a lock on his new digs.

"Alexis Price, I was having a nice little day there, looking at the ocean. Why am I in a dead man's skin suit?" Frank hollered.

John and Chad stood mostly still behind Jack, having much more experience. Mia hung back, watching the enemy. She didn't need her legs; she had her magic to transport her from point A to point B.

"Great googly moogly, who'd you stuff in those?" Bria asked as I marched the crazier spirits off to the side, jerking and screaming and trying to beat on the walls, themselves, or each other. Only I could hear the screaming, since they were spirits and their dead bodies didn't have working voice boxes, but their movements sold the effect.

"A few who will provide great distraction," I said. "What do we do now, wait for a whistle?"

"I don't want any part of this," Frank grumbled. "How do I get out of this thing?"

"We raise hell," Thane said, standing in the back with his arms crossed, as calm as could be. He wouldn't be going full Berserk, I had faith in that. He knew better than to turn when we were trapped with him.

"Okay, then," I said, raising my voice. "Take 'em down!"

I set the bodies loose, and they sprinted forward, or to the side, or jumped around and waved their arms.

"Where's Kieran?" Jack asked, not going active yet. He clearly hadn't looked up.

I shoved him at the enemies behind Chad and John, who'd already started to run forward. "Give 'em hell, Jack!"

One of our opponents stalked to the center, an enormous man with muscles for days, blond hair, and a cleft in his chin. His biceps were so big that I wondered how he scratched his face.

He bent at the waist and flexed, like a bodybuilder. I couldn't help cocking my head at him in confusion. Was this a battle, or a muscle show?

"Someone from Hercules's line, I bet," Bria said, pulling out her knives. "They can pose a problem in hand-to-hand combat, but they're not good for much else. That fool doesn't know what he's gotten himself into. What a gas."

Mia disappeared, and I heard tables and chairs scraping against the balcony, people leaning forward in surprise.

"I got this." Red ripped out a knife, but before she could start forward, Mia reappeared beside the big man. She threw her arms around him, barely able to wrap those dead limbs around his big waist. He had little time to startle before they disappeared again.

"He's got an Apporter, too?" I heard one of the surprised leaders exclaim.

I could barely hear Magnus's answering drawl. "The Apporter is a spirit—a powerful one—and the Spirit Walker has it under her control."

One flowering vine rose into the air, then another, reaching out toward Thane, who was leaning against the wall. He watched their progress but didn't move.

Mia reappeared fifty feet above the ground. She opened her arms and disappeared again.

"Ohhh shiiiit!" The muscular man's arms windmilled. His curse turned into a high-pitched scream.

Jerry sent a rock flying through the air. It smashed into the woman hiding behind the solitary bush. She cried out, slammed backward. The rock rose and smashed into her a second time. The vines dropped from the air, one of them having nearly reached a very unconcerned Thane.

Darts sprayed through the air as the Hercules man slapped against the ground. His head bounced and his body went limp.

Mia popped back next to me, sagging. That had taken a lot of her energy.

"You better not have just killed that man, Mia," I said through gritted teeth, knowing those in the balcony would think I'd instigated the attack, since Magnus had claimed I was in control.

"He'll heal. Another ten feet and he would've died," she replied. Hopefully she was correct.

Donovan knocked the darts to the side with his telekinetic magic, now standing in front of Daisy. Mordecai was pressed against her leg, not allowing her to shove him off.

Dylan lifted his hands, and for a moment, everyone visibly quailed. Lightning crackled, slicing from the parallel walls, catching two of our opponents in the crossfire.

"A Demigod is blocking me from gathering the clouds," he yelled, making lightning zip across the ground, something he'd said was incredibly difficult. He was showing off. It fizzed across the pool of water and reached a man who stood with his hands out and fingers splayed, like a sorcerer. Electricity sizzled up his leg. He screamed, convulsing, as a second wave of darts sprayed from his hands. I didn't know what kind of magic that was, but he wasn't going to use it any more today.

Donovan already had the first round of darts

pushed out of the way, and he quickly went to work on the second. Boman sliced light across a guy in the far back who hadn't shown us any magic yet, burning a hole in his chest. The man screamed and beat at himself before Boman hit him with another.

A bright flare lit up the sky, so intense I had to rip my eyes away. It beat down on us, turning the world white, blocking my vision. When the light finally faded, I was confused to see a desert oasis under my feet, as if Mia had transported me somewhere else.

This wasn't my first hallucinogenic rodeo.

I pulled power from the Line and grabbed up all the opponents' souls.

"Lexi, we need to see," Boman yelled.

Power pumped through me. Unseen eyes turned my way, spirit watchers hanging out behind the veil, just outside of my field of vision. I ignored them. This had happened a lot since the showdown at Lydia's place. I'd always assumed it was my father, but since he was currently staring down at me from his table on the balcony, probably not.

I took a deep breath, tempered my power so I didn't kill anyone, and softly *yanked*. Souls clattered against casings, and in a one-two punch, I sliced the outsides of said casings. These people were getting it in two different ways—both horrible, both painful, neither life-threatening.

Shouts and screams filled the arena, and the illusion of the desert cut off immediately. The opponents fell to their knees or sides, clutching their middles and rolling. Not one of them still stood. No one even looked our way.

Havoc roared, and I knew the effect would be flapping those souls in their casings. Chaos bounded forward to use his claws.

"No!" I shouted as another wave of shouts and screams filled the arena. The guy with the darts screamed so loud and long that his voice turned hoarse. He kicked at an invisible enemy. "Havoc, Chaos, desist!"

I could barely hear myself over the man's screaming, though the cats obliged, looking back at me. Still the man screamed, now clawing at his chest, his face.

"Knock him out—he's consumed with fear," I shouted.

Red was there in a moment, happy to oblige. Bria jogged forward, knives out, still on the offensive. The guys, too, were readying for another attack.

"Stop! What are you doing?" I shouted. "They're down. It's over."

Bria paused over a man curled in on himself, ready to poke holes in him. One of the crazy zombies ran by, screaming for no reason. A man sobbed in the corner. A woman rolled back and forth, whimpering, clutching her chest. Not one of the opponents was trying to get up.

"We need to take the rest of them out to prove our victory. That's how it's done," Bria said.

Over the din I could hear seats groaning from the balcony as people moved around. They'd come for blood and wouldn't be satisfied until we gave it to them.

They could suck it.

In a real battle, when the enemy was subdued, that was it. You walked away. You didn't continue to fight for the fun of it. You didn't have an audience. Hell, you were just happy to be alive.

I elevated my voice so everyone would be sure to hear. "Leave them. They don't need to be bloody to prove who won. They've had enough."

"Finish them!" someone yelled from the balcony.

I turned and faced the bloodthirsty Demigods and leaders. "No," I said in a clear voice. "The battle is decided. It's finished."

"We say when this battle is done, not them. We rule," another shouted from the back somewhere. "Make them finish it."

"The battle is over." Kieran stood, his eyes on me for a moment before they swept the balcony. He was late to the party, but he was finally showing up to do the right thing. "Alexis enacted a punishment far worse than physical wounds. It will stay on their minds long after they have healed. This battle is done. If she continues, those people down there will lose their minds. I've seen it happen. They would have to be killed. She is not showing them mercy—she is protecting their lives, as the rules clearly state she should."

I was totally showing them mercy, which he knew, but if this was the way he needed to spin it to get the leaders in line, more power to him, especially since he wasn't wrong. Dart Fingers might already be too far gone.

Silence greeted Kieran, the people in the back not pressing their thirst for blood.

Zander's voice rang out. "Agreed. The battle is done."

"Agreed," his wife said quickly.

"Agreed," said the very regal lady we'd seen last night, sitting on Zander's other side.

"Agreed," Magnus added.

Others took up the call, everyone stating the word plainly or mumbling it. The door opened and the clipboard-carrying dickface reemerged.

Thane pushed away from the wall. "I say we get all the people in the halls to move out to the garden so I can play, too."

"Lexi, whoa, whoa, whoa…" Bria pointed at the zombies still running around the place like wild men. "Put those back."

I marched them back to keep Jerry from having to help load up the bodies. I didn't want him throwing up in front of all those Demigods.

"Was she controlling all of those while doing her magic?" someone asked from the balcony.

I didn't respond, letting them think that I did. It made me look cooler, probably.

"Oh my stars, look at all those Demigods," Frank said, marshaled back to the cart with everyone else. "I would like to mention that I detest wearing one of these skin suits, Alexis, and I am not the fighting type, but wow is it impressive to see all those Demigods. Look at them, all prim and proper and dressed nice. You should take a lesson, girlie, they—"

I ripped him out of the body and flung him back toward home. My nerves were already frayed—I didn't need him adding to the irritation. I got the rest of the bodies packed away and sent the rest of the spirits back, getting nods from Chad and John, a tired wave from Mia, and a demand from Jack to let him stay. He didn't care about the danger, but I did. Not gonna happen.

Tired, I headed toward the others, sparing a glance for Kieran as I left. He was sitting again, staring down at me intently. A waiter interrupted our view, and I noticed Aaron and Lydia were also looking at me from opposite sides of the second row. Both of them stared down at me with mingled hatred and desire—they wanted me for their arsenal now more than ever.

I shivered, knowing in my bones that one or both of them had something nasty planned for me. Would I meet their teams in the halls? Or would I meet them in person when I didn't have the protection of a Demigod at my back?

Chapter 10

ALEXIS

"WELL, THAT WENT about as expected." Bria pulled the bodies along behind her as we trudged toward the halls, the treacherous labyrinth at the outskirts of the large building. The middle of the building, I was finding, was reserved for the Demigods and the staff they brought along for protection, their second-string people in many cases, with only a few of their top tier. Demigod-on-Demigod crime was very rare at a Summit. The more experienced staff did what we were doing now—looking for a fight.

"We were chosen specifically to fight in front of the Demigods," Dylan said, his eyes constantly scanning. "That's a big honor in most situations." He paused, giving me a side-eye. "Most people realize the Demigods want to see blood. They look more favorably on those who give them a grueling, bloody fight."

Donovan laughed. "Lexi's not the type to fall in line, brother."

"I need to grab a few rocks before we get where

we're going, by the way," Jerry said. "What are we doing with these kids? Can we drop them off? I don't like the idea of the princess being with us without superior healing. She shouldn't have been in that battle just now."

"You're big, giant. If you keep using that nickname, soon we'll find out how hard you fall," Daisy ground out.

Jerry's wide grin made me smile with him. He might not partake in the razzing with the guys all that often, but he loved to push Daisy's buttons. He probably wanted to see what she'd eventually do in retaliation. I wondered myself.

"That battle was light," Henry said. "I didn't have to do anything. I wonder why they didn't put us with someone of higher caliber."

"They don't have any idea what we can do," Boman responded. "They probably thought we'd be evenly matched. It's like Dylan said: the Demigods prefer longer, bloodier battles."

"Ours was beyond quick," Bria said. "I didn't get to do anything either. The Soul Stealer stole my shit."

"The battles will get harder. All the more reason for the kids to stay out of it," Jerry said.

Mordecai growled softly.

"Yes, Fido, we know you want to fight." Daisy patted his head and his ears flattened back. He was not happy with the treatment.

Donovan's smile at their antics was short-lived. "The kids need to come. Daisy has to prove she can exist in a magical environment—the summit's words, not Kieran's. I don't entirely disagree. They technically can't attack her, since she's under eighteen, but she's expected to take part."

I nodded, knowing all that. I'd hoped the kids could sit out the more organized fights, but that had effectively been cleared up for me. This was a sink-or-swim situation.

"I can handle myself." Daisy patted her breasts, and I knew there was a knife hidden in her bra.

"It's the healing issue that is the sticky wicket." Donovan frowned, glancing down another hallway. A couple of people in office attire stood chatting, computer bags slung over their arms. We had a ways to go before we reached the battle area, clearly. I hadn't even known part of the area was used for clerical work.

"A blood oath can be applied to a non-magical, can't it?" Dylan asked.

"I will *not* be taking a blood oath," Daisy said.

"It can, yes. But any work she'll do in the magical world will have to be as an independent contractor." Zorn's arms flared with muscle. "She will never fit into our world. Nor will she ever fit into her own. Just like Lexi, she'll always be a misfit. Unlike Lexi, though, she'll need to stick to the shadows, to the night, like a black widow."

"Or a bat." Thane gave her a small shove.

"What about a raccoon? Or a skunk?" Boman grinned. "Her breath some mornings…"

"A varmint, definitely. Some kind of varmint," Henry said, as though considering it carefully.

The only one who didn't crack a smile was Zorn, whose face was as serious and resolute as always. Daisy currently matched him.

"Let's veer right for Jerry to grab some rocks, and then it's go time," Henry said, his humor falling away.

"I have an awesome idea." The ledge of Bria's cart scraped against the corner when we turned. "Let's put rocks in a cadaver or two, and Jerry can throw bodies at people."

Jerry afforded her a look of death as we walked.

"Think about it. That would really confuse everyone," Bria prodded. "Limbs whipping around, heads wobbling, flying by the middle…"

"Something is terribly wrong with you," Jerry told her in a gruff voice. I had a feeling he was trying to control his stomach. "Terribly wrong."

"Yeah." She grinned.

Once we'd gathered rocks from the garden—judging by the divots already there, we weren't the only ones to have done so—we found our way to a hallway like any other. This time, though, Henry stopped, looking down at his phone. "We're here. Apparently."

We all looked around, the way clear for fifty feet in each direction before corners or dead ends closed off the view. No blood splattered the walls. No burn marks or anything out of place.

"Has it started yet?" I asked, feeling a solid weight settle on me. It wasn't from the situation, it was from those damn watchers in spirit. When I turned to look, they were just smears of black on the murky ultraviolet plane of the Line. This time, though, their gaze felt heavier—not oppressive but focused. I hadn't felt it this strongly since our showdown at Lydia's place.

If my father wasn't watching me, who was? Aaron and Lydia had been present at the courtyard fight too.

"We're at the very outskirts." Henry put away his phone. "And we're dealing with the best of the best. Keep your wits about you; things are going to get hairy."

All humor gone, we walked slowly down the hall. The doors were closed, but I'd be able to feel anyone in the rooms we approached. The stagnant air stifled the noise of our advancement, except for the soft squeal of one of the wheels on Bria's cart and the muted thuds of Jerry's rocks rolling along on the thin carpet.

"Are you sure we're in the right spot?" I whispered.

"Yes and no." Henry didn't take out his phone again. "We're in the right place per the phone app, but I have no idea where people generally fight. Amber was the encyclopedia on all that."

"Something you might've mentioned before I sent her away."

"I thought you wanted to access your mother's magic."

"I don't know how to access my mother's magic," I hissed. "Mostly. I think it happens sometimes by accident, but I never actually try."

"I think our best approach is to embrace the unpredictability of the situation," Daisy said. "These magical types are all so buttoned up. They might think they are wild and crazy, but their world is governed by a very slowly changing set of rules with a tightly defined gray area. If it's a public fight, there should be blood, check. Less experienced fighters stick to the garden, please, out of sight." She stuck up her nose, mimicking what she clearly thought of the Demigods in this place. "The most experienced can have the hallways, which we can pretend is a dangerous maze with lots of hiding places. Bonus—it affords a fantastic ability for observation."

"There is no recording in the battlegrounds," Henry said.

Daisy huffed and Zorn shook his head.

"You were sharper when you were thinking for yourself," Zorn said. "Amber doesn't know everything. We've passed two cameras so far."

Henry looked upward. "What? We weren't told there would be surveillance."

"It's better if people don't know they are being watched," Daisy said.

Henry dug out his phone, probably to text Amber. They'd want to try to hack into the system. Something told me it would be much harder here than it had been at Demigod Lydia's mansion.

"Battling Flora on an unknown mountain in the middle of nowhere was ten times more dangerous than this." Daisy shook her head exasperatedly. "That garden would be a much better place for the more experienced fighters. The environment is another unknown, and if manipulated correctly, it could be as deadly as the enemy. You could hide in the branches or in a hole, or lay a tripwire in the bushes. *That* is a real test. This is just a well-regulated training exercise. No one is battering down walls here, I bet. It's lame."

"Tripwires?" Thane asked. "Like the kind the Chesters use?"

The hallway we walked ended at another. Henry pointed right, toward the edge of the building. We turned that way, only momentarily hindered by Bria running into the corner again and getting the cart stuck.

Once we successfully took the corner, Dylan answered, "Yes. When I was in the Chester lands, one of my acquaintances was a former special ops in the...Army? I can't remember what branch of the military, but he was special forces and taught me all manner of tactical non-magical warfare. Some of the things he could rig up for an enemy were crazy. I thought Daisy might need all the combat knowledge she could get, magical and otherwise, so I've been teaching her what I know."

Daisy ran her fingers across the strap of her cross-body bag.

"Wait..." I braced my hand on her shoulder. "Are you telling me that you have explosives in that bag?"

Her wide eyes and innocent look told me all I needed to know.

"No." I put my finger out. "No explosives."

"Why not?" she, Zorn, and Henry chorused.

"Because you could kill people! Because we don't need it. Because you'll ruin these lovely unmarked walls." I could see I wasn't getting through to them. I had to get creative. "Because...don't you want that to be your secret weapon if you get in dire straits in the real world? If you use it here, people will know to expect it."

Everyone turned thoughtful. Henry finally nodded. "That's a good point. Magical people don't use Chester tactics, thinking it is beneath them. But those who can do magical tripwires are heavily sought-after. Seems silly when any Tom, Dick, and Jane could create them."

"Who are they?" Jerry asked.

"It's a figure of speech, *Jerry*," Donovan said.

"Missed the context of that one, eh, *Jerry*?" Thane murmured, his bearing hunched a little, like he was expecting danger to pop out at any moment.

A soul popped onto my radar up ahead. Dylan put out his hand, his forearm connecting with my chest like a mother slamming on the brakes and trying to protect her child in the front seat.

"Zeus?" I asked him.

He lowered his arm, slowed, and everyone slowed with him. "Yes. Five of them, all strong."

More souls popped up after he said that. His magic had a better range than mine, but he could only sense Zeus types. "Eight people total, off to the side. In a room, I would gather."

"Awesome. It's *go* time." Daisy rubbed her hands together excitedly.

"No, you're not—"

"Only a few Demigods would have that many Zeus types working for them," she said. The cats rubbed against her legs, clearly on her side, whatever that side was. "So Zander or Flora, but we put a big hole in Flora's ranks, and she hasn't had time to assemble a new, stronger staff, so I'm guessing this is Zander's crew, on the outskirts of things and taking a break. Otherwise they'd be in the center of the hall yelling, *You shall not pass*, right, Mordie? Like your friends in *Lord of the Rings*?"

"What's the best course of action?" Zorn asked her.

Adrenaline coursed through me. "Really? We're taking a break from a dangerous situation in order to engage in a training session?"

A growl rumbled deep in Chaos's throat, and I got the distinct impression he was telling me to be quiet.

Daisy ran her lower lip through her teeth, thinking. "We'll obviously barge in and scare the bejesus out of them, and then we'll take them out for the remainder of the day. That's a given. How is the question."

"Thoughts?" Zorn prompted.

"We want to make a positive impression on Zander, so we can't use Lexi to take them down through the wall. Zeus people would think that's cowardice. They might have a defense against Dylan, so we need to send the giant in first, in rock form. He'll take the brunt of their attack. Then we send Red and Bria around him to stab a bitch. Get one in the neck. That bleeds a lot. I'll throw some knives as well, just to treat them like pincushions. Mordecai, rip into a throat, just don't kill. Tear out a stomach if you want—let's give it some flourish. Who else—Oh! Boman, flash some light and blind them. Dylan, do the thunder. What a ruckus. Henry and Thane, hang back and look pretty. The room is only so big. Chaos, you rip up a… Where are some cool places to have scars? Because your shit doesn't heal.

Sorry, Lexi, I get to swear in battle. That's a given."

"The back is good for scars. Those'll get a sympathy lay, right, Zorn?" Donovan grinned.

"Good call." Daisy nodded. "Chaos, rip up a guy's back, not a girl's—guys are superficial, and she *won't* get laid because of it. We're not tryin' to ruin lives here. At the crescendo, Havoc, you do the roar that flaps their souls. That's a real mood killer. For an extra flourish, Lexi, you stand just outside of the commotion with your hair blowing in your weird fake breeze." She clapped. "Yes? Sound like a plan?"

"What about me?" Donovan asked, respect twinkling in his eyes.

"You stand by in case they throw something at us we don't expect, which is highly probable. Three of those buggers aren't Zeus—who knows what they could be."

Daisy ended by looking at Zorn for approval.

"You forgot me," he said.

Her face colored. "Oops. Sorry. Drift in as gas around Jerry, figure out who is the most dangerous, and put them out early. A few kidney shots and a loss of consciousness should do."

Zorn nodded, and so did everyone else. We'd be going with Daisy's plan.

I couldn't help but feel a glow of pride. A non-magical teenager was setting the strategy for a Demigod's crew. That was pretty amazing.

My pride quickly turned to worry. "You should hang back," I told her as we jogged for position.

Dylan pointed at the door harboring the enemy, two up and on the right.

"I'm just throwing knives," she whispered. "I'll be hiding behind Jerry. I'll be fine."

Excitement lit her eyes and filled her voice. If she'd been any other teenager, I might have thought her eagerness would wear off as soon as she got a look at the action. But she'd seen plenty of action so far, right up close, and she'd been left behind more times than not. Her excitement was to finally fight with her family.

On some deep level, I felt like I'd failed her. She should be safe at home, far from anyone who might want to kill her for being non-magical, but this was no time to dwell. Wallowing in guilt would distract me and potentially get someone killed. We had to fight through this if we ever hoped to find a future of safety.

"They will be highly organized and excel at their magic," Dylan whispered as we neared the door. Murmuring came from within. No souls moved position. Those inside were probably sitting and chatting, or maybe gearing up for round two. "They will be used to structured battles. They won't like being caught off guard."

"Then they certainly will not like the absolute clusterfuck of crazy we are about to throw their way. Great heavens, I love my job." Bria's grin was jubilant.

As Jerry's skin turned into a stone crust, Red stepped up and, with a practiced movement, rammed her foot against the door near the handle. It cracked open like a nut and swung wildly, banging against the opposite side.

All eight of the people inside looked up with wide eyes, momentarily freezing. Their inactivity was short-lived. A blast of electrical current zipped from the front runner's palm and slammed into Jerry's chest with enough force to knock a normal person on their ass.

Jerry was not a normal person.

He barely bumped back before advancing again with slow, deliberate movements.

"Zorn, take out the rear," I said, seeing how their formation had altered in a blink, those in the front administering the assault. The weak had fallen behind—they weren't used to people fighting dirty.

Welcome to battling a person of Hades.

A woman on the side put out her hand, aimed at Jerry. She probably had the magic to force Jerry to shift back into his skin, but if Demigod Flora hadn't been strong enough to do it, this chick certainly couldn't.

Bria and Red darted in, Red faster than thought and Bria not far behind. They slammed into the magical workers, knives slashing and sticking in practiced, brutal movements. Blood splattered a polished wood table and the recipient of Red's vicious attack groaned, grabbing his neck. Blood oozed between his fingers. She'd done as Daisy had suggested.

Dylan stepped out from behind Jerry, and in a move I hadn't seen yet, he slapped his hands together and then flung them out like he was playing patty-cake. Lightning rode the rumble of thunder, the sound muted for those on his side, electricity spitting and blistering in a wave. The enemy visibly quaked.

A spark died between the palms of a woman who'd been about to unleash her magic on us. Daisy saw an opportunity and dashed out with her throwing knives. Three of them rammed into the woman's chest in quick succession, the placement a perfect triangle. Daisy darted back behind Jerry as a sliver of lightning zipped toward her from a man on the left.

I almost brought the male lightning slinger to his knees, but I held back. It was a gut reaction and unnecessary.

A woman screamed in the back before a man slid to the ground. Oops—I was wrong, the scream had come from him.

Zorn popped out of existence, his disappearing act startling the hell out of the woman next to him. It was like she had no idea what magic Zorn had. Her hands came up and the air shivered near her fingers. Zorn appeared again, his face screwed up in confusion, lowering his hand as though he didn't understand what was happening.

A fierce growl vibrated through the room. Mordecai streaked past Jerry, darted around the edge of the group, and launched himself at the woman, blasting through the wavy air. His form went limp for a moment, but his heavy wolf body slammed into the woman. She must've been using some sort of mind control, because it wasn't a force field she'd erected. They tumbled back together and she yelled out in surprise.

Mordecai rolled off, shook his head to clear it, and, before the woman could get her hands back up, attacked her throat and chest. I hoped to hell she had blood magic.

Zorn, freed from the woman's magic, pivoted and pushed forward, aiming for a guy in the middle of the group. I didn't see where his machete went in, but I saw the tip come out, through the other end of the guy's shoulder. I grimaced as Zorn pulled the weapon free and the man jerked, his mouth rounding and his face turning pale. His eyes swung around wildly, looking for the source of the attack.

Trying to add the flourish Daisy had suggested, I waved at him and gave his soul box a little squeeze.

His eyes widened and he froze. Zorn stabbed him

again, in the other shoulder. I slashed his soul box and broke one of the prongs keeping his soul in place, trying to scare the bastard and give him a story to tell his friends.

Instead, his eyes rolled into the back of his head, and he dropped to the ground.

"Oh shit," I breathed, spirit rolling around me like a tornado.

"What happened?" Henry stepped forward. "What went wrong?"

I checked the guy's soul to make sure it was still in its casing. Strangely, his spirit felt kinda…watery. Like it was going to slip right out of its confinement. It was like I'd pushed him past his point of no return, and he was easing himself out of the world of the living.

"Stop!" I yelled, ignoring Henry and stepping into the room. I pushed Jerry, trying to get some space. When he didn't budge, I went around and put out my hands. "Stop. Everyone stop! I might've accidentally killed someone. Hold on so I can see if I can fix it!"

"That's not how it works, Lexi," Dylan said, slamming those still standing with thin bands of lightning from his fingers.

"What do you mean that's not how it works?" I gripped the man's soul, not letting it slip out of the casing. At the same time, I mended the prong I'd broken. "Dang it, why are Zeus people so easy to scare with my magic?" I ducked under Jerry's arm, which had come out to try to push me behind him. "All I did was rattle him a bit. He wasn't anywhere near death, but now it feels like he's trying to abandon ship." I crouched by his head and put my hands on his temples.

"Red," Henry called.

"Got it." Red leapt over me and grabbed a guy scrambling up off the ground, his clothes smoking from where Dylan had gotten him. She flung him across the room.

"Shh, it's okay. Everything is okay." I rubbed a thumb across the hurt guy's forehead. His soul was still trying to escape. It was the craziest thing—I'd never felt it before.

"You don't just stop a battle because someone went down," Dylan yelled, and lightning jumped from his hands again.

"This isn't a real battle," I yelled, "and he didn't just go down—he is dying."

"Lexi, accidents happen." Donovan batted the air with his hands. Red spun, and something just missed her and slammed into the wall.

A rock flew up from outside, crashing through the window and slamming into one of the two enemies still standing. Glass rained down, and I ducked my head. The woman had fallen to the floor, and Bria descended on her, stopping her from getting back up.

Dylan redirected a buzzing ball of light, and Daisy jumped onto the back of the last man, wrapping her legs around his upper body, trapping his arms to his sides. She reached around and raked her dagger across his jugular. When he tried to jerk away, she unwrapped her legs, pushed off with her hands, and kicked her feet against his back, helping him fall forward. She hit the desk and rolled off, landing on her feet while he crashed down through two chairs, grasping at his throat. It was as incredible as it was gross. Also highly distracting.

"Get Daisy out of there. I don't want to use my magic on that guy; these people are very fragile," I hollered.

"I sure do hope this room is being monitored," Donovan said with a grin as he magically lifted the last man, whose hands were glued to his profusely bleeding neck, and tossed him out of the window.

"Well, that's…" I huffed and turned my attention back to the man on the ground. Everyone else would heal (I hoped), but this guy just didn't want to. His soul was trying to escape fast. "Hang in there, buddy. You're okay. Everything is okay."

"What'd you do?" Boman looked down at me, and I realized he hadn't gotten much of a chance to fight.

Thane stepped into the room. "We got five coming down the hall, all dressed in black. Probably Hades."

Boman's eyes lit up. "Lexi, we'll call you if we need

you," he said, and jogged out.

"We won't need you." Dylan winked at me, following him.

Bria dropped down on a knee next to me. "Lexi, they won't penalize you for an accident if we get lost. Let's go."

"I have a feeling that one guy in the last fight isn't going to find his way back to rational thought, which means this would be my second 'accident,' Bria. What if they keep happening? I'll be called in, you know I will. This guy isn't that hurt—there's a chance he'll be fine if I can get him to hang on."

She sighed. "Fine, okay. If he isn't hurt, then what'd you do?"

"Nothing I haven't done to all of you. Just rattled his soul cage a little, no biggie. But now he's trying to die on me. It's really weird. I don't know what to do."

Bria felt his pulse. "Slip into that other plane and see if your dad is there. If not…fuck, let's sing him a lullaby, I don't know. Want me to light a nice-smelling candle or something? Rub his feet?"

"Be serious."

"It's hard when you act like this."

I fell into a trance, just enough to peek into the spirit plane. I didn't want to leave my body for any reason, not with Lydia and Aaron hanging around this place and Hades players out in the hallway.

Amazingly, Harding waited in a foggy mist. Since I'd only dipped a toe into spirit, his appearance was gauzy and only half realized, but it was him all the same. I could feel his soul.

Relief flooded me at his presence, immediately followed by fear. He shouldn't be here! With the Hades Demigods well able to move through spirit, he could easily get found out.

"Oops, you found me. Hello." He squatted, making his head level with mine. "How are you? You do realize you're doing something I haven't taught you yet, right? This is an entirely different plane of spirit, one very few ever use. And here you are. You really do rise to the occasion in a crisis. What a marvel. You're going to go really far—"

"Yeah, yeah, later." I quickly told him what I'd done and what was happening.

After I'd finished, he looked at me gravely for a moment.

"Bad news?" I asked, fear kindling within me. Despite what everyone said about accidents, I knew I had less room for error than most. My magic was already scary, and I was undoubtedly seen as a troublemaker. Two of the Hades Demigods had a vendetta against me, and if Demigod Zander ever caught on to who trained me, he'd be wary as well.

I was skating on thin ice, and I knew it.

"Bad news for you? Not so much. For me? A bit." He looked both ways, although I had no idea what he was seeing. From my perspective, there was nothing but hazy gray. "I've been watching you from afar so I wouldn't be discovered. Dang, lady, I wish you weren't so helpless and naive and likable and hot, all at once. Move over."

"Watching me from afar? You're the…things that are always just out of sight?"

"Yes and no. I said move over."

I tried to scoot over, forgetting that I was still half in spirit. The act sent me reeling out of spirit. I sucked in a startled breath and nearly tipped over, out of balance.

Harding *stepped* through the spiritual plane like it was a window, his foot touching down on the spot I had just occupied—the one I'd used to peek through.

Bria's eyes pulled together and her body went rigid. "What is that, Alexis? Who's here?"

"Ah, my favorite Necromancer. Fantastic." Harding crouched down beside me, over the prone man, whose lips had started to turn blue.

"Maybe Zorn pierced his lungs or something?" I asked, hovering my hand in front of his mouth to feel for breath. "Why else wouldn't he be breathing? Maybe he doesn't have a blood oath."

"Zorn knows what he's doing. He wouldn't have pierced anything vital," Bria said.

"It's not his body that's the problem." Harding tsked. "Poor Zeus. He thinks he's so mighty, and yet he's so easily knocked off his high horse. Egos, you know. When they get too big, they are highly unstable." He ran his hand down my arm, and it felt, for all the world, like a real hand. I shivered beneath his warm caress.

"What—"

"*Shh,*" he said softly, wrapping his strong fingers around my wrist to prevent me from pulling away. "Watch. *Feel.* This is advanced magic. *This* is the kind of good you can do."

He guided my hand over the chest of the prone man, our touch warm on his unnaturally cool skin.

"You have literally scared the life out of him." Harding chuckled.

"Not funny." My voice was barely louder than my heavy breathing.

"This is what happens when the will to live leaves a person. The soul goes…soggy, for lack of a better term. The body is intact, but the soul has no interest in residing. The good news is you can heal his soul. That is a powerful thing. Do you see how amazing our magic is? You can actually *will* a person to keep living. You are life and death, all in one."

With his guidance, I pulled power from the line, twining it with spirit.

"You are a favorite. This magic is a favorite. It will protect you, Alexis, for all eternity, with or without a body."

He sounded so sweet, so reverent, that I didn't remind him that he hadn't been protected in life and still wasn't safe in death, his presence at this Summit being a prime example. We weren't favorites—just like Dylan wasn't a favorite. We were coveted. That fact made us vulnerable.

My hair tingled as a violet strand crawled into existence, connecting my palm with the man's chest, burrowing deeper until it reached his soul. It was the same sort of string that Lydia had used to siphon energy from spirits, only I would be using it to pump energy in.

"Close your eyes," Harding whispered, his voice both around and within me, folding over itself like cake batter and sliding across my skin like a ghostly touch. "Surrender yourself to the magic."

The power of the Line fizzed through my blood, and a substance like quicksilver glinted along the velvet string. It carried something pure and light from me to the dead man—my will for him to live. *My* will, not his. But as it wrapped around the violet string, strengthening it, bolstering it, the feeling manifested into a desire. Then into an action.

Live! Live!

It coated the soul box, strengthening it, keeping the

soul from slipping out, and then filtered inside.

Live! Live!

"Yes, Alexis. A little bit longer. Just a little more… I couldn't do this when I was alive. I couldn't use this part of the magic, because I couldn't open myself to it. I didn't desire people to live, not after what they'd done to me. But you are pure. You can love. You have the full spectrum at your disposal."

The soul shied away from my quicksilver touch at first, but then it started to drink in my offer. It regenerated, stronger and stronger until it filled the casing once again, like a flower blooming in the sun, more vibrant and alive than I'd found it.

"There you go. Now you must pull back gently. Very gently." Harding's touch coaxed me, his magic tracing mine and showing me what to do. "That's right. Here we go—you must pull back without scaring him again, the silly little Zeus boy. So fragile after you get past all the hotheaded blustering."

My magic retreated, ever so slowly, and I opened my eyes as I dissolved the remnants of the violet thread. The man blinked his eyes open, looking at me for one long beat before he sat up slowly and rubbed his head.

"Where am I?" he asked.

"Ta-da. Good job." Harding patted me on the head, of all things. "Okay, gotta go. I shouldn't be here. I do *not* want to get noticed, as you know. And don't learn how to scare away my watchers. I like to know your progress."

He stood and stepped back through the window into the other plane, disappearing into the swirling gray mists. Once he was through, reality pulled back down. He hadn't even turned to wave goodbye.

I stared at the man I'd helped, trying to process everything. He stared back at me.

"Okay. Well." Bria clapped the man on the back. "You're alive."

"What…" The man reached his hand up, probably to run it down his face, and then flinched. He touched the blood oozing down his chest. "What happened?"

"You got stabbed, but you're good. You're okay now." I stood and braced my hands on my back, seeing a couple of the others rouse, lying in pools of their own blood. No spirits had popped out, though, and I could feel their souls bright and happy in their casings. "You would've died had I not intervened, so save me from the effort of having to knock you out, would ya? Take the loss. That was strangely taxing, even though I had help."

He blinked at me a few more times, and I figured that was probably a yes. He was too confused to use his magic.

"Okay. That was anticlimactic for me." Bria bounded up. "But that certain someone should *not* be here, Lexi. You can't risk someone finding out."

"I know, but...well, he offered, and I didn't have any other choice. He's the one who's been watching—"

A muted thunderclap rang through the hall. I belatedly felt the enemy souls doing battle with our guys. "Dang it. Today is going to be a long day."

Chapter 11

ALEXIS

BY MIDAFTERNOON WE had four hall battles behind us. The Hades people Boman and the others had engaged after our battle with Zander's team had been an easy win. They'd used a bunch of stuff that probably worked on other people but didn't faze my crew, not when they'd trained with me and I could literally scare someone to death. The third had been a nice reprieve. Jerry had turned to stone and handled the flares of sunlight and zips of light magic (Apollo magic, clearly) without effort. He'd then flattened everyone with rocks. That guy had been worth the hassle to get him.

The fourth had been a little hairy. The magic was more diverse, with some Hades, a Zeus, and a few others I didn't recognize. They rattled our cages, so to speak, one reaching me with an invisible blade that opened a thick gash down my arm. Another got to Dylan with mind control, making him punch himself in the face three times before bashing his head against the wall. Jerry couldn't walk forward because of a very precise windstorm. He bore it in stubborn silence.

While we were indisposed, Boman sliced through their line with his light and Donovan picked a couple of people up and slammed them against the wall. Henry stepped in front of Dylan, got the blast of mind-control magic, and reflected it while Daisy and Zorn and the cats sprinted down the hall after the enemy.

Daisy leapt at someone as if on springs. The girl was like a little jungle cat. She landed on him legs first, wrapped her thighs around his middle, and stabbed his breastplate, both hands gripping the hilt of the knife. The guy dropped like one of Jerry's stones. Zorn disappeared, then reappeared, stabbing someone. Chaos clawed someone's leg, and then let loose a roar that had everyone scattering from him like their asses were on fire.

He clearly had the ability to roar fear, one of Hades's traits. That had been a nice surprise.

Havoc followed that up with her roar, moving spirit and flapping souls.

The battle hadn't lasted much longer. Thane had watched the whole thing from ten feet behind us, leaning against the wall with this arms crossed over his chest.

Patched up with Boman's help, we limped and trudged down the hall, looking for more trouble.

"When do we get to go home?" I asked, wiping my

forearm against my forehead.

"When we have to be carried." Donovan rolled his neck. "Have you noticed the majority of these teams only have magic from one god?"

"Wow. Look at you, professor. Good work." Thane clapped Donovan on the back.

"Shut up, dead weight."

"Dead weight? No, I prefer the term *audience*. Better yet, peanut gallery."

"That's always been the way." Dylan rubbed a large lump on his head. If he didn't have accelerated healing, he'd be in a hospital with a concussion. "Demigods—actually, most of the leaders—tend to look for talent like their own. That seemed perfectly natural to me before I met you guys. I felt like a traitor for not choosing Zeus over Poseidon. But we are *ten times* stronger with a mixed crew. Maybe more. We have something for everyone. The team we just battled was the hardest yet, and it wasn't because of their magic or ability. It was because they had a bunch of different types of magic, too. Mark my words, people will take notice. Other Demigods—the smarter Demigods—will start to break tradition after this. They'll look for the diversity Kieran—sorry, Demigod Kieran has."

"Ew, really? You can't just call him Kieran at this point?" Daisy rolled her eyes, her silken complexion marred with a streak of blood.

"We have a teenage Chester taking down experienced magical people." Dylan laughed, and a lot of us stopped and gaped for a moment. The guy didn't laugh often. "What a circus. Yes, we'll be noticed. Zander doesn't like to lose. I bet he'll be the first to make changes. He almost lost someone today, though he probably won't hear about that."

"He won't have to. He'll see it." Henry's mouth formed a grim line. "Daisy was right about the cameras. They're all over this place. New tech—tiny, well-hidden cameras, and a firewall that is hard to crack. They have an excellent team behind that firewall, too. The second Amber is in, they kick her out."

"Well, boy genius?" Boman held his hands out in a *what the hell* gesture. "What are you waiting for? You don't need her to figure this out."

Henry gave him a scowl.

"Yes," I said, feeling a soul blip onto my radar, stealing my focus from the conversation. It made me a bit blunter than usual. "You aren't as useful magically as you are doing your infiltrating thing—"

"Sure felt useful when I was banging my head against the wall," Dylan muttered.

"Go find a way to get some intel, or mess with them, or whatever it is you do," I told Henry.

"She's got a point, brother," Donovan said as that one soul turned into a group.

I sighed. "We got another one, just about to turn the corner."

"Okay. Good luck!" Henry gave me a thumbs-up and took off in the other direction.

"Well, he didn't need much convincing," Jerry murmured.

"Not Zeus," Dylan said, straightening his shirt for some reason.

The first person came around the bend, a woman with a grim expression and strange hat with a little tassel on it. She stopped and held up her hands. "We have heavily wounded. We are on our way out, but we would offer you our Necromancers, if you'd like to duel them."

"Lexi, don't you dare." Bria dropped the handle of her cart and marched up to the front. "This is mine, do you hear me? I've got some new tricks up my sleeve I want to try out."

"She said Necromancerzzz, plural," I said.

"Yeah, I heard. Bring me the bodies, Jerry. Just carry them on up here, one by one. Hold them really close while you do."

"You're out of your fucking mind, woman," Jerry said.

"You disappoint me, *Jerry*." Bria grinned and motioned for Donovan and Thane, who obliged with smirks and long glances at Jerry.

"I accept the challenge," Bria called, unslinging her backpack and dropping it to the ground. She hovered over it. "You call it out."

"What does that—"

"Shh!" She waved her hand at me.

I felt Boman's hand on my shoulder, pulling me back. "It's a Necromancer thing. They don't usually get as much fighting time as Bria does. She's a bit crazy for her faction. Just let her work."

"Okay, but…I'm here if you need me," I said to Bria. "Because they have more than one."

She waved me away again.

Two men came forward, one pulling a cart like Bria's. The woman fell back around the corner with the other souls, most of them lowering to the ground, probably sitting or lying down. After the men had laid the bodies out, they set up little trays for their supplies.

"Really, guys? *Mobile stations?*" Bria called down.

They didn't respond, organizing their bells and whistles and stinky incense with quick, practiced movements. Bria took that opportunity to pull out her similar supplies, placing them in loose clusters that lacked the organization of the setup across the hall.

"This is how they do it?" Dylan leaned against the wall. "A chat as they set up to battle with dead bodies?"

"Didn't the Demigod you served come here?" I asked him. "Why don't you know more about how this place works?"

He gave me a tight-eyed glance. "She didn't bring me to the Summit."

"The belle of the ball had to stay home in bed," Jerry murmured.

Everyone turned to him wide-eyed and jaws slacked. A grin spread across Donovan's face and his shoulders started to shake with suppressed laughter. Thane covered his mouth and turned away, his eyes tearing up. Boman guffawed, his face pointed at the ceiling, unabashed. Even Zorn allowed himself a smirk.

Dylan's face turned beet red, but some of the tension left his shoulders. For someone who didn't joke around often, Jerry sure knew how to make one land.

"Five," said one of the other Necromancers, a man with a grisly gray beard and a ring of chub around his middle. "Four…"

Bria braced herself, her hands out, ready. I crossed my arms and leaned against the wall as the countdown continued, happy for the break.

"Go!"

Bria burst into action, moving faster than her opponents as she grabbed up black stones that looked like onyx before backing up behind the bodies, shooing us back as she did so. She dotted the carpet from wall to wall with the stones, then hopped over the line to grab a set of purple rocks. Those got lined up behind the black stones, the two rows staggered.

"I've never seen you do that before," I said.

"When I was researching how to trap a spirit because of a certain...guy who has been training you, I found all sorts of interesting things. There are some lesser-known texts full of old-school Necromancy teachings. It's almost like witchcraft. Given you've stolen my thunder and made life boring, I've been playing with this stuff. We'll see if it works."

"The Soul Stealer can't help you," Gray Beard called down, lighting a candle. The other guy had a tchotchke in hand, and I knew he was about to stuff a spirit into one of their very fresh-looking bodies.

"The Soul Stealer *can too* help me," Bria yelled back, fashioning a semicircle of candles in front of the stone and rock line. She grabbed incense next, arranging them in a diamond shape within the semicircle. "She is a type of Necromancer, she is just way better at it."

"This is a Necromancer duel, not a *type* of Necromancer duel."

"And you have two against one, you feeble-minded, goat-milk-drinking whore of a dingleberry." She sprinkled some ash across the entire setup before jumping out in front and sprinkling ash there as well. "But don't worry the hairs on your ass; I told her not to help. I'll beat you fair and square. Underdog always wins."

"Only in movies," Gray Beard replied.

"Welcome to the movie of my life, sweat pea. Get ready to lose."

The other Necromancer huffed out a laugh, smiled, and shook his head. "I forgot how distracting you can be in these things," he said.

"Yeah. It's not just about working the cadavers." She paused for a long moment, looking over her setup. "Oh shit." She snatched up her backpack and rooted around in an outside pocket. "That would've been a disaster."

A man drifted through the hall, his brow furrowed and his fists balled. He joined the Necromancers at the other end of the hall, but he was not happy to be there. I said as much.

"I'm sure they use the same spirits repeatedly." Bria pulled out a little silver marble and placed it in the center of the diamond. "It's easier to control spirits when you're familiar with the ways they try to revolt. Easier to call them, too, actually. It's a common practice." She pulled out a handful of items from the front pocket of her backpack, and I saw that they belonged to the spirits we always had hanging around. "It's even easier when you trust the spirits, they aren't pissed at you, and you don't actually need to control them to get the job done. Thanks for that."

A woman drifted through this time, pulled faster than the last, her face as calm as a quiet spring day but tension making her body rigid. Hate fueled her, I could tell, kept on a tight leash until she could exercise it properly.

These spirits were as trapped as those in Lydia's house. As trapped as those in Valens's air and spirit cages.

Trapped for the last time.

Although I'd promised not to intervene in the fight, I hadn't said anything about what happened afterward. This crew would have to find some new spirits. Good luck calling this bunch back after I sent them to the farthest reaches of beyond.

Jack drifted in like the others, not appearing as quickly as he would've if I had called him.

"Hey, guys," he said when he stopped moving. I relayed what he'd said.

"Hey, Jack." Donovan nodded, looking at the wrong pocket of space. "You're more help in death than Thane is in life."

"But is he more encouraging and supportive of your wins? That's the real question," Thane said, crossing his arms over his chest. His large biceps flared.

John flew in next, right behind another pissed-off spirit heading to the other side. John looked at me, annoyed.

"That wasn't as pleasant of a ride," he grumbled.

I pointed at Bria. "She's in charge. I'm not allowed

to help."

"He better not be complaining, that bastard." Bria grabbed up a button—Mia's.

"I hadn't properly appreciated how quickly Lexi can get bodies animated," Dylan mumbled, sinking down to a crouch.

"Trust me, I have," Bria said. "It's more fun to stop messing with all this stuff and just stab people."

In another fifteen minutes, the duo down the hall started lodging spirits into bodies. Bria waved her hand at her collection of spirits, all of whom were standing around, waiting for direction. This was the difference between working with spirits and controlling them.

"Climb into the body of your choice," she told them, pulling a lighter from her pocket. "I will secure you as best I can, but it won't feel as snug as when Lexi does it. You might need to make some adjustments."

"What if I just fastened one prong on each?" I said, biting my lip. "That's not really helping."

"Don't need it," Chad said, choosing one of the less-mangled bodies. "They won't tear me from this body if I don't want to go." I told Bria what he'd said as the rest chose bodies and climbed in.

"He's great. He was a good find." She flinched then sucked her thumb, which she'd probably burned on the lighter.

Candles and incense lit, she shooed us away a little

farther and took up residence between the lines of stones and rocks. Out came the bells, and she kneeled in place.

"If you're in and ready, rise up." Bria's face turned red, and I knew she was helping them.

The bodies flailed, like turtles on their backs. I shoved my hands in my pockets, really wanting to help.

"When did you get so dramatic?" said the non-Gray Beard guy, a man in his forties and with dyed black hair and a matching mustache. He muttered something, and three of his bodies rose, shaky and jerking, very well controlled, especially because they were probably trying to fight him. "And so wild? It looks like you barely have a handle on them."

"I am their battle commander. That's the beauty of working alongside a Spirit Walker: she makes friends, and those friends are an extension of the team. You won't be battling the will of one person, boys—you'll be battling a half-dozen minds, all doing whatever they want."

"That's absurd," Gray Beard said. "Commanding cadavers? Allowing spirits to think for themselves? What New Age bullcrap is this?"

"Bull*shit*, Jim," Dyed Hair said. "You sound stupid when you say crap."

Both teams were up and ready now, the cadavers staring at each other.

Jack turned back to look at Bria, his upper body randomly leaning left. "What are we waiting for?" he asked. I relayed the question.

"Them to make the first move." Bria set up a second station, and I recognized the tools in this one. These would help her pull spirits from the bodies controlled by the other Necromancers. In a whisper that wouldn't carry to the opponent, she said, "It gives me more time to start working on their cadavers. I won't have to do two things at once, but they have twice as many as we do. I have to work fast."

Their collection of bodies started forward in a loose formation, three at the top and the rest spreading out wide behind them.

"What's the goal here?" Chad asked, keeping the others from walking to meet the challenge. "Take down the controllers, or take down the bodies?"

"If you can get through the cadavers to get to the controllers, take them down. Just don't kill." Bria raised her voice. "Mia, did you hear me? *Do not* kill. You came awfully close that last time. I know you hate magical people, but it'll reflect poorly on us if you kill someone."

"Child's play," I heard from Chad. He stepped to the front of his line, taking over, barking commands. Time to fight.

"Don't you need them to defend you, though?" Dylan said, rising. I wasn't the only one who wanted to help.

"No. Hopefully not, anyway. Why do you think I spent so much time on this old-school demon worshiper line?" Bria got to work, ringing a bell, muttering some words.

Thane leaned forward, trying to see. "Demon what? What did she say?"

Chad and John barreled into the first zombies they reached. They ripped and tore even as they ducked out of the way, slipping free of the next rank of cadavers. Mia disappeared, then reappeared next to Gray Beard. She grabbed his head and spun. If she'd been stronger in that body, she would've broken his neck. As it was, she must've sprained it, because he cried out, dropping the bell in his hand.

"Jesus," Boman whispered. "She'd be terrifying if she were alive. No controlling that one, I bet."

"She's terrifying in death," Jerry murmured.

Jack picked up one of the opponents' cadavers. He lifted it up and then brought it back down, breaking its spine over his knee.

"Yes!" Donovan fist-pumped the air. "Brutal!"

Cadavers ambled toward Bria, all of them consumed by a single purpose. One of the bodies on the other side of the battlefield fell. The spirit popped out and looked around, confused. That must've been Bria's handiwork, because the spirit Jack had accosted still hunkered in its body, trying to rise back into the air, controlled like a pawn.

I grabbed the spirit Bria had freed, pulled up the Line, and launched it as far beyond the barrier as I could. As it went, I felt a supreme sigh of relief. Of letting go. She was leaving this world, finally at rest.

Another popped out, and I shoved him the same way, feeling years of anger and frustration melt away in an instant. Warmth filled my middle. I was doing my job, as nature intended. I was giving people the freedom and closure they'd longed for. It felt good. It felt *right.*

Zombies ran at Bria now, ready to swarm. When their feet reached the ash, their bodies jerked and swayed, slowing down. Forced on, they neared the half crescent of candles, punching through the plume of stinky incense.

The controllers jerked on the other side of the hall, as though they'd been shot. The bodies continued to push forward, but it clearly cost the Necromancers. With each step, the controllers bent over a little more, winded. In pain, maybe. Those stones Bria had set up were doing their job.

Another soul popped out of one of their cadavers, and then another. I sent them across the Line. John ripped the head off one zombie and threw it at another. Both bodies fell and he was through, running at the controllers.

Mia popped out of her body, their doing. I clenched my fists, wanting to shove her back in. Instead, I murmured, "Mia is out."

Bria swore under her breath and switched tools, working on getting Mia back into the body. Mia was a VIP—she was worth the effort.

John didn't tackle Dyed Hair like I thought he might. Instead, he grabbed the lip of the small table holding their supplies and tossed it.

"Smart," Bria muttered, having chanced a quick look. "No one does that. Why do no Necromancers do that? Very smart."

Mia, back in her body, disappeared off the ground and reappeared by Gray Beard. She dragged the exposed bone of her fingers across his neck. It opened up nasty gashes, and he screamed, probably more from fear and disgust than pain. She grabbed his head again and ripped. Her energy must have been flagging, because the attack was weaker than before, but tweaking his already sprained neck was enough to bring him to his knees.

"He healed fast—he must have a blood oath," Jerry said.

"Yeah. He's the resident Necromancer. He's got the oath," Bria replied.

The zombies in front of Bria stopped, stuck as though the air had turned solid. One fell and the spirit popped out. Then another. I grabbed them up and shoved them across the Line.

Chad reached Dyed Hair, convened for a second with John, and then they both grabbed him, Dyed Hair flailing in their grasp. They flung him at the wall. He hit headfirst and fell to the floor.

The rest of the zombies fell with him.

"Yield," Dyed Hair yelled, his hand up. "*I yield!*"

"Yield," Gray Beard said, his voice pained. He lay down on his back, his hands on his neck.

"Okay, Alexis, you can help now." Bria sighed and sat back, her forehead glistening with sweat.

Dyed Hair, blood running down the side of his face, sat up against the wall. He touched his forehead and winced.

I grabbed up all the remaining souls, our people included, and yanked. Without any prongs securing them, the souls popped out with next to no effort. Bodies fell into heaps and Dyed Hair's eyes widened, as big as saucers. Jerry gagged and turned away.

"Anyone who wants an eternal resting place, raise your hand," I said. The Line throbbed off to the side, its ultraviolet light leaking into the living world. A presence waited just behind the veil, and when I turned to look, the shadowy being, a blotch of liquid night, gave me a little wave. No soul pulsed for me to feel, but I knew it was Harding, watching again. I'd been too preoccupied to notice his scrutiny during the zombie battle, but I felt it now. He wasn't in spirit, but he'd found another way to keep tabs on me. I still had so much to learn.

I also hoped he wasn't getting too cocky. He was great in spirit, but he didn't have the power of a Demigod. He needed to watch himself or he'd get plucked right out of spirit and thrust into a body. The last thing I wanted to do was face off against him.

The opposing spirits looked around in confusion, not used to being seen or heard by the living.

John tapped one of them and then pointed at me. "She means you. We can leave at any time. She doesn't control us."

Heads turned slowly. Eyes found me. Hunger and desperation sparked to life.

"If you want an eternal resting place, please raise your hand—"

"What are you doing?" Dyed Hair asked, struggling to stand. He swayed, like he was dizzy, and braced himself against the wall.

"She's doing what her magic was designed to do, ol' boy." Bria began gathering her supplies. "Protect spirits. Hope you brought a good collection of spirit items, because this bunch is about to run out of your stables."

"No, wait—"

Spectral hands rose, slow at first and then shooting

upward. The Line throbbed. I sent them sailing away, shoving them too far for someone of lesser power to retrieve. Harding's shape seemed to nod in pride as I pushed the Line away, its strange colors leaking from the world. All our spirits stood waiting, probably to see if we needed anything else.

Cleanup was fairly quick, mostly because I shoved all the spirits back into the bodies and they helped by walking to the trailer. They climbed in and lay down, and then I sent them home where they could lose track of time like normal.

Bria took longer to pack up her arsenal, and I realized she was stalling. I was grateful. I was tired of fighting. The competitions in this place seemed pointless; I was used to fighting for a cause. I would've rather settled down with a book and waited for Kieran to finish up.

"You go on, I'll clean up," Dyed Hair said to Gray Beard as the rest of their crew limped out from behind the corner and headed past us down the hall. Another team passed in front of us, not bothering with the crew who clearly had up their white flag. I hoped they'd meet someone else so there would be one less team to take on.

"Thane, Donovan, help him." Bria jerked her head at Dyed Hair. "He doesn't have a blood oath. That slam to the head probably smarts."

"It does, yes." The man put his palm to the wound. "Quite a lot." He took a step away from the wall and winced. He motioned to me. "She can really load up cadavers and empty them that fast, huh? Without much effort?"

"Yeah." Bria zipped up her backpack and snuffed out the incense with her boot, smashing the ash into the carpet. "The stuff she can do without much effort would blow your mind. You'd need a whole army of cadavers to take her on. She's no joke."

"I've never seen that." I pointed where the rock and stone barrier had been. "You've really upped your game, and you were already one of our best."

"Yeah. Boredom, it does things to a person." Bria slung her backpack over her shoulder as Thane and Donovan finished piling up the other guys' bodies. "You going to make it?"

Dyed Hair walked slowly to his cart, nodding his thanks at the guys. We all stopped near him, needing to pass him to continue into the fray. "Yes. I just need to make it back and then I can lie down."

"Well, if these were all the spirits you had at your disposal, you'll be off for a few days." Bria hooked a thumb at me. "She scattered them beyond your reach."

"Those were all the menial spirits, yes. Listen…" He looked around before leaning closer to her.

"Nope. Nope, nope. Wait a moment." She held up

her hand to stop him and looked at Zorn, standing next to Havoc and slowly stroking her head. "The cameras," she whispered. "Do we know if they have sound?"

"Cameras?" Dyed Hair barely kept from looking upward, I could tell. "No mics on those. They are surveillance cameras only. Unless there is sound recording somewhere else, but I doubt it. I haven't seen even a hint of that."

"Go ahead," she said to Dyed Hair, "but don't look sneaky."

"This is the first I've heard of cameras," he said with a rumpled brow. "I can't imagine the Demigods will be into that."

"I doubt the Demigods are being recorded. This setup is to watch their lackeys, I bet," she replied.

He nodded and sat down at the edge of the cart, palming his head. "Christ, this hurts. Your spirits are powerful. Anyway, listen." He lowered his voice again. "You didn't hear this from me, but we go way back. You've had my back plenty, so I'm returning the favor. I've been called in to help with a particularly strong spirit. Two level-five, experienced Necromancers, one with a blood oath, to handle just this one spirit." He paused, not looking up.

Bria put her hand on his shoulder and peered at his wound in a performance for the cameras. She had no knowledge of patching people up. "What's the nature of the spirit?"

"When they hired me, they didn't say. I just know it's an incredibly dangerous level five. Calling it will apparently be tough, and controlling it will be even tougher. Probably like that Apporter you have."

Boman stepped forward and moved Bria out of the way. He reached into one of his cargo pant pockets and came out with disinfectant wipes. He did have experience patching people up, and apparently he'd decided to help this guy because he was giving us information.

"Two level fives, one of whom is outrageously expensive, means Aaron means business," Bria murmured.

Ice slid down my spine. "This is Aaron's crew?" I asked.

"He's been desperate ever since Alexis came on scene. You probably shouldn't have taken this gig, bud," Bria told Dyed Hair, ignoring me. "If he is saying it is dangerous, it probably means it is also very stupid, no matter how many Necromancers you have."

"As you said, we're both very experienced level fives—I think we can handle anything. But..." He winced at Boman's ministrations. "From the whisperings I've heard around the lodge, it sounds like Aaron had to steal the item to call this spirit. Getting it was supposedly incredibly tough, and he's tickled with himself for pulling it off. I heard someone drop Zander's name as I came around the corner, but then everyone zipped their lips and scurried away. Aaron wants to make a big splash. He's going to battle with this spirit, and he doesn't think he can lose."

The cold claiming my spine spread to the rest of my body. I shivered and saw my thoughts mirrored on the others' faces.

Aaron was going to try to wrest control of Harding away from me, and I hadn't brought the pocket watch. Was that why Harding was hiding? Did he know?

It was entirely possible Aaron could do it too, and once he had control of Harding, he would set his sights on me. Harding knew more than I did about this magic—plenty more. And he also knew plenty about me.

If Aaron managed to control him, I might end up being another "accident," my death excused when Aaron's people ran. There would be nothing Kieran could do about it.

Chapter 12

ALEXIS

"HE WON'T BE able to control Harding," Thane said as we trudged down the hall, out of steam and completely over this whole thing.

It was five o'clock, the shadows outside were starting to lengthen, and still we kept going. We hadn't been taken down, so leaving prematurely would make us look weak. Or maybe afraid? I didn't know—the code didn't make much sense to me, but everyone else agreed we had to keep going for a while longer. We'd barely even been hurt. Dylan absolutely couldn't believe it.

He couldn't stop crying right now, however, so he wasn't thinking clearly.

He and Thane had been hit with some sort of empathic power that forced emotions on people. Dylan had gotten sadness, or something that translated into sadness. He'd burst into tears and sunk in on himself, hugging his middle. It had rendered him completely useless for the entire battle.

Thane hadn't gotten sad. Not at all. The guy who

had been useless all day had suddenly become incredibly dangerous. Rage would do that to a Berserker.

Maybe she'd seen those YouTube videos and knew what he was. If so, it was a hell of a risk to take. He would have been just as likely to tear through their group. Trample them. Use them as bowling balls. Tear them in half.

Thane hadn't broken, though. His face had turned a bright shade of crimson, his fists had balled up, and thick cords of muscle had stood out all over his body. He'd fought the urge to change, and he'd beaten it, an incredible feat for a Berserker. His control was beyond compare. Unheard of, even.

While the others combated the rest of her group, I went after that woman with every non-life-threatening trick I knew. She was tough, too. She'd clearly battled other people with Hades magic.

But she hadn't battled a Spirit Walker.

I'd scared the Empath so badly that she'd blacked out. I was no Harding, but I was good enough for the likes of this place. Most of it, anyway.

One lady did give me a run for my money. This particular team leaned heavily toward Ares, and she'd stood in the back with her bow and arrow. She didn't miss. Not ever. We had to hide behind Jerry in his rock form so as not to be stuck like pincushions. Donovan had already been hit three times, all of the hits in locations on his body that prevented him from moving his limbs.

I went to work, slashing and tearing at her soul casing. I broke two prongs. I poked her actual soul. Her tanned face lost a few shades of color, but she did not buckle. She did not relent. If the ceiling had been taller, she would've been able to arch arrows over Jerry to hit us. Boman got hit that way and had to push in closer.

Zorn was the one who'd brought her down. He'd gone into gas, puffed into a human right next to her, and stabbed her through the stomach. He'd then slammed the hilt of the knife onto her head and knocked her out. Within that tiny slice of time, she'd put two arrows into him with her bare hands.

Pulling all those arrows out was so gross that I'd nearly gone home right then and there. That shit was for the birds.

So now, countless battles in, Dylan still sobbing in the back—the magic had worn off, but it had tapped into something inside him—we walked like the zombies I never really controlled, trudging and jerking and not having complete control of our bodies. Magnus had been right—at the end of day one, we were utterly exhausted. At least we hadn't lost anyone, though.

"Aaron's Necromancer is one of the best in the business," Bria said, picking our conversation back up. Blood splattered all down her front and across her exposed forearms. She'd had to do some serious knife work in our last confrontation. "Noah, the hired gun, is also one of the best in the business. He partially trained me, and we've been professionally circling each other ever since. We've gone head to head a bunch of times. The two of them working together might be strong enough, and savvy enough, to get the job done."

"But can't Lexi just grab control right back?" Donovan asked, swinging his left arm. "Damn that chick. Was she hot, or was she hot? She had the pressure points down. I wonder what other pressure points she might know." He paused to shake out his leg.

"She was hot," Boman said, nodding.

"Lexi doesn't need an item to call spirits." Donovan checked the gauze on his arm, soaked through with red. His healing ability aside, two Advil couldn't have been enough for that puncture. He was good at hiding pain.

"Depends on how strong they are," I said. "I can probably do it, but if they have a firm hold, I'll need to be close. Maybe close enough for them to attack me. Harding showed me how to ward off an attack on my soul, but this pupil is far from becoming the master."

"Yeah, but he's not as strong as you, right?" Red asked, a trail of dried blood on her arm. Four Advil couldn't have been enough for her, either, especially without the blood bond. We needed to head back, and not only because Thane was uncharacteristically quiet.

He hadn't even picked on Jerry the last time he could have.

"He would've been a strong level five in life," Bria said. "If they don't scramble his head to make him easier to manage, and I assume they won't, since they brought in a very expensive Necromancer to help the already expensive Necromancer on staff, he would be probably a mid- or lower-level five in a body."

"A highly experienced, very technical mid- to low-level five." Fear clawed at my guts. Harding could handle things I couldn't—and do it with ease. Earlier today, he'd *stepped* through the planes of reality as if it were nothing.

I shook my head but didn't say anything, worried I might open my mouth and throw up instead of speak.

Silence filtered down between us, and when I could no longer stand it, I voiced the thing everyone was probably thinking.

"If they lose control of Harding, and he's in a bad temper because he was forced, it might take me a while to calm him down. Within that time, how many souls will he rip out? How much carnage can he do?"

"Can you..." Dylan took a shuddering breath and wiped his nose with his shirt—not a good look on anyone, but he was so hot he could get away with it. "Can you go to... Maybe Kieran can go to Zander with your concerns? If the object was taken from him, he has an investment in the situation. Plus, Harding isn't likely to look kindly on him."

"All Aaron has to do is hide the evidence." Bria slowed with me as I saw a man at the other end of the corridor, standing in the middle of the space, facing us. "No one is going to do anything without proof, except maybe caution him. Our biggest issue, though, is that Aaron is out to lunch. He hasn't been thinking clearly for a while. He's not going to listen to anyone cautioning him, and since Lexi just scattered all his on-call spirits, the only way he can beat her is with his own offspring, or so he'll think. No, if that's the railway the train is on, it has already left the station. There is no stopping it."

"That was a serious railroad metaphor," Thane said, and cracked his neck. "We need to talk this over with Demigod Kieran. Get his input. Right now, though, we have other stuff to do. That's a Berserker up there, I bet you. Someone is very stupid. I could yank his arms off and…" Thane scrunched his eyes and flexed his arms out to the sides, enormous even in his human form.

The man down the way continued to stand there, waiting for us, or maybe just waiting for a challenge from anyone. A little closer and Dylan pointed out a woman standing behind him a ways. She had fisted hands, and the door to her right stood open.

"She's of Zeus," he said.

Thane started to laugh. "Stupid. Stupid and horribly ignorant."

"Maybe explain a little more?" I kept walking, mostly because everyone else kept walking, even though usually we'd stop about now and come up with a plan.

"That guy has the look of a Berserker, and the little miss behind him probably has the kind of magic that forces someone to change back to human. The guy will change, the woman thinks she'll force me to return to human, and the guy will thump me. That's their whole plan, I bet you a hundred bucks. I doubt he's changed in such a confined space before. This is no place for a Berserker. You saw what I did at Lydia's place, and there was a lot more room to maneuver."

"And you still made a few new doorways," Boman said with a grin.

"Exactly." Thane took a steadying breath. "Take him down, Lexi. I won't let my other form loose in here. But we gotta go soon. My energy is flagging and my other half wants to come out to play. Soon I won't be able to stop it, especially after this bastard changes. Another Berserker is like a battle cry—it's hard to resist."

"Hi!" I lifted my hand and took the lead. I swore I heard Daisy mutter, "Nerd."

The man stared at me, watching my approach. I could just make out the muscle working in his jaw, his teeth tightly clenched.

"Thane—our Berserker—knows better than to change in here." I hooked a thumb back at Thane. "You probably should, too. We can either take this out to the garden so he can play too, or we should just let bygones be bygones."

The man's face turned red.

"I can see you're going to ignore me." I looked back for the cats. They came forward without being called. "He's still not going to change, so if you do, you'll be tangoing with me. I just want to warn you: I am not pleasant. It would be best to head to the garden or just go home. We're tired. We'd rather go home."

The man started to laugh, his voice deepening slowly, his size increasing. Fear wormed through me. Berserkers had always terrified me. Didn't matter that I'd seen Thane change more than once, or that I'd subdued him a couple of times. The primal feeling would probably never go away.

"You think you can stop me, Soul Stealer?" His eyes tinged red.

"You mean, because I'm not supposed to kill you?"

He didn't answer, just continued to grow larger much more slowly than Thane would have if he'd decided to make the change.

"Well, either way, the answer is yes, I can stop you," I said. "It won't be pleasant for you. Or me, actually. I really dislike dealing with your kind. No offense,

Thane."

"You can't kill me. Only a Demigod can take down one of my stature." The guy roared, the sound filling the hall. My legs started to shake and my heart ramped up. *Here we go.*

"Young hotheaded clown," Thane murmured, his voice strained. He was fighting the change.

The Berserker in front of me grew, larger and larger until he took up half the space between the walls and topped my height by four feet. For all his size, he wasn't as big as Thane.

He roared again, sending tendrils of fear winding through my gut. I braced myself as he bent, about to charge.

My heart ramped up. "Here we go. Who's on knife duty? Donovan, you can keep those whips off me, right?"

"Those whips come with age, and this kid doesn't have them," Donovan said, almost sounding bored. Unaffected. "He's nothing to you, Lexi."

"Okay, but what if you're wrong?"

The Berserker thudded his feet on the ground, coming at me. Ready to bowl us all down. His enormous, grotesque muscles bunched and coiled. He swung his arms a little, side to side and then in front of him. If it was part of his strategy, I didn't understand why.

"I'm tired," Bria said, not moving forward to stand

with me.

"I got this, if she needs me." Thank God at least Red was still on board to help out.

I didn't have time to chastise anyone. That manic red stare bore down on me. My heart tried to punch a hole through my ribcage.

I punched his spirit box with everything I had, while simultaneously rattling it. Havoc roared, sending a blast of spirit right through the Berserker's middle, shaking the soul I had in my magic's iron grip. Chaos darted forward, batted a sparkly little item he'd found on the ground, somersaulted in the air for no reason, then darted away behind us again—distracting but not helpful.

The Berserker staggered, ramming a hole in the wall with his huge shoulder. He howled, flailing his hands and then beating at his chest. He took two more steps, his guttural wail one of agony. Before I could slice at him, he took a tumble, not having gone very far.

He kept wailing, now rolling around on the ground. He kicked the wall, another hole. He banged the ground with his fists.

Chaos ran back in, pounced on the Berserker's back, and charged the woman with the Zeus magic. She screamed, threw out her hand, and, when that didn't yield results, ran into the room next to her and slammed the door behind her.

The Berserker shrank, quickly turning human. Once done, he curled up into the fetal position and groaned.

I stared for a moment.

"Oh," I said. The tension slowly draining out of me, I looked around in confusion. "Is that it?" I narrowed my eyes at the others. "Is this a trick?"

Everyone chuckled behind me. Thane let out a ragged breath.

"You just rang that guy's bell. Let's head home." Thane turned, his hands still fisted. "Thanks, Lexi. I don't have much left. I would've pounded the shit outta that guy. I would have—"

"Whoa, big guy, keep it together." Bria patted his flexed arm. "How about a lovely, cold bath? Or, I know, why don't you have a nice, big cry with Dylan? He could use a little company."

We made it around the corner, back toward the exit, before we all stopped dead. Magnus's pack strolled toward us, confident, arrogant, and clearly still going strong. They'd been too far away for me to sense. The leader, the small-statured woman with tight curls and a nice disposition hiding a mean personality, gave us a chilling smile.

Thane groaned, and I had the feeling he didn't have enough left to resist punching some holes through these very white walls.

Chapter 13
KIERAN

"DEMIGOD KIERAN, A word."

Kieran slowed, trying to keep his head from drooping in exhaustion. He was well and truly spent, but he'd gotten a better handle on things as the day progressed, and had even jumped into the fray a few times.

The last meeting of the day had been a closed-door talk among the high-status Demigods, invite only. It had floored him to get an invitation. Humbled him, too. These people had an awe-inspiring grip on their territories, plus years of experience dealing with and, when necessary, manipulating non-magical governments. It had been like a master class for him. He'd taken notes like a demon.

"Yes, Demigod Zander." Kieran offered a bow, a show of respect that was genuine and not just for show. He admired the way the other Demigod had spoken so unguardedly in the meeting, and his concern for those he ruled.

Zander picked a moderate pace as they left the meeting room. "I wanted to congratulate you on your win."

Lesser-status Demigods watched them with wide eyes. They probably wondered how in hell Kieran had gotten so many perks on his first day. Kieran wondered the same thing. Part of him even wondered if he was being set up.

"Which win is that?" Kieran asked.

Zander glanced at him. "You haven't been told? Your team has been working through the halls. Last I heard, they were still there, taking very light damage. Very light. One of the first teams they took down was mine. It galls a little, I must say."

Zander's grin was teasing, but his tone wasn't entirely light. It did gall, clearly, and he wasn't bashful in admitting it.

Pride welled within Kieran. He hadn't been actively monitoring Lexi or his people, his mind whirling from the constant meetings.

He wondered how Zander had gotten the scoop—he and his co-leader wife had been in all the same meetings as Kieran, and phone calls weren't allowed in the halls.

"I hadn't heard, no," he said, keeping his tone level. "Thank you. I'll be sure to pass that on."

As they wove through the building, making their

way toward the exit, more looked at Zander and then Kieran. Eyes widened, like before, and some people stopped to murmur to each other. Kieran's skin started to tingle in warning.

"My team was taking a break and yours happened upon them," Zander said, not looking at anyone they passed. "They were in a room with a closed door, you understand. Most people can't see or feel through walls. Your little Soul Stealer could've taken them down from the hallway, I see that now. She chose instead to come at them face to face, with honor. She directed your crew in and hardly engaged at all. Just enough to nearly kill one of my guys, and then…somehow bring him back to life. The details are very hazy to me; I only heard this secondhand. The man in question has professed he will never fight her again. That he is in her debt." Zander chuckled softly. "I can make him fight her, of course, but I found the exaltation…most odd." He paused for a moment. "Possibly this is due to her flouting of our customs. Your little Soul Stealer helps the enemy rather than finishing them. We saw it before us in the courtyard. My team saw it firsthand. I thank you for that. I would've been grieved to lose him. Usually he is exemplary in battle. I'm not sure what happened."

"She doesn't help the enemy on a real battlefield, I assure you," Kieran said, his heart pounding warmth through him. "She's not used to battles being games.

The first time she used her magic was against my father. She fought an experienced Demigod's army right out of the gate. With all due respect, to my people at this point…fighting inside an office building isn't real fighting. It is like training, and when you train, you don't aim to kill others."

"Quite right, yes. Just so." Zander fell into silence for a moment as they continued to walk. They were both still the objects of scrutiny, although Kieran noticed people seemed to be watching him for longer than his companion. "This thing with bringing people back to life… I'd thought she was the bringer of death. I haven't heard about this other facet of the magic. What is it?"

"It's not bringing someone back to life, it is more…keeping them from dying. She cannot heal a body, but as long as the body is sound, she can heal a soul. After Magnus and Aaron attacked us, her male ward was left clinging to life. I helped repair his body with my…magic, and she rebuilt his soul so that he would live. I could try explaining how such a thing is possible, but it—"

Zander waved him away. "Of course, of course. Broad strokes are fine."

"Anyway, when it comes to spirit, she is a killer *and* a healer. She can take a life, or save a life. Her magic, when used with a sound mind and good heart, can do a lot of good. That is why I must keep her safe from those who would use her for mindless killing. She's more than a blunt instrument, but she could be an extremely potent blunt instrument."

Zander turned a little as they neared the exit, his eyebrows raised. "You must be forgetting who finally stopped the last blunt instrument."

Kieran bent his head a little. No, he had not forgotten—none of them had—which was why he was trying so hard to help Zander see the good facets of Lexi's magic.

"That young man—the last Soul Stealer—was not capable of doing any sort of healing," Zander said, pushing open the door. His protection detail ran in from the side, perfectly in line. Kieran's people came right after them, equally organized but giving precedence to Zander's people. "He would not spare a life if he could help it. He was…corrupted. Mind and body, that young man was not right. Death was a blessing for him. If your Soul Stealer was anything like that…"

"That's not the sort of person I'd want on my team," Kieran said in a firm tone.

"Good, good. Yes. You have a level head on your shoulders. Your father and I didn't see eye to eye on many things, but he was good at what he did. He was effective. I see he passed that on, and then some." Zander stopped near his collection of golf carts, parked right in front. "You have a long way to go, let's get that straight."

"Quite a long way, yes. Today has humbled me in ways I wasn't expecting."

"As well it should. You are smart for realizing it. Tomorrow won't be so packed. If you show well again, perhaps we will have you for dinner. Juri is incredibly taken with… What is her name? Your Soul Stealer?"

"Alexis."

"Yes, Alexis. Juri is quite taken with her. She's fascinated. Miss Alexis is so strange in her customs, and between us, I think Juri would like to take her under her wing." Zander's look turned severe. "That is, if you pass the formal investigation into that mark she wears. Your past with her is convoluted. We must protect her if that mark was placed without her consent."

Kieran schooled his expression, keeping it neutral. He knew full well Zander didn't give two shits about protecting a rare level five. He mostly followed the rules and laws, it was true, but not out of any softness of heart. The law was important because it helped keep order—if one Demigod was allowed to mark someone rare and special against that person's will, it would open the floodgates for the rest of them to get greedy.

Thank heavens Kieran's Soul Stealer loved him.

"I'd also hate…" Zander paused for a moment, looking out at the trees, as if wondering if he should go on. He straightened up, his shoulders tense. "I'd hate that Soul Stealer to fall into...the wrong hands. The last one's owner was not as sly as he could've been. A Soul Stealer in...different hands would be...quite a situation."

Kieran feigned indifference. He pretended not to know Zander was talking about Magnus. From the closed-door meeting, Kieran had picked up some conflict between the two. Conflict they didn't advertise in the more public meetings or places. They were both masters of their craft, Kieran could tell, with a firm handle on their territories and their political goals, but they were coming at it from opposite points of view. Magnus was interested more in what he could financially gain, and Zander seemed to favor the overall wellbeing of his territory, money as well as general citizen prosperity.

Kieran wasn't going to lie—he would've preferred if Alexis's personal connection had been to Zander. Magnus was certainly the trickier of the two. However, if he could get an alliance with Zander, and Alexis could secure the cooperation of Magnus, maybe Kieran would find himself in a good (though incredibly dangerous) spot between the two.

Thinking like a true Demigod.

Kieran gritted his teeth and pushed his father's voice away.

"Well. See you tomorrow, then." Zander turned away and lifted his chin somewhat, arrogance on full blast. Kieran bowed, knowing his place, then bowed again to Juri, who exited the building and sauntered after Zander, having clearly stalled to give them time to chat.

Once there was some space between them, Kieran headed back to his collection of golf carts, Amber closing the distance between them. "Sir, you are the talk of the town."

"They probably can't believe I was pulled into that last meeting. It was obviously an afterthought, but I don't care. I'm fucking awe-struck. I never expected to gain this much status so quickly. What do you think the odds are that they're trying to take me out in some way? Could they arrange that here, or just plan for it and do it when I got back to San Francisco?"

"Um…" She frowned at him. "No, they likely don't plan to take you out. They wouldn't have pulled you into a very prestigious meeting if that was their plan. Your crew has just now headed home after a long day of battling. Technically they lost to Magnus's team. Alexis forfeited."

Kieran stalled at his golf cart and checked his watch. Nearly six in the evening. "I didn't think they allowed forfeits unless a team was badly hurt and leaving the grounds."

"They usually don't, but in this case they made an exception. Alexis judged that Thane would not last another fight on the sidelines. He'd lasted all day, despite being magically flooded with rage and challenged by another Berserker. His incredible level of control is being whispered about throughout the Summit. The man will be a legend among Berserkers. Even still, he was spent. Magnus's people were at Lydia's. They saw, firsthand, what Thane is capable of. They weren't willing to risk it."

"Still, they lasted this long and Zander congratulated me on my win. That has to count as a pretty good showing."

Amber stared at him for a moment, her expression flat. She shifted her weight, just a little, and it seemed she was annoyed about something.

He rubbed his face. Thane wasn't the only one who was spent.

"What am I missing?" he asked, sitting in one of the carts. He'd been sitting all day, but still he was too tired to stand.

"There are only a few teams that lasted the whole day, all of them belonging to high-status Demigods, but those other groups took breaks. From what I'm hearing—not from your crew, who hasn't contacted me all day—your people didn't take breaks. I don't think they knew they could."

She paused, and guilt ate away at him. He hadn't told Lexi, assuming Amber would. But they'd sent her back to him.

"No one could hide from them, either," Amber went on, and Kieran wondered if her pause had been a deliberate attempt to make him feel guilty. "If they passed a room with someone in it, they barged in and took the team out. Ran into someone? Took them down. Not one of them had to go back to the lodge. They worked together better than any other team—that has been acknowledged by all. No grandstanding amongst them. No arrogance. Lexi could so easily be a diva with her magic, as could Dylan. You know, of course, that they are not. Bria took on two highly experienced level-five Necromancers, without Lexi's help, and won. Daisy fought beside the rest of them." Amber laughed, the first indication she had a sense of humor. "A teen Chester without a blood link took down experienced, level-five magical workers. The cats, Jerry—your crew is exactly as effective as we've been working toward. Exactly. The risks to get them were not in vain. Your crew's success is the reason you got pulled into that last meeting. They've impressed people, Demigod Kieran. Greatly. The hearing about Lexi's mark has been fast-tracked. They know they need to button up her involvement in the magical world, because there is not one person at this Summit that wouldn't slit a throat to get her on their team. Dylan is amazing, but she is absolutely priceless, even without her healing abilities and those strange cats who follow her command. Guard her with your life, sir, because she gives you an incredible amount of status. She was the find of a lifetime, and her mother should be revered for preserving her and not letting the magical world corrupt her."

Kieran found his way to the house in a fog. He'd had no idea the battles counted for so much. He'd thought they were mostly ridiculous, truth be told. He understood the practice in theory—their people's abilities reflected on their leadership—but fighting in a hallway? Taking breaks? What was the point?

Well, now he knew. He hadn't even applied any pressure. The opposite, in fact. He'd told Lexi to play it safe and let him work the political side. Instead, she'd bumped him up a crapload of levels just by being herself. By being amazing…and human. Honest and empathetic. By swallowing down her fear and letting her kid take people down. By refusing to let people die.

Priceless. That was what Amber had said. He'd always thought so, but now everyone else could see exactly what he did.

He found his way into the lodge, as everyone was calling it. The warehouse-house. The cats lounged in the living room, curled up together. Havoc lifted her head as he entered and slowly blinked those luminous eyes. She dropped her head back to its position on Chaos's neck as Kieran passed.

"All I'm saying is, we did damn well for beginners, you know?" Donovan leaned against the kitchen cabinets, his arms crossed, and a half-drunk bottle of beer beside him. "We lasted in those halls longer than most. That has to count for something."

Thane sat at the island, his elbows propped on the granite and his chin planted on a fist, looking downward. "Yeah, until Lexi had to forfeit because I couldn't hold it together."

Boman rooted through the fridge, and Jerry sat in the corner on a stool, leaning against the wall with his head back and eyes closed. The rest of them were out of sight.

"She could've just sent you away, but she didn't," Donovan said. "She was tired. We were all tired. At least we had a good excuse and didn't have to go home bloody." He looked Kieran's way. "Hey, sir." He shrugged. "We gave it the ol' college try. There's always tomorrow."

Kieran felt Lexi in their room, starting to head his way. He summoned the rest of his people through the blood link and texted Bria, Red, and the kids. One by one they trickled in, weary, with their spines bowed and their lids drooping. Alexis's eyes lit up when she saw him.

"Hey, babe. How'd it go?" She slipped her hand in his.

He looked down at her beautiful face as everyone waited for him to speak. "I had a damn good day. My status, right now, is at a level that doesn't even make sense, it's so high. Zander walked me outside and congratulated me on my win. *Your* win. You all turned heads and broke the mold. Even you, Daisy." He turned to give her his full attention. "Especially you, a non-magical teenager with no blood link protection. You showed courage beyond your years." He looked at the others, taking in their surprise. "You didn't just do well for beginners, you did well for experienced magical workers who have been together for lifetimes stacked on top of each other.

"Thane, keep your head high. You've turned heads with your superior control. Forfeiting usually isn't allowed, but they let you do it because they didn't want you bashing their heads in."

Boman grinned and clapped Thane on the back.

"No violence yet, please," Thane said calmly, rage not far from the surface. Kieran could feel it boiling. Even now he was working on his control.

"Excellent work, all of you. You did me proud. Sleep in tomorrow—you earned it." Kieran swooped Lexi up into his arms. She squealed and wrapped her hands around his neck. "I need to speak with you. Alone. For a while."

"Ew," Daisy said, and turned away.

He rushed Lexi to their room, needing to explore this feeling of victory.

Door closed behind them, he ripped into her clothes. Her shirt dropped to the floor as he tore at the button on her pants. Her shaking hands were just as hurried as she reached into his undone belt and captured his hard length.

"Hmm, Lexi," he said, his breathing fractured. He bent to capture a taut nipple between his teeth, pinching softly and then sucking. She pushed his jacket off his shoulders.

He straightened up, lifted her again, and unceremoniously dumped her on the bed. She giggled in delight, but her eyes didn't lose the glimmer of hunger. He stripped out of his clothes, standing naked before her, staring down at the woman who held his heart in an iron fist. A woman he would claim, over and over, for the rest of their lives.

"Amber called you priceless," he said, crawling onto the bed slowly, like a predator. Her eyes sparkled with excitement, and she scooted back, squeezing her thighs together to tamp down on the desire he felt pumping through the soul link. "She said they wanted to button up your situation because everyone in this whole place would love to add you to their team."

"Amber has a tendency to be dramatic." Her voice was a purr and her words were a deflection of a topic that clearly made her uncomfortable.

He allowed himself a loose smile, running his palm up her ankle, and then pushed her knees wide. She gripped the sheets in tight fists, her chest rising and falling quickly. Her back bumped against the headboard. She watched him advance, and he felt her anticipation building.

"I will have the belle of the ball as my wife. Only the ball will be a battlefield, and you will lead an army instead of a dance." He grabbed her by the knees and dragged her closer. Her hair fanned out above her and her face flushed. "Nearly running you over with my car was the absolute best thing that has ever happened to me."

He bent and ran his tongue up her wetness, her arousal tightening her body while her kaleidoscope of emotions—lust, love, desire, passion, a thread of anticipatory fear—soaked through him. She was responding to the ruthless side of him, the Demigod that controlled and protected his territory with everything he had. The side that would break the world to come to her aid if she were ever in harm's way.

He sucked in her nub before swirling it in his mouth.

"Oh *God*, Kieran. Hmm." She arched back, falling into his ministrations.

He kept up the suction and worked her with his fingers, plunging and retreating. She gyrated her hips and grabbed his hair, moaning. Calling his name. His cock pounded with need; he was desperate to feel her warm depths.

He worked her faster, reaching up and teasing her nipples. His Selkie magic coated her skin and wound through her body, spreading sensual desire to heighten her pleasure.

"*Oh!* Oh gaw—" She pulsed beneath him, her orgasm making her body shudder.

He was on her in a flash, pushing her into the plush mattress. He lined up and thrust in one fast movement, plunging to the hilt. She cried out, probably still sensitive from her orgasm with no time to come down.

He pulled out and thrust into her again, desperate to be closer, falling into the push and pull of her body. The bed beat against the wall. His cock pounded into her.

"Yes. Oh yes. Yes, Kieran," she exalted, wild now, clutching at his flesh with her nails, squeezing his middle with her thighs.

Control fled. Love throbbed. He pushed harder, needing more of her. Needing to go higher. The Line throbbed to life in the room, her magic searing across him and driving sensation to unbelievable heights. He reciprocated, burning her with his mark, something only a Demigod could do. His Selkie magic pounded in time with his body. Pleasure beat within their frantic movements.

An orgasm crashed into him, dragging him under. She cried out and shook beneath him.

"I love you," he said against her lips, tension easing from deep within him. They'd proven today that their team was more than qualified to protect her. There wasn't a living person who could come between them.

Chapter 14

ALEXIS

"YOU READY?" BRIA asked as she ducked into the room.

I stood at the island in an empty kitchen with the golden summons on the table next to my nearly empty mug of coffee. It had come yesterday evening after dinner. It had ensured talk of strategy ceased—all of us worrying about what was on the line—and that I didn't sleep a wink.

"I guess. How do I look?"

Bria squinted at my face before glancing over my formfitting pale pink dress. Daisy had said the color would soften me and make me look more feminine. People were slower to think girly-girls were incredibly dangerous, I guess. It was worth a shot, though I doubted people would forget what I could do. The guy who'd freaked out in the open courtyard battle hadn't recovered—his mind had been too messed up by the combined power of my magic and Dylan's. I'd suspected that would happen, but it still sucked. The end result had widened a few eyes. At least I'd prevented Zander's guy from chasing the white light—which, of course, wasn't actually white, but more of an ultraviolet bruise color.

"Good, though that outfit enhances the mark. I'm not sure if that's a good or bad thing, given you are on trial for the thing."

"Daisy said it's a good thing because it shows I'm not trying to hide it. The opposite, in fact."

The corners of Bria's lips turned downward, and after a moment, she nodded. "Kid's got a point. Come on, it's time to go. Kieran is waiting out near the limos. He called them in for this."

This being the trial that would decide my future in the magical world. Despite everything, I was still worried someone would find a way to take me away from Kieran.

"It's going to be fine." Bria patted my shoulder. "It really is. I'm more concerned with what happens after you're declared legit. People aren't used to your type of shenanigans."

I gave her a flat look, grabbed a cute little handbag that had certainly cost way too much, and headed out to meet Kieran and his people at the limos. They'd all be coming for this, standing guard outside the Summit's equivalent of a courtroom, ready to step in if things went sideways. According to Amber, only two types of teams would be prowling the halls today—those who wished to regain lost status and graduates from the garden. Everyone else would be resting.

Kieran had enjoyed some great benefits of status yesterday, but today, he was ready to fight the very people who'd given him a hand up, if need be. When it came to me, he didn't care about bureaucracy.

Warmth filled my chest.

"Ready?" he asked when I met him at the lead limo, his hair styled, his suit perfect, and his bearing and confidence mouth-watering.

Not trusting my voice, I nodded and slipped into the limo. He climbed in after me, and the driver shut the door, closing just the two of us inside. The kids weren't needed for this, and I didn't want to worry about them getting caught up in the melee if things went south. They were staying home.

"What kind of questions should I be expecting?" I asked as we got underway. I kind of wished we'd taken the golf carts—they moved slower.

He stroked my hand comfortingly with his thumb. "I'm not sure. It might depend on my answers. I'll get called in first and questioned independently of you. I will answer truthfully and honestly. I have nothing to hide. You'll be called in next, on your own. Just stick with the truth and everything will be fine."

Easier said than done. I wasn't used to being interrogated. I'd probably go on the defensive without meaning to, and it would make me seem guilty.

But I kept my reservations to myself and held my head high as we entered the Summit building and made our way to the correct room.

Rows of bench seating, almost like church pews, lined the pathway to large, ornate double doors. Carvings of gods peered down at us from the wood. Guards stood to either side of the doorway, their suits pressed and devoid of wrinkles or lint, their hands clasped in front of them.

A broad-shouldered man with short legs met Kieran halfway to the double doors. A wire led from his earpiece to somewhere behind his neck.

"They are ready for you now, sir," the man said, motioning Kieran on.

Kieran checked his watch. We were fifteen minutes early. He nodded anyway and squeezed my hand.

"Just tell the truth," he murmured to me, and then he was striding away.

A short woman I hadn't noticed stepped out from behind the man, giving me her rendition of a smile—a tight-lipped affair that set me on edge. She gestured to the front of the mostly empty benches.

"You can wait here."

I took a seat at the edge and Donovan slid in beside me. Thane took the seat behind us and reached forward to massage my shoulders.

"This is just a formality," he said. "You are very clearly on Team Kieran. They just want to make it official, no biggie."

Zorn stood just off to the side, and when the same woman tried to get him to sit, she ended up backing away slowly, as if sensing a predator.

"They have to know we wouldn't let anyone take you from us," Zorn said, clasping his hands behind his back. Somehow, his freshly pressed and expensive suit made him seem more dangerous rather than less. It was obvious he'd be plenty happy if things went sour so he could operate without rules. "Even if they bamboozled Demigod Kieran with their prestige, they could never sway us. We know what's right, and we'll fight for it."

Time slowly ground by. Each minute lengthened into an hour. My gut churned, my stomach queasy.

"Think those battles in the halls would have gone down differently if we'd been out for blood?" Boman asked.

"We *were* out for blood," Dylan replied.

"No, I mean, actually fighting. Fighting to kill."

"Yes, the fighting would've gone much differently." Amber's voice was a low hum. She'd sat behind me and to the side, a little removed from everyone else. "You should know that from when you battled Valens. I believe this team would've still done exceptionally well.

You have recent experience in do-or-die situations. However, some of these Demigod crews have been around since time turned over. They are cunning and brutal and specialize in killing. Fighting here is a game. When you strip away the rules, you reveal the true nature of magical people. It's why we have the rules in the first place."

I stared at the large double doors in front of me, sick with worry. I had no doubt the ruthless crews Amber had spoken of were within striking distance. If this went south, there'd be a blood bath.

"Ma'am."

I nearly jumped out of my skin, so wound up that I hadn't seen or felt the short-legged man approach. His grim expression did nothing to pacify me. Was I about to walk into a hostile situation?

"They're ready for you." The man motioned me forward.

"You'll be good," Boman said, standing as I did, followed by the rest of the crew.

"No sweat, Lexi, just be yourself." Bria winked at me, which might have been reassuring if I hadn't seen her fingers turning white where they held the back of the pew-like bench in front of her.

Breathing was difficult. I should've brought the kids to calm me down. We'd been through hell together—they were used to putting a good spin on things.

The door groaned as it opened, echoing into the cavernous space within. High ceilings and muted tones of wood and cream greeted me, along with seven men and women in black robes seated on a high bench. Had they stolen this getup from the non-magical world, or vice versa? Either way, their elevated presence was incredibly imposing as I took a seat in front of them, my table average height but seeming so much lower.

Kieran was absent, which meant he must've exited through a side or back door, out of sight. Someone had set out a glass of sparkling water for me, and I contemplated taking a sip. My intensely shaking hands would have given me away, though.

"Alexis." Zander sat in the prime position, directly in front of me. Magnus sat beside him, leaning back, his face unreadable. The stately woman I'd seen on the first night's walk was next in line. I recognized a few other faces, but thankfully, no other Hades Demigods were present.

"Yes." I nodded, my fingers digging into the backs of my hands where they were clasped.

"Do you know why you've been called in?"

"Yes. Because of the mark Kieran put—applied to me. Put on me, rather." I wiped away the sweat collecting on my brow.

"Correct. We are going to ask you a few questions to get to the bottom of it. Now, do you know the significance of a Demigod's mark?"

I took a deep breath so I wouldn't pass out halfway through my explanation. "In the past, Demigods marked people to claim them as property. Now marks are usually only used in love connections, which is to say they're not used very much at all. It is basically branding a person with the Demigod's signature."

Zander clasped his hands on the desk. "In essence, yes, you get the gist of it. How did that mark come to be placed on your skin?"

I explained my version of events, revealing that I'd actually known about the mark (from the guys) before Kieran had, and that I had also established a permanent soul link between us. While it didn't show on the surface, it claimed someone just as thoroughly. Maybe more so.

Throughout my explanation, Magnus leaned against the arm of his chair, watching me silently.

"Can you prove this soul link exists?" Zander asked, and a man I did not know at the far right grinned, his eyes hungry. He thought I couldn't.

I used air magic to whip his tie, and then let it blow across the others. "The soul link allows us to share some of our powers. I can feel a person's power level now, too, not just their soul. Kieran can use my magic enough to see spirits."

"Yes, but we've seen your magic move the air as

well," Zander said, squinting. "For those that don't know, what is the difference between what air magic and spirit can do?"

I blew spirit across them, sucking power from the Line to do it, making sure they felt it. When their souls rattled in their casings, every Demigod but Magnus sucked in a startled breath.

"Looks the same, but feels different," I concluded.

"Yes. Quite." Zander visibly shivered.

"The soul link also swells her power. Surely you can feel her elevated level," Magnus said, his finger draped across his upper lip.

Zander turned a little to look at him, as though surprised.

Magnus answered the unspoken question. "I've known she must have a soul link for some time. I am familiar with them, though I no longer have one."

"Oh right, yes. The reason for the…" Zander made a circular motion with his finger. "The child issue." He turned back to face me. "Fine. Now, Alexis, I do know Demigod Kieran has asked you to marry him. He has *said* he wishes to make you co-ruler once you marry, which would make the mark immediately legitimate, but here you are with nothing but a promise. I can't help but question this. It would be a good strategy for him to mark you, offer to share the leadership, and then never go through with it. He would…have his cake and eat it too, so to speak."

I chuckled. I couldn't help it.

"Something is funny?" the woman beside Zander asked.

I schooled my expression. "It's Kieran who wants to share the leadership role, not me. I have no desire to step up to the plate, but I will because he wants me at his side. Look, the mark has nothing to do with that. I love him. I want him, forever. I don't care if he's in charge of a territory or not. I like the way it feels when he burns his mark across my skin and claims me as his. I ask him to do it often. I like being tethered to his soul. Everything else is just politics, and I don't much care for that. There's nothing else I can tell you about it."

Silence trickled into the lofty room, all seven pairs of eyes beating down on me.

"One last question," the woman beside Zander said. "Why not marry before coming here? You have pledged yourself to him—why not button it up and make it official?"

"The mark and the soul link *are* official. It's more official than a few signed pieces of paper and a rubber stamp. A legal partnership can be undone, but the ways we have united cannot be dismissed. With us, it is until death do us part, *literally*. One of us will have to die to undo what has been done.

"As for your question, I haven't decided what kind

of wedding I want. I don't know where I want to have it. I couldn't waste time thinking about it before this Summit because I had too much to prepare for, and..."

I sucked in a breath and wiped my forehead again, trying to stop the flow of words. I couldn't imagine they were helping at this point.

Silence filtered through again, all those eyes making me nervous, their judgment turning my blood cold. The assembled didn't seem to like my answers.

"Look, I love him," I said. "I love him with everything that is in me. I wouldn't go back and change anything that has happened between us. I trust him to keep me safe, and I'll support him in all things. We're stronger together. I don't know how else to convince you, and I certainly don't know how to make you butt out."

The woman looked down her nose at me. "You can marry him now and finish this up. That will make us...butt...out."

I responded without much consideration. "A person only gets married once. Kieran and I will marry when and *how* we want, and I guarantee you, it won't be a rush job in some oversized office building in front of a lot of humorless magical people who have a shaky hold, at best, on morals."

"Have a care, Alexis, on how you speak to your betters," said a woman beside Magnus, and I gritted my teeth to the point of pain, trying to hold back the words that wanted to bubble out. These clowns weren't my betters, or even my equals. They had more power, that was it. That was all. If we were on equal footing, I'd push and shove until I could inject a little humanity back into his group of tyrants.

Pressure settled on my shoulders and bit into my shoulder blades, the feeling of being watched oppressive. The Line throbbed into the room, unbidden, and shadows zipped all around it. Magnus jerked, seeing it.

A shadow lurked within, staring into the room. This wasn't Harding—the shadow being exuded menace. It pulsed with vengeance.

Panic welled up in me. Would Lydia or Aaron dare to make a move in such a public place, before Magnus?

"Fine, fine." Zander banged the gavel, and I jumped. Still that shadow stared. "I move to a vote. Will the mark be classified as valid, yay or nay?"

He turned to get answers, but I couldn't look away from that shadow. If I did, I feared it might step into my plane, like Harding had done. Something about that thought had cold creeping through my middle.

"Nay."

The coldness turned to dread. I dragged my eyes away from the shadow long enough to see who'd spoken. The guy at the end, who'd doubted the soul link earlier, smirked at me. He'd just added himself to my "enemy" list.

Chapter 15

ALEXIS

WHEN I SWUNG my gaze back to the Line, it abruptly disappeared, and the shadow with it. Colors returned to normal. The freezing grip that had squeezed my middle relented.

Magnus's gaze was heavy on me, his eyes analyzing—or maybe accusatory?

A "yay" came in, then another, my heart still hammering despite it.

"Yay," Magnus said when his turn came, his stare intense.

"Yay." Zander banged the gavel. "Passes, six to one. The mark is valid. Now, Alexis, let's move on to other business."

Magnus's brow rumpled and he finally looked away, peering over at Zander. Apparently he hadn't realized there would be other business.

"I have questions about the Thunderstroke," Zander said, and Magnus's look went from confused to flat and disinterested.

The sound of the doors opening echoed through the lofty hall.

I didn't have time to relax before my body wound up again. Dylan's shoulders were tight and his eyes panicked, but he walked in with his head held high, as befitted one of Zeus.

"What about him?" I asked, dread squeezing me a second time. I wasn't the only valuable one the Demigods wanted to get their hands on.

Dylan sat in the chair beside me, which he scooted a little closer until it was touching mine.

"The situation surrounding him is highly unusual." Zander leaned forward, and hunger sparked in his gaze. Despite his reputation as a rule follower, it was clear that even Zander wasn't above scheming to acquire a rarity for his collection. "We need to make sure that he wasn't…cornered into the position he now holds, you understand."

"All due respect," I said, "that's rich, coming from the lot of you. You grilled me about my very legitimate mark, but you didn't bat an eye at the bogus mark he was forced to endure in the past."

"He was not brought before us, therefore his mark could not be called into question."

"Why do you think he wasn't brought before you?" I waited a moment, my cheeks hot. "Because he was confined while being physically and emotionally abused by his captor. He was sufficiently *cornered* there, yet no one showed up to help him. Now that he's in a good situation for once in his life, he's the subject of scrutiny? Do you only go after those who don't require your help, or what?"

"Just a moment, young lady," Zander said, his voice dropping an octave and his intensity making the hairs on my arms stand at attention. "I ask that you have a little patience." It was entirely too clear that he wasn't asking. "Gianna kept that boy under lock and key. We didn't see him. Out of sight, out of mind."

I clenched my fist. What a sorry excuse.

"Now, Mr. Maccini—"

"That is no longer my name," Dylan cut in. "I started a new life. I've chosen a new name."

Zander braced his forearms against the desk surface. "Did Demigod Kieran urge you to take a new name?" he asked.

"I chose a new name when I landed in that Chester town in the hills. Demigod Kieran accepted the name I offered him."

"Yes, let's talk about how you ended up in that Chester town. Demigod Gianna was poisoned. You were both poisoned—poison was found in your bowls and in your blood work—and you were both pronounced dead. I inquired at the time and had it on good authority that you were *thoroughly* dead. The person responsible was never found, but given you'd gone down with the ship, so to speak, we had no reason to suspect it was you. But now, here you are, strong as a lark. I find all of this highly suspicious."

"I couldn't have poisoned her, if that's what you mean. Not with the blood oath." Dylan fidgeted with his shirt.

"Maybe not you, but certainly an accomplice isn't out of the realm of possibility."

Dylan laughed without humor. "An accomplice? I wasn't allowed to speak to anyone without supervision. I wasn't allowed to have any friends. If I could've poisoned her and granted my freedom, I would've, believe me. If I could've found a way to end my own life just to get away, I would've. But I was trapped. Thoroughly trapped. Granting my own salvation was impossible."

"Then how did you escape?" Zander pressed.

Dylan shrugged. "To this day, I still don't know. I remember my throat closing up and the taste of bile. I remember clawing at my neck, desperately gasping for air but not getting any. Gianna was beside me, doing the same thing. Magic exploded around the room. The pain was excruciating, and given Demigod Gianna's fancy for whips, nipple clamps, hot wax, and strap-ons, that's saying something."

The accusation in Zander's eyes dulled somewhat.

His face twisted in disgust. “I see.”

“Pardon my bluntness, sir, but no, you do not. I lived in hell on earth. Trapped, like I said. Caged, like an animal, at times. I longed for death more than once. Dying itself was excruciating, but as the blackness blotted out my vision and the pain lifted, I was honestly happy to be released. The last memory I have of the attack is lying on the floor on my side and seeing the door open. My last thought was *Please let death release me from this life.* That’s all I remember.”

“And yet you haven’t been released at all.” The guy at the end leaned forward this time, his eyes alight. “That pretty little Soul Stealer—”

“I would ask you to refrain from using the words *pretty* and *little* when speaking about a woman with superior status and a highly advantageous magic, if you would be so kind,” the stately woman said pompously. “It is degrading.”

“Agreed,” Magnus drawled, leaning heavily in his chair now. He was clearly bored. “Not to mention disrespectful when speaking of your colleague’s daughter. Or didn’t you get the memo, Rufus?”

“Ah yes. Now that you mention it, I did hear somewhere that you are getting soft in your old age.” A sneer covered Rufus’s face.

“Men, please, enough.” Zander frowned, keeping his gaze on Dylan. “Rufus, what was your point?”

"I find it interesting that a Thunderstroke essentially came back from the dead and ended up with a Spirit Walker. Didn't she bring one of yours back from the dead yesterday, Zander? Seems suspect."

Magnus sighed so loudly that it was clear he meant to be heard. "The incident in question happened fifteen years ago. Alexis was eleven. Even if she'd been in training at the time, she wouldn't have been able to travel to the other side of the country without being noticed, let alone use the sort of magic necessary to bring a man back from poisoning. I doubt she could do it now. She can only repair the soul—she cannot repair the body. Try again, Rufus. We do so love when you speak out of turn about things you have no knowledge of."

"Yes, yes, quite right, Magnus, quite right. Hmm." Zander rubbed his chin, the sound like sandpaper. "And then what happened, Mister…Dylan?"

Dylan relayed the story about how he'd woken up in a morgue all by himself, cold and alone, without a mortician or guard nearby. He filled them in on how he'd snuck out, creeping past sleeping guards, and found an unoccupied van. He'd later ditched the car and gotten a ride from a truck driver, who'd brought him as far as the Chester town.

"So you had no contact with the magical world for fifteen years?" Zander asked, his confusion evident.

"None. I read the news, but that was it," Dylan responded.

"Then how did Demigod Kieran find you?"

I held my breath, and Magnus's eyes returned to me. I had a feeling the guy could read me even though I was trying to keep all my emotions bottled up.

They couldn't know Harding had told me about him.

"They said they noticed the pattern." Dylan scratched the side of his head. "I wasn't as subtle as I'd intended to be with my magic. I tried to use it as sparingly as I could, but…"

"The weather has been increasingly strange these last years. Even the last decade. You expect me to believe Demigod Kieran's people just…happened to notice more lightning than normal?" Zander's gaze fell on me. "What is it you are hiding, young lady?"

How'd he know I was the one hiding something? Was my face as red as it felt?

"We heard a rumor that Dylan's grave was empty," I blurted, trying to play it cool, like Daisy always did when she lied. Thank God they didn't have an Authenticator here to magically confirm that I was lying. "The plot was there, but nothing was in it, basically. Amber found it on some conspiracy theory chat room or other, I think. Some guy used one of those sonar machines or something, I don't know. I was only half listening." I shrugged. "She is great at her job. She and Henry did the research, and the evidence seemed to fit, so we checked it out."

Zander leaned back in his chair, clearly getting agitated. "A conspiracy theory chat room… Have I heard of this site?"

"There are as many of those as there are souls in the beyond," Magnus said. "I'm sure Amber could show it to you."

"I'm still unclear on what it is that we are trying to assess," the regal woman beside Zander said, her patience clearly thinning. "Are we trying to ascertain if he killed Gianna? The reason for his escape is pretty clear—anyone in his situation would've run if they'd had the chance."

"We are trying to assess how Demigod Kieran was able to find the prized Thunderstroke and Demigod Zander was not," Magnus said with a little smile playing across his lips.

Anger infused Zander's expression. "As I see it, there are two issues on the table. The first is who killed Gianna. The fact that Dylan is alive and has been in hiding makes him a suspect. The second is the legitimacy of the blood oath he took with Kieran. I would hate the Thunder—Dylan to be subject to a bad situation a second time."

"Why didn't we question Demigod Kieran about

this when he was here?" a woman at the end asked.

"Because it is easier to badger the hired help." Magnus's smile burned a little brighter. The guy at the end grinned, leaning on his forearms. It was clear only Zander cared about this issue.

Zander's jaw clenched, and I wondered if maybe he and my father weren't the best of friends. I needed to mention it to Kieran.

"Look..." Zander paused. "I'm simply trying to assess how he ended up in Demigod Kieran's employ when he was presumed dead. It is one thing to follow up on a cloak-and-dagger story and quite another to find a living Thunderstroke hiding in a Chester territory. Something isn't making sense here. Something is missing."

"As I see it..." the regal woman said slowly, and suddenly all the air dried up in the room. It wasn't magic, it was her intensity. "Someone who's trying to escape doesn't attempt to kill himself in the process. But if you want to open up an inquisition regarding Gianna's death, fine. I propose you do it on your own time, however. That situation is of little importance to me."

"Agreed," Magnus said.

"Agreed," two others chorused.

"Fine, fine," Zander cut in, clearly seeing the writing on the wall. "But what about—"

"I chose Demigod Kieran," Dylan cut in, and lifted

his chin. I knew it wasn't easy to admit that to someone of Zeus given the way Zeus people traditionally stuck together. "You can question the Chester townspeople, or simply check the timeline. There is proof to back up these claims. I went to Kieran. I accepted the oath from him. I'm satisfied where I am."

"Yes, there. See?" The regal woman checked her watch. "Genuine. You can tell these things. I don't think there is anything more for us to do here."

Zander's stare beat into Dylan, and I knew the holes in the story were still bothering him. He wasn't about to let this go, not when it concerned a magic he clearly wanted.

"All who think his testimony is valid, say yay," Magnus said.

"Wait a moment." Zander held up his hand. "Wait. I am not clear on the whole story. I wish to think about this some more. Something isn't adding up."

"I am satisfied with the testimony and I have places to be." Rufus braced his hands on the arms of his chair, getting ready to stand. "You lost out on a precious Thunderstroke. Magnus didn't get to kill his kid… You guys can have drinks about it and remember the good old times before you instituted these tedious hearings. Now, if you'll—"

"I vote we table this for now until I can get to the bottom of the discrepancy," Zander said, his voice booming. Nervousness exploded in my belly. I'd come in here thinking *I* was under fire. I hadn't known Dylan would be tossed into the flames with me.

"Fine. Yay. Whatever." Rufus stood.

"Yay." The regal woman stood as well.

The rest muttered their assent, eager to be gone.

My heart was beating too quickly. I could sense the concern from Kieran through the link.

Now we'd have Zander poking into our affairs, and if he found out who'd really told me about Dylan, he'd be none too pleased. We'd first summoned Harding with a pocket watch originally stolen from Zander, after all, not to mention I was being trained by someone Zander had killed. There were all sorts of skeletons in my closet, and I didn't want Zander knowing about any of them.

"DYLAN, RIDE WITH us." Kieran pushed open the door to the Summit building and paused for me to go through. Anger and annoyance burned through the soul link.

"Yes, sir," Dylan said, walking out after me, the others following.

The limos waited where we'd left them, each of the drivers standing beside an opened door. I got into the lead limo and scooted over so Kieran and Dylan could follow me in. As soon as we got moving, Kieran let out a big sigh.

"Tell me what happened. Start from the beginning," Kieran said.

Working together, Dylan and I recounted what had been said, pausing for more precise questions and left turning occasionally to explain what the other Demigods had said and done. When we were finished, Kieran stared out the window for a moment in silence.

"That is…surprising," he said softly as we neared the lodge. "I hadn't picked up on his concerns. I had no idea he would try to pull Dylan in. Damn it, some of these old-timers are wily."

"He's not happy with the story," I said, bracing my hand to my stomach as nervous butterflies exploded through my ribcage. "He sees the obvious holes."

Kieran nodded slowly, still staring out the window. "The holes in Dylan's half of the story have nothing to do with us. He can look into that all he wants—maybe he'll even uncover the killer, who knows. It won't have anything to do with us. Or Dylan. Your story…"

Another wave of butterflies fluttered in my stomach.

"Still has nothing to do with me," Dylan said softly.

Kieran leaned back and slung his arm across the seatback. "Exactly. Alexis working with Harding has nothing to do with you. There are absolutely no grounds to take you from this team. Zander can scratch and sniff all he wants; he won't come up with anything, especially since the other Demigods will surely cock-block him if he tries to get sneaky."

"But the thing with Harding will *not* look good for me," I said, now feeling a little sick. "It'll make him question me all over again. Your mark won't mean a thing if they think I am too dangerous to live."

Kieran brushed my hair away from my face. "It'll be okay. We'll handle this. He'll never find out. Tell me about the spirit that peered in during the proceedings. You only mentioned that in passing. It wasn't Harding?"

I shook my head as we pulled up in front of the lodge, a smear of red catching my eye. Dylan leaned closer to the window and his mouth dropped open. "Oh crap."

"What is it?" I asked as he pushed open the door.

The second the limo stopped, he was out, jogging toward the lodge. Kieran got out next, and a flurry of emotion rolled through the link.

"What is it?" I asked again, taking his hand and letting him help me out.

Shouts made me glance right, and I caught Thane and Zorn running for the lodge. The rest of the guys and gals hurried out of their rides, their faces grim and movements urgent. In a moment, it all came together.

The walkway was awash with blood. It dripped off the concrete and into the dirt. Drops of red had splattered across white and yellow flower petals. A dark smear ran down the wall near the gaping door. The guys had charged in too quickly to bother closing it.

Just beyond the puddle of blood, *Chester* had been written in a red, shaky scrawl.

My chest constricted as I noticed a lump of flesh off to the side of the path, so mutilated it was unidentifiable.

"Oh God," I said, tears prickling my eyes and panic clawing at my mind. "Oh God, Da—"

"She's good." Thane appeared in the doorway and gave us a thumbs-up. "She's good. They're both good. They didn't even know this had happened. They've been inside the whole time."

"We got a pig, people," Bria said, kneeling by the lump of flesh. "This poor porker lost his life for a hate crime. Ain't that some bullshit."

"I'll check the cameras." Henry jogged toward the house, stomping on a couple of flowers to avoid the walkway. Amber followed, taking more care to leave the plant life intact.

Red looked down on the dead thing. "Is it fresh? We have a barbecue out back. Might as well cook it."

"Yeah, good call." Bria stood and looked over the blood-scrawled word. "Think this is a threat, or a prank?"

Kieran took my hand as I veered around the mess

toward the house, wanting to check on Daisy. "We'd have to have some sick friends for this to be a prank," he said. "Thane, call headquarters and get someone to clean this up."

Jerry pointed at Bria. "Maybe her kind did it. They have a thing for corpses."

"Nah." Bria followed us into the house. "My kind would carve 'Chester' into the side of the animal, stuff a spirit in its carcass, and make it dance on the front porch. Which is exactly what I'd do to the assholes who did this if that pig was in anyway useable. It's too chewed up, though."

"Sorry I mentioned it," Jerry grumbled.

"I figured you would be."

Inside, the house was as we'd left it, calm and quiet.

"They got as far as the door, but didn't cross the threshold," Red said.

"Crossing the threshold would have been a territory violation, and I could have dealt with them myself," Kieran growled. "Which they would've known."

"We need to keep that little gremlin with us at all times," Red said. "This was a threat, and if they get a chance, they'll follow it up with steel."

Chapter 16

Daisy

DAISY SAT IN the wood chair overlooking the crystalline ocean, the white sands of the public beach not three feet from her chair. Mordecai waited beside her, not wanting to leave her by herself. Who knew what could sneak along the beach and snatch her from the edges of Kieran's territory?

Daisy was only out here because she was curious.

"We shouldn't be out here without one of the crew," Mordecai mumbled, only the third time he'd said it since she'd snuck out of the house.

"The lodge is just a hop, step, and skip away, Mordecai, we'll be fine. No one is going to get us."

"Except maybe whoever left the dead pig for you earlier."

"Oh my God, are you serious? Did you hit your head and lose a few brain cells?" She scowled at him. "Those people came by when Kieran and Lexi were away. They very clearly did not want to get caught sneaking around a Demigod's territory. No way are they going to come by when the whole crew is here, are you mad? *Think!*"

He huffed and looked away down the beach. He knew she was right; he was just worried. That was his problem—he worried too much. It would make him gray before his time.

The people that had left her the unimaginative pig's blood love note had been smart enough to hide their identities from the cameras mounted on the front porch by wearing nondescript hooded brown robes. But they hadn't been smart enough to hide their shoes or take off their jewelry. One had a distinctive silver ring, another wore runners, and the rest of the group had on boots in various colors and styles. Any of those characteristics wouldn't stand out much on its own, but she'd be looking for a group of people.

Lexi better not keep Daisy from going after them. She knew Zorn would be down to help her.

"You're not going like that, right?" Mordecai pointed at her hoody. He was trying to light a fire under her butt.

They were going to Magnus's house in a bit, the invite delivered soon after Lexi and Kieran had returned from the hearing for the mark.

"No, I am not going like this. I have to change into a dress that cost over two grand." She couldn't help laughing at that. "Did you ever think, in a million years, we'd have the money to buy such pricey clothes?"

"It's a waste. Fabric doesn't cost that much. Neither does honest labor."

"True. But it does have a label, and the people here notice those kinds of things."

"They're idiots for not noticing what a waste it is. Think of how many people you could feed with that money."

Mordecai might play nice, but so many parts of this world disgusted him. He wasn't overly enthused about hobnobbing with important people.

Honestly, neither was Daisy. The crew Kieran had assembled was awesome, but a lot of the other magical people in this place were self-important snobs. She couldn't stand their voices.

Daisy sighed and squinted up at the falling sun. She *did* need to get dressed and ready to go.

"Today was boring," she said, and stretched for no reason.

It took her a moment to realize Mordecai had gone rigid. She followed his gaze down the beach, where two stocky characters glided along, their movements fluid and graceful despite the sand.

"Have you seen any shifters yet?" she murmured, keeping her voice down so their superior hearing wouldn't pick up her words. They were too far away now, but moving quickly. They weren't just out for a stroll.

"No, not in the teams we've battled."

"But those are shifters, right?"

He didn't answer for a moment before looking out at the ocean. "Yup. They must've heard about the shifter kid that got kicked out of his pack. Jack warned me when he was alive that shifters act funny about someone that was exiled. Some get aggressive toward outcasts, some view them as easy pickings and want to bully, others are curious why they were cast out, which often turns into a challenge… If they're out here looking for me, they have an agenda."

"But you were a kid. A sick kid, at that. Holding you responsible for being cast out by a shit alpha is crap."

"The type of people that would pick on an outcast aren't the type known for their thinking ability," Mordecai said dryly.

A thrill arrested her. *Such* a good idea to sneak out.

"What are you thinking?" she asked, leaning back and taking on an unaffected pose.

"We are underage, alone, and it would be stupid to engage. We let them go by."

A good idea to sneak out, a bad idea to bring him.

"But what if you can take them?" she asked. "Aren't you curious what it's like to take on an enemy shifter?"

"They aren't our enemies."

"I can make them our enemies in, like, two seconds

flat. I got a way with words, Mordie, don't you worry. You want a fight, I'll get you that fight."

He gave her a flat look. "We both know which of us wants to fight." Looking at the ocean again, he added, "You're reckless."

"Tell me you aren't curious. Tell me, I dare you. No, don't even bother, you'd be lying. You want to know how you stack up against your own kind. It's only natural."

"And I suppose you wonder how you'd stack up against your own kind."

"Give me a break—I'd rock any Chester's world."

His sigh was slight, but it spoke volumes. Oh yeah, he was curious. He hadn't gotten much action yesterday. Neither of them had. The taste they'd been given hadn't been enough to satisfy the craving their training had developed. It hadn't been enough to really show where they stood.

"Can you smell them?" she whispered excitedly. A shifter could glean plenty of information from watching and smelling an opponent. Powerful shifters smelled powerful, and they held themselves a certain way. Daisy was still learning the nuances, and obviously smell would forever be a blind spot to her dulled senses, but she had a pretty good handle on how these things worked.

"Yes. I'm downwind."

"Aaaand?" She watched his body language. Excitement bubbled through him, she could see it. Anticipation. "You're more dominant, aren't you?"

"I won't know unless I fight."

"Estimate, jackass."

"I remember when I saw Will Green's man in that strip mall a year or so ago. He scared the crap out of me. He was by far more dominant. Everything in me wanted to turn and run. It was Lexi that handled things."

Daisy nearly sat forward, riveted. Mordie never really opened up about this stuff—he was too levelheaded and boring. She could see the drive in him right now. She could see the light bulb clicking on.

"These guys are stronger than that other guy, I'd bet my life on it. I doubt they are as corrupt or brutal, but they are more experienced. I can see their intensity in their movements. I can see how dominant they think they are."

She lifted her eyebrows, not hiding the grin working up her face. She knew where this was going.

Everything in his posture stayed loose when he said, "I'm half their age, but I could take one and a half of them. Individually, I'm more dominant. I'd have to prove it, but…"

He didn't finish because he was humble, but he didn't have to.

Daisy's grin turned into a full smile. "Damn right

you're more dominant. I don't hang out with no chump." She patted the dagger hugging her hip, something she always took with her now. This was Mordie's chance. He needed to take on a shifter and win. He didn't just need to prove his dominance to another shifter—he needed to prove it to himself. He'd never fought on his own, and he'd certainly never fought his own kind for dominance. Until he could spend more time with his kind, he wouldn't, either. Unless she helped.

"I'll play beta. I'll distract one of them for a few moments while you get to work. Don't worry, I'll let you run the show. I'll just help out."

Mordecai glanced back at her, his hazel eyes sparkling with the challenge. In a moment, though, the call of battle dulled. His posture sagged a little, like someone putting away their knives.

He turned back around. "You don't have blood magic or backup, Daisy. I'm here to protect you, not put you in needless danger. We stand down."

Her mouth dropped open. "Are you serious? You know I'm good for this, Mordecai. You know I'll stay out of harm's way. All I'm going to do is distract the guy, not properly fight him. I could do it in my sleep!"

"All it would take would be one thing to go wrong. One unexpected thing, like stepping wrong and twisting your ankle, or flinching at the wrong time. Without healing magic, you're too fragile. You should've taken Kieran up on his offer for the blood magic, but you didn't, and now here you are."

Anger and frustration boiled within her. Kieran had made that offer yesterday evening, approaching her in private so she wouldn't feel pressured. He'd known what she was going to say, but he'd given her the choice anyway. It was a good move, but in vain. If Kieran one day turned into Valens, Daisy needed to be the level-headed ejector cord. The healing magic would've been nice, and whatever gifts came with it, but the price was too steep.

She hadn't expected Mordecai to penalize her for it, the douche.

"There is no way I am letting that Demigod have a piece of me, Mordecai, you know that. I don't need him. I'm good without it."

"Not right now, you're not. We stand down."

The guys approached them, their eyes firmly on Mordecai, as though they were walking by strictly to see if he wanted to come out and play. Daisy wished to hell he would.

"What's this, Roy?" the guy on the right said, a block of muscle with a square head, a buzzcut, and huge ears. "A little bitty wolf cub without a pack."

Roy, taller and leaner but with plenty of power in his movements, grinned maliciously. "Heard you got kicked out of your pack. What kind of sad sack gets kicked out of a pack as a kid? You must've been utter shit."

If they'd expected to get a rise out of Mordecai, they were sorely mistaken. He had way too much confidence and pride in his past for that.

Daisy waved her hand a little to grab their attention. Only Big Ears glanced her way. She pointed at herself, then flicked her eyes to Mordecai.

Big Ears scrunched up his face, looking confused.

"Not a thinker, huh?" Daisy murmured, leaning her forearms on her knees and staring him down. Hopefully that would register as a challenge.

Mordecai needed to get his feet wet. She'd be damned if she would hold him back. Or let him hold himself back.

She couldn't just leave him to it, though. There was that half to think about.

"You're going to hide behind your age like a little—"

"What are you looking at, Chester?" Big Ears asked, cutting Roy off.

Daisy smirked and straightened, slipping a little arrogant condescension into her gaze. She didn't respond, though. She didn't want Mordecai to know she was instigating this.

"Disgusting." Roy spat, the glob landing dangerously close to Mordecai's shoe. "A shifter hanging out with a filthy Chester. He's a disgrace to his kind."

Daisy flashed a thumbs-up.

Big Ears snarled. "Look down, Chester, or I'll *make* you look down. Realize when you're being approached by your betters."

"No thanks," Daisy said flippantly.

"I bet you're a dirty girl. Do you get on all fours and beg to mate?" Big Ears said, turning slightly so his chest was pointed at her. She couldn't tell if he was taking the hint and going after her in order to incite Mordie, or if he was just small-minded and super gross.

Mordecai tensed, and so Daisy didn't respond, though she really wanted to.

"Chester whore," Roy spat, clearly incapable of any sort of independent or creative thinking.

Daisy leaned back and yawned, feigning boredom. Roy turned a little, his full attention on her now, too. Oops. Maybe she'd been a little too zealous in her dismissal of their presence. She'd read that shifters *really* hated that, but she'd never actually put it to the test. Verdict: true.

"You stupid little bitch," Roy said, his face screwed up in anger. "You shouldn't even be here. We should do everyone a favor and drown you in the ocean."

Big Ears looked at the invisible but very clear territory line in front of them—one step over it and they could grab Daisy. They could wrestle with Mordecai.

The adult shifters glanced around, looking for witnesses. Their eyes narrowed, each clearly thinking the same thing—they could kill these two teens, stash the bodies, and get out of here. Who would know?

Daisy barely dared to breathe. These guys weren't too far gone to see reason. Mordecai was the soul of reason. He could remind them it was against the rules to challenge a minor, back them down, and make an exit.

Or they could fight.

Mordecai stood, smooth and graceful. The two guys braced themselves. When Mordecai turned, Daisy nearly sagged with annoyance.

"Take the half." And then Mordecai was shrugging out of his clothes.

He'd accepted the unspoken challenge!

Daisy was up in a flash. Freeing her dagger, she launched herself at Big Ears before he could even get out of his boots. She was a non-magical Chester; she didn't have to fight fair.

He startled and clamped his hands around her shoulders. The bastard was strong.

Arching back, she pulled her knees up—her flexibility and wiliness were her biggest strengths. Her weight slammed into him suddenly—unexpectedly—pulling his top half with her as he struggled to hang on. She pushed out with her arms, arching more, and yanked her feet around. The force was finally too much, and he let go. The soles of her feet hit ground instead of her head. *Phew.* She hadn't properly accounted for his strength with that maneuver.

No time to stall, she launched forward, dagger up, jabbing. The business end pierced his stomach. He grunted and reached for her, ignoring the painful wound. She was already moving. To stay still in this situation was to be overpowered and die.

Dodging his reaching arms, she took the hilt of the dagger in both hands and slammed the blade into his body. It squelched as it came back out, and then she jammed it in again, aiming for a kidney. Her aim on this part of the body was terrible—she knew she'd miss—but it would hurt like hell, and if he knew what she was going for, it would freak him out. A couple of shots to the kidney would kill a shifter, and now he knew that she knew.

Welcome to being mind-fucked, my friend.

A fierce snarl nearly pulled her focus. Mordecai was engaging. She couldn't watch, though. One slip and she'd be toast, as he'd said. She'd be damned if she'd die and give him a complex.

"Stupid bitch," Big Ears wheezed.

Big ears…

Maybe she'd cut one of those off, just for shits and giggles.

Ducking behind him, she bent and stuck her knife in his inner thigh, *really* close to his nut sack. If the kidneys didn't freak him out, this would.

His high-pitched scream made her smile. She jumped, slammed her blade into the top of his shoulder, and climbed him like a tree. He spun while reaching around, trying to throw her off. But this was why she'd embedded the knife—as a handle.

He spun the other way, slowing a little. It was too good of an opportunity to pass up.

Working faster than she ever had in training, she scrambled up to his shoulders, wrapped her legs around his head, clutched the knife, and spun her upper body down and to the side, ripping her legs with her. Gravity helped her to the ground. Before she hit, she pushed her arms wide so the knife didn't end up in her middle.

The impact cracked something and knocked the air out of her. Her execution of that move needed a little work, because that had hurt like hell.

Struggling for breath, she scrambled up. To give in to the pain was to give in to death—or so Zorn always said. Right now, she believed it.

A black animal went rolling across the white sands, leaving a trail of bright red in its wake. Was that a panther? Cool. Mordecai was on it a moment later, his fierce snarl sending a jolt of uncontrolled, primal fear through Daisy's middle. She'd never heard that note in

Mordecai's growl before. She'd never felt this sort of unbridled intensity when they'd trained. It was a little daunting.

Mordecai still busy, she took two side steps, spun, and attacked, dagger ready. The shifter hadn't gotten up and certainly hadn't changed, so she pounced on his back and dug the knife between his shoulder blades.

She yanked it free and bounced off, waiting for his movements to determine where she struck next.

But he didn't so much as twitch.

A howl of pain grabbed her attention. Mordecai ripped across the panther's belly with his claws before going for the jugular. The panther struggled feebly, beaten.

All Daisy had to do was stall before Mordecai handled the other half of hers. Well...probably more like a quarter at this point. She'd stuck him pretty good. He hadn't been as quick as the people they'd faced in the halls.

The man still lay prone, unmoving.

Worry crept through her. She really hoped he was playing dead so as to surprise her.

Except...shifters didn't play dead. They were like Zeus in that way. Their egos couldn't handle standing down.

"Shit," she whispered, kicking one of his arms out of the way. It was heavy and lifeless. "Oh shit. Mordie...I think I fucked up."

Mordecai padded over, leaving the panther on its side, its bloody, glistening body rising and falling as it struggled to breathe, its jugular ripped open and freely bleeding into the sand. Mordecai had taken that fight, hands down.

"Is that one going to live?" she asked, pointing at the panther.

Mordecai sniffed Big Ears's face before his head came up, his intelligent hazel eyes meeting hers. She knew the situation without having to ask. That crack hadn't been her back—it had been his neck. She might've executed the move poorly, but she'd done it well enough to be effective, something Zorn had said she didn't have the strength and precision to do yet.

Well, joke was on him, because she had enough precision to crack someone's neck, she just didn't have the landing down.

Maybe the joke was also on her and Mordie, because now they had a body on their hands.

"Zorn will help us get rid of it. Should I go get him? This is really his fault, anyway. If he'd had more faith in me, I wouldn't have tried to practice on this guy." Only an asshole blamed herself, after all.

Mordecai changed back into himself, breathing quickly from the fight and the change.

"That wasn't half," he said, bending to take the

man's pulse.

"Right, yes. I know. Sorry, but honestly, I didn't mean to kill him. I was just going to stab him a whole bunch until you were ready."

He grinned, and she paused.

"I knew you weren't going to settle for half." He straightened again. "I also knew you weren't going to settle for standing down."

"I…would've…"

"You were intentionally egging them on, Daisy, I saw you. You can't tell Lexi about this. She would kill me if she knew I let you fight a shifter twice your age, size, and experience level. *Kill* me!"

Daisy couldn't help laughing. "Who's the good kid now, huh?"

His eyebrows pinched together. "You're still not the good kid."

"Yeah, okay, fair enough." The panther still panted, bleeding heavily, not trying to get up. "I mean…should we just throw them into the ocean, or… Zorn will keep the secret. I still vote we go get him."

"Yeah, okay," Mordecai said quietly, heading to his clothes. Though he was clearly ready to take challenges from experienced shifters, he was not ready to hide a body. Nobody was perfect.

A strange feeling rolled over Daisy. They weren't alone anymore—a…presence had joined them. Beautiful and wicked, like a unicorn had slid down a rainbow, trotted over to her, and then crapped on her shoe. The dichotomy delighted her. Excited her.

Called to her.

This wasn't the first time she'd sensed this particular…thing watching. She'd felt the same presence yesterday before the courtyard battle. It had stood just off to the side, noticed by absolutely no one, a spectral brilliance that not even Zorn could manifest on his best day. But this being was one of Zorn's people—she knew that much. Dark fae.

Not many people knew about Zorn's magic. He didn't speak of its origins, not ever, and neither did Kieran. There were plenty of Jinns in the magical world, after all, and Zorn was connected to water, so why should anyone question his link to Poseidon? But a little research had revealed the truth: if you went far enough back, all Jinns originated from the land of the dark fae. A twisted place where nothing was as it seemed.

She still didn't know how Zorn had come to be in Ireland all those years ago, but he or his parents must have made it across the fae borders that had been erected to protect the human world. The fae weren't supposed to cross those borders unless they had a binding contract that permitted them to carry out their business in the human world. They were incredibly dangerous, she'd heard. Treacherous. One might befriend you, save you, make love to you, only to turn around and stab you in the heart.

Who in their right mind would employ the dark fae?

Lydia had made a pact with them, but that pact had surely been broken, had it not? Lexi had gotten away, and so had Kieran.

The panther lifted its long tail, distracting her, before laying it down again. His paw slid across the sands. The bleeding had slowed.

"He's going to make it," Mordecai said, shrugging into his shirt. "I clearly have more control than you."

"Fine, yeah…" She'd meant to say *hurry up* so they could get Zorn and deal with her *faux pas*, but the words wouldn't come. If anything, she wanted Mordecai to slow down so she could think. So she could continue to observe that transparent rainbow sheen in the air. She was sure someone waited there, watching. Analyzing. Thinking he/she was hidden behind the glamor of their magic.

Would it be bad to bring Zorn out here when one of his kind was hanging around? Probably, since she got the distinct impression the being lurking at the Summit was there for a reason—and that it wouldn't be pleased if she got in its way. That was the main reason she hadn't mentioned its presence to anyone else. She wasn't trying to get on the bad side of the fae.

"Should we cover up the blood in the sand before we get Zorn?" Mordecai asked, slipping into his pants. "In case someone else is going for a stroll? Or…maybe we need to just pull them into the garden to get them out of plain sight?"

The panther's breathing had slowed to normal. It wouldn't be long before he could hobble away. His friend wasn't going anywhere. At least he wouldn't tattle on them—he wouldn't want to admit to instigating a fight with two teenagers.

"It doesn't really ring as *accident* if we hide the body in the garden," she said, debating the wisdom of turning away from that shimmer. It wasn't wise to turn's one back on the fae, but they needed to get help. This wasn't something they should probably hide from Kieran, as horrible as that conversation would go.

Daisy glanced at the sparkling shimmer. For just a moment—a brief, mind-confusing moment—a pair of vivid green eyes, with a burnished gold ring around the pupil, flared into existence. She saw a flash of sharp cheekbones but nothing of the body. Even still, something about the presence rang male.

Her world lit up, sparkling with gold and color and light-like confetti. It dazzled and danced in her vision, exploding through her middle. Something deep inside of her sparked and then burned, her breathing fracturing. She couldn't tear her eyes away, wishing a body would manifest. Wanting him to speak.

The arching black brows pinched together, as though confused. The face tilted, a nod of sorts. A subtle kind of hello.

Her belly danced. Breathing became difficult.

In another moment, everything vanished. The eyes, the presence, everything. Magic too incredible, too potent, to feel or track or maybe even acknowledge blinked out.

"What was—what..." Mordecai took two quick steps forward, shock on his face, and looked at the beach.

The bodies were gone. Both of them. The blood, the messed-with sand—all of it. It was as though the skirmish hadn't happened and Daisy hadn't killed someone five feet from where she stood.

"What's going on?" Mordecai turned to her, and then his eyes flicked to the spot where the person had revealed himself. Mordecai had probably seen the eyes. Daisy couldn't imagine how anyone could've missed them, as beautiful and green as they were.

She opened her mouth to explain—

Shh, little dove. It must remain our secret, or it will become your group that I must silence.

It was as if the sentiment had been left behind like a landmine, triggered when she went to speak about him. The voice was silky and smooth and flowered in her mind. It should've scared the hell out of her, felt invasive. Instead, all the worry over what his presence might mean to Lexi melted away. Daisy had no idea if that was magic or what, but she felt in her blood that if she didn't remain silent, they would have hell knocking on their door.

Chapter 17
ALEXIS

"IT'LL BE FINE. Amber and Henry are constructing that conspiracy theory website right now." Kieran held my hand as we drove slowly through the darkness, on the way to Magnus's lodge for dinner. We'd brought the kids and the crew, just in case, plus our fleet of golf carts, but Kieran and I were leading the way. "Amber has a good tech team working on it back home. They'll get it all sorted. Zander hasn't changed with the times enough to recognize a hastily thrown together website. He's also stepping on my toes. I might be new, but he fucked himself by giving me the time of day. He has to go about this delicately unless I royally screw something up. We're good. We've got this locked down."

But it didn't feel like we did, and I could tell he didn't, either. Fear of what Aaron had in store for us ate through my gut, not to mention the presence of that shadow in the trial room. Logic dictated it must have been a Demigod. It hadn't been Harding, and no one else had that kind of advanced spirit magic. But what

Demigod in their right mind would have risked showing up in full view of Magnus? It didn't make sense. There had to be another explanation.

I worried I would not like that explanation.

I wanted so badly to talk to Harding about it, to ask if he'd seen anything, but earlier I hadn't been able to cross that weird plane. I'd only managed to stick my head in normal spirit, freak out in case one of the other Demigods was lurking and caught me, and ducked back into reality. I would get no help from him.

"How's Daisy faring?" Kieran asked as he glanced to the side, his brow furrowing. Uncertainty bled into the link.

I followed his gaze, but didn't feel or see anything in the night. "She called it a love note. I think it must be bothering her a little, though. She was flushed when she stopped in to borrow some jewelry earlier, when I was getting ready, and she's been abnormally contemplative."

He nodded, turning away from whatever he'd been looking at. "She'll be fine. We'll keep an eye on her. What about you? How are you taking all this?"

"I want her to go home. She doesn't even have healing magic, Kieran. Not even experienced magical people without healing magic belong here. She has the nod of approval—it's time for her to go."

"We can't send her home. She's making a name for

herself right now—she's finding her place. If we send her home, we'll send the message that she can't handle it. Besides, she wouldn't leave. She's sneaky—she'd find a way back in. Zorn is almost positive she and Mordecai snuck out when we were all discussing this dinner."

I crinkled my brow, thinking back. I hadn't missed her. Then again, the formal invitation to dine with my father had had me plenty distracted.

Kieran took a deep breath. "I wasn't going to tell you, but…I offered her the magic last night. She wouldn't take it. She doesn't want to be tied to me."

I jerked my head toward him. It was unusual for a Demigod to give his blood to someone who hadn't offered him an oath. Kieran clearly didn't care much about the norm, since he'd given his blood to both me and Mordie, but it was unheard of for a Demigod to offer such a boon to a perfectly healthy, non-magical person. And she'd said no.

Tears filled my eyes. "I can make her see reason."

"Which is why I didn't tell you. I don't think you should push her, Lexi. Daisy is in a very precarious situation in a world she doesn't belong in. She's trying to find her way. With all due respect, I think we need to let her. I won't force an attachment on her if she doesn't want it. We'll just keep her with us at all times. With you or with me, she's covered."

I nodded and blotted the wetness under my eyes.

Stupid eye makeup. It was so fragile.

"She's tough, though," he said with a grin. "I have to give her that. We've always known it, but…wow. Henry made…friends with a woman who works for the surveillance team." Friends meant they were bumping uglies. Apparently Henry was excellent at pillow talk. "He showed me some of the clips he smuggled out. Daisy is every bit the gremlin we've always called her. She's like a flying squirrel but with razor-sharp teeth and claws. It's kind of fun to watch."

"What if she is actually crazy instead of tough? That is my fault."

"And all the hassle you're going through is my fault. It'll be—"

"Don't." I held up my hand. "Don't say fine."

Wisely, he listened.

He turned the golf cart and crossed the sidewalk. A path that took us through grassy knolls retreated every so often and gave way to a little patch of garden. It probably said something about my mindset that I paid less attention to the fragrant flowers in deep red, canary yellow, or cerulean blue than I did the decorative rocks Jerry could use to smash in a face.

"Remember, Demigods might appear casual and friendly, but they are always looking for information," Kieran said. We hit a bump, and I reached out to grab the metal bar at the side. "Watch what you say around

Magnus. This dinner is part of some sort of game that probably has nuances we won't realize for years. I have a new appreciation for strategy after dealing with some of these guys. Keep your head. If you need a breather, don't be afraid to take it."

My father's warehouse loomed up ahead—larger than ours, it sat with its back to the beach, no more than a hundred yards from the Summit building. Fairy lights suspended on poles dangled above red rosebushes, creating a twinkling walkway to the entrance. A blood-red carpet led to the open door, flanked by two men in formfitting white coats and black pants. One of the men stepped forward to help me out, and the other bowed deeply to Kieran and took his place in the golf cart.

Huh, valet golf cart parking.

Daisy and Mordecai, sitting at the back of a four-seater with Thane driving and Boman riding shotgun, pulled up behind us. As the kids disembarked, Kieran held out his arm for me to take and then escorted me slowly along the carpet. The others handed over their ride and followed.

"This entrance is on *point*," Daisy whispered to Mordecai.

"I approve," Bria muttered somewhere behind us.

"The high-status Demigods get to choose how their accommodations are presented," Amber murmured, "so this is all to Magnus's taste. So far, he has a very subdued palette."

"In the real world, we call that *refined*," Bria said.

"Good evening." A woman greeted us at the door, bowing deeply. She'd stuck to the same dress code as the others, but her clothes had a more delicate cut. She gestured, and a man stepped forward from the side with a silver tray laden with various drinks. "We've taken the liberty at guessing what you might be in the mood for, but please, let me know if I can get you anything else."

I took a glass of champagne and Kieran took a whiskey straight. At Lydia's, Kieran and I had been waited on differently than the others in our crew, but the tray holder moved on back to serve the rest of our people. He tsked at Daisy for trying to take a margarita, nodding when she settled for a Coke instead, and lifted an eyebrow when Bria took a beer instead of the Jack and Coke. They'd done their homework.

The woman stepped back within the arching entryway. "Please, Alexis, if you wouldn't mind taking your party into the sitting room and awaiting Demigod Magnus? He'll be along shortly." The lights were down low on the chandelier, giving the setting just the right amount of glitter, and the candles in sconces placed strategically along the hallway gave the space a sense of intimacy that made me feel more comfortable.

"Oh yeah, his sense of style is *on point*." Bria sipped her beer, looking at the art and furnishings.

The woman hadn't gestured right or left. Her hands stayed tucked behind her, and she stood in the center of the foyer, allowing me to choose.

I glanced left first, expecting to see the gaudy gold décor from Kieran's sitting room in our lodge, and finding instead leather seats, an artful rug, and textured wallpaper with a really interesting design. The room on the right had fabric chairs, a rug that didn't look so fine, and a piano in the corner.

"Does anyone play?" I pointed at it.

"Thane." Boman stepped to the side, allowing Thane to come forward. "He's a miracle worker on that thing."

That was odd. I'd never heard him play.

"Would you mind?" I asked. "Just while we wait."

"Not at all," Thane said.

The woman stepped toward the room of choice. "You will find the piano perfectly in tune. If you need any other instruments, please let me know."

Kieran escorted me into the room and followed my lead to a loveseat facing the piano. He settled in beside me, taking my hand.

Thane took a seat at the piano as everyone else got comfortable except for Zorn, who stood in the corner so he could see the whole room. He rarely relaxed in a strange setting.

"This is *swank*," Daisy said, dragging her fingers

across the back of a couch before walking around to the front of it and sitting. It faced another couch separated by a little table. Mordecai sat opposite her. "Ew, I don't want to look at your mug. Go somewhere else."

"What are you going to do, stare at the wall?" he snapped.

"Do you actually mean the really cool painting behind you? Because yes, that was the plan. *Move.*"

"Kids, just for once, would you stop fighting?" I said through clenched teeth.

"Why won't you tell me?" Mordecai said.

"Mind your business," Daisy replied, and I gave them the look of death.

Mordecai caught it and skulked to the other side of the room.

The music filling the room scattered all thoughts of the kids' bickering from my head. As Thane played, he swayed with a beauty I couldn't put into words. It was like the tune had infused his whole body until he himself was alive with the sweet sound curling through the air. It whisked me away to sun-drenched hillsides of swaying grasses. The tune ebbed and flowed, filling me up and carrying me along, so in rapture that at first I didn't notice Magnus entering through the rear, walking slowly, as though taking this time to analyze the people who looked so at peace in his temporary home. Even Zorn had relaxed, his shoulders loose and easy, his eyes fixed on Thane as he soaked in the melody.

Kieran rose elegantly, and though we'd never been on a dance floor, I knew in that moment that he'd be as good at that as he was at everything else. He nearly glowed with the music.

"Demigod Magnus, thank you for welcoming us into your home." Kieran bowed low, lower than I would've expected, given his status boost.

But it struck me that he wasn't here as a Demigod—he was here as my date. And he was acting accordingly.

The gorgeous music stopped, and it felt like a hole had been punched through the moment. I took a deep breath and let Kieran help me to standing, doing a quick check that everything was in place before facing my father.

"Magnus," I said, grimacing when I realized I should've added his title. "Demigod Magnus." I didn't know if I should bow and I didn't know how to properly curtsy—I'd failed that lesson and neglected to practice. I settled for nodding awkwardly.

"Alexis, welcome." He put out a hand, and I shook it, very formal. "Thank you for joining me. If you agree, let's head back to the dining area."

I didn't know what to expect, but the place we ended up in surprised me all the same.

The kitchen was similar to ours, with the stools around the island, a small table in the corner, and various items simmering on the updated stove. A fan ran with a low hum, sucking away the steam. Both the island and the small table held place settings.

Magnus stepped up to the island and undid the button on his navy-blue suit. He peeled off his jacket before draping it on the back of one of the bar chairs.

"Please." He gestured at the other chairs. "Have a seat. I'm just finishing up. Here." He wrapped a large hand around the delicate neck of a wine bottle and handed it off to a silent and watchful Mordecai. Mordecai took it with a start. "You're sixteen, right?"

"Yes, sir," Mordecai responded without a hitch.

I, on the other hand, definitely had shock written plainly on my face.

Magnus pulled open a drawer, took out a wine opener, and handed it off. "It's time you learned a very important element of a dinner party. Or do you already know how to open a bottle of wine?"

Mordecai walked to the counter, a grin tugging at his lips. "I think I can figure it out."

"Good lad." Magnus lifted a white apron from the counter. "Daisy, correct?" He showered her with his singular focus. She met it unflinchingly, not nodding or responding to his question in any way.

My face heated. "Daisy, he's speaking to you."

"He also nearly got me and Mordecai killed," she said. "I hold grudges."

She needed to be coached in dealing with people like Magnus, or she wouldn't be able to go to dinners and meetings like this, but this wasn't the time to tell her. I needed that lesson myself, given how I'd reacted to Aaron that first night.

Magnus surveyed her for a moment. "You are exactly right," he said finally, looping the apron around his neck. "I was ultimately in charge of the Possessor. He went off course and kidnapped you when he shouldn't have, but the fault can only be traced back to me. I see I will have a long road to gain your trust."

"You will never gain my trust."

"*Daisy*," I said through clenched teeth. "You are a guest."

"I apologize. I was too blunt. Excuse me." She lowered into a curtsy, and when she came up, it was with a stare that could slice a sheet of silk in two.

Magnus shook his head slowly. "It is too bad you aren't magical. You have an inner fire that would serve you quite well in the field. It might need to serve you here—I heard about the note written in swine that you received. It seems a challenge has been laid on your doorstep, quite literally. But you saved yourself when Aaron's woman tried to kill you, did you not?"

"I did, yes. You left me no choice."

The corner of Magnus's eyes creased, a smile lighting his eyes but not curving his lips. "Well. Miss Daisy.

You will cause me no offense if you'd prefer to eat with the crew."

"No, thank you, I will dine with my family. Thank you for your…hospitality." She curtsied again, not so low this time.

Now the smile did reach Magnus's lips. He laughed, a deep, hearty chuckle that filled the room. "You are one to watch, Miss Daisy, magic or no. Well. I have taken the liberty of making dinner for you all." He tied his apron behind his back and nodded at Mordecai, who pulled glasses from the cabinets. "Alexis, I know that your mother never liked ceremony. She absolutely detested when I put on a big show for her. She'd unleash her magic and everything I'd planned would fall apart. Dinner would end up on the floor. Staff would be covered in spilled sauce or wine. A chandelier fell once, splintering the table. The more I tried to impress her, the more frequently I lost precious treasures hanging on my walls or lining my shelves. I finally took the hint and toned down my courtship."

"Your…" My tongue felt too big for my suddenly dry mouth. "Your courtship?"

"Yes." He pulled a lid off a pot and stirred the contents. "It was short but incredibly intense. I lost myself when I was with your mother. And then I lost her entirely, as I'm sure you have guessed."

"Do you need help?" Kieran asked.

"That would be great, yes. Check the roast, if you wouldn't mind. I assume you all eat meat? I know the young shifter certainly does. How about the contrary teen?" He looked at Daisy. "If you hate everything I have prepared, it would be my pleasure to make something that would dazzle you. Figuring out meals from a random list of ingredients is a fun pastime when I need a challenge."

Magnus's charm filled the kitchen like a delightful fragrance. There was no way it wasn't built from lots of practice.

"Magnus, I wondered if I could ask..." I bit my lip, not sure what the protocol was at a dinner party. Was I allowed to talk business? Because I was going to. "Have you seen Demigod Lydia? We haven't seen her around much."

He hummed. A saucepan flared, fire kissing the sky in front of him. He leaned back gracefully until it died down, and continued working. "I saw her yesterday in passing, yes. She seems quite troubled, and no wonder. She has lost a great deal of status because of the events at her...homestead. Her face is a mess, as well. Plastic surgery has only helped a little. Your cat...is not a cat."

I put up my hands. "Honestly, those cats are literally from normal cats. I have no idea what happened."

Magnus looked back at me, his eyes calculating. "I do believe you are telling the truth, Alexis, though I can't help feeling there is a missing piece of the puzzle. Speaking of puzzles, I hear Zander's technical man got into a scuffle earlier today. It sounds like he was jumped. When they looked for footage, they discovered the live surveillance feed was down—something to do with a virus. Most odd. I guess no one will ever know what happened."

"I wasn't aware cameras had been incorporated into the grounds this year," Kieran said smoothly. "Huh."

I could just see Magnus's ear lift, indicating he was hiding a smile. I had a feeling it lacked any humor. "Didn't you? Hmm. In any case, the man will live, I hear, but he's slow to heal despite the blood bond. He'll be out of commission for a while. Zander is most grieved by this, of course—the injured party is the only person on his team with any knowledge of the web and websites and things like that."

Healing took energy. If someone was siphoning energy from the man, he would indeed be down for the count for a while.

Was this Magnus hinting that he was helping me?

I dropped into a light trance, looking for a little violet string connecting Magnus to the ailing man. The Line pulsed, feeding me with power, but I didn't find what I was looking for. He was clear.

"Spirit isn't the only way to keep a man down, Alexis," Magnus said softly. "Given you suspect me, though, it seems you don't know the answer. Interesting. Also, my dear, you must look for spirit connections without drawing notice. You have enough power to exert your magic without calling additional power from the Line. You mustn't always reach for it. Doing so in the presence of those who can feel or see it might come back at you in unpleasant ways. You need to be better at holding your cards to your chest. I can help you, if you like."

"The roast is ready to rest." Kieran pulled it from the oven.

"Fantastic. I'm almost ready." Magnus's hands moved quickly and expertly as he finished up the sauce and plated the potatoes.

"Why would you suddenly want to help her, when not so long ago you wanted to kidnap her?" Daisy asked, and I didn't call her down. I was wondering myself.

"Yes, the kidnapping. I admit, that was shortsighted." Magnus gave me a look, as if expecting reproach. "I saw an opportunity and rushed to take it before Aaron did. I wanted to control a situation that could not be controlled. I should have known better. But in answer to your question, I have always wanted to help her. Given the situation, however, it was impossible. I have a history with children, as I'm sure you've heard." Magnus carved the roast and added portions to each of the dishes. "Let's sit down to dinner, and I can give you a small history lesson, Alexis, if you'd like."

After everyone took a plate, Magnus led a toast to good health, and we all tasted the food. It was delicious, and I said so, which was when Magnus casually dropped his bomb.

"I loved your mother, Alexis. I loved her like I've only loved one other. Unlike the other, my love for her was just budding. It was new, without roots. It was fast and furious, and before either of us knew it, she was pregnant." He took a moment to chew and then sipped his wine. "I have a reputation, as I've said. A reputation I believe in. I've known horrors you couldn't imagine at the hands of my own children. It was a lesson I learned soundly."

"So then…why am I alive?" I asked through a constricted throat. My mind was whirling. He'd known about me the whole time? I could scarcely believe it. It didn't make sense.

Magnus looked across the flickering candlelight at me, the lights in the chandelier above us low and intimate. The setting was homey despite the obvious wealth surrounding us. He looked lost for a moment.

"It was hard to say no to your mom. When I found out she was pregnant, I left, hoping she'd see sense. Then she sent me a picture of the ultrasound, proclaiming it was a girl…" He put his forearms on the table, bowing his head over them. "All those sons scattered across time, but you're my first daughter. Something about that…" His eyes fluttered and he turned to Kieran. "There is something special about a little girl, you'll see. Maybe it is because you hope they will take after the woman you love. Or maybe they are God-kissed, I don't know." He returned his gaze to me. "I made a deal with her. If she hid your lineage and kept you out of the magical world, she could keep you. I would not harm you—indeed, I'd forget you existed."

"You helped me before Kieran exposed me to the world," I said with a shaking voice.

"Yes. I've kept tabs on you, over the years. At first it was to make sure your mother kept her word. Then because I was fascinated that she wouldn't take any money. I'm sure it was because she didn't want me in her life at all—she worried I'd eventually harden and fall into…old habits. And it might have happened, who's to say? She lived a life of poverty to keep me at a distance. She kept you safe better than anyone else could." He paused for a moment. "Even from me."

"Did you know what she was all along?" Kieran asked, his plate finished and his hand on his stomach.

"No. I doubt even her mother knew. When you entered her life, Kieran, I watched much more closely. I saw her bud, I saw her magic flower, and then the truth was revealed to me."

"Yet you didn't try to grab her then." Kieran wasn't asking a question.

Magnus let out a breath and leaned back in his chair. "I will be honest with you… I have no idea why. Shell-shocked, maybe? Set in my ways? I didn't know you'd move so quickly? Or maybe I thought it would be in my best interest if you defeated your father. Take your pick."

Surprise flitted through the soul link but did not show on Kieran's face. He hadn't known there was beef between Magnus and Valens.

"I should have taken her, though." Magnus pushed his plate away. A woman bustled in, starting to clear. He gestured at her. "Forgive me—I love cooking, but I hate cleaning up. She is oath-bound to silence. She cannot repeat anything she hears."

"Why should you have grabbed her?" Mordecai asked.

Magnus studied Mordecai for a silent beat before answering. "Because I am the best equipped to train her. Given she has no interest in ruling, she would've been a perfect addition to my team. No one would begrudge me letting a Spirit Walker live. No one has. You all know why, of course. You've fought with her. Not even Zeus's prized Thunderstroke can compare." He rested his elbows on the table this time, steepling his fingers in front of his mouth. "I thought you'd eventually have to come to me when you hit a wall. I thought wrong.

Please, Alexis, answer me this: who has shown you the way? I know it is not Aaron—he is losing his grip on sanity. Lydia…well. We know it is not her…"

I remembered there was one other Hades Demigod, though he wasn't active in politics. He was old and removed from the fast lane. Maybe Magnus would think it was him. Whatever he thought, I didn't plan on telling him the truth.

His eyes sparkled as they beheld me. "'Secrets, secrets are no fun,'" he recited softly. "'Secrets, secrets can hurt someone.'"

Cold bled through me. Did he know?

"Come. Let's have some dessert and then hear more of that fine music. Who knew a Berserker could create such a melody? Perhaps you can join me in my study later. I have some pictures you might like to see."

Dessert was probably delicious, but I couldn't taste it.

Later, as Zorn sang in accompaniment to Thane's playing, a sweeter melody than I'd ever heard, Magnus led me to his office with Kieran in tow. The leather-bound album he produced was filled with pictures of my life, starting in childhood. Many had been taken from a distance, and I recognized a few of the chaotic moments that had been captured. He'd been there, through all of that. He'd watched from a distance, taking snapshots of my life—or, more likely, having someone else do it.

In the very front, on the first page, was an ultrasound of a swimming white blob amid blackness. Under it was a note written in my mother's scratchy hand proclaiming, *It's a girl!*

I didn't know what to say.

I didn't say anything.

A fog settled over me as I tried to figure out where this left us. I wished the politics of the magical world weren't standing in our way. I wished some of his past behavior had been different.

I wanted to ask him if he'd ever felt love for me as a father would his offspring, but I was too terrified he'd say no. Given the circumstances, I was also scared he'd say yes.

As the night drew to a close and everyone prepared to leave, Magnus pulled me aside.

"I must ask, Alexis. Who was the spirit you called today during your summons?"

I frowned at him, the question eating through the fog. "I didn't call it. I didn't recognize the presence, either, but it seemed menacing. It wasn't another Demigod?"

He studied me for a long moment, and something flickered within his eyes. Something uncertain, if I wasn't mistaken.

"Not even Aaron would be so stupid. Watch yourself, Alexis. There are always shadowy dealings at these things, but I have a feeling you will be affected by this one. Guard your back at all times."

I nodded slowly, although he hadn't told me anything I didn't already know.

"And one more thing," he said, his voice low. "I realize that it is all hearts and roses with your Demigod right now. That's to be expected. But if ever you find yourself in a lonely castle on a forgotten island, I am always here. My door is always open. You'll have a place of your own and a team to lead. You will never be trapped like Valens's wife was. You will always have someone who can free you."

My heart melted just a little more. Daisy would never, in a million years, let me take him up on that, but the sentiment was nice.

I nodded, my eyes misting.

He spread his arms, as though going for a hug, then dropped them again before sticking out his hand.

I laughed. He'd hidden it well, but clearly there was some degree of social awkwardness there. It made me feel better about my own shortcomings.

"Remember," he said as he walked me to the door to meet Kieran, waiting to escort me out, "watch your back, Alexis. I've effectively made it so that if I can't have you, no one can, but that doesn't mean *accidents* won't happen. Your mother sacrificed a lot to keep you safe. Don't let her sacrifice be in vain."

Chapter 18

ALEXIS

THE NEXT AFTERNOON I stood in the kitchen in my finest dress, with my hair and makeup done *just so* and a sickening feeling in my gut. My father's warning had infiltrated my dreams, one nightmare twisting and turning into another. Sometimes it was just me facing off against a terrible, faceless foe. In the worst dreams, I was fighting in front of my kids, backed up against a wall. In all the dream sequences, I was in over my head, outmatched if not outnumbered. They were so vivid that they almost felt like a series of premonitions, inescapable.

I leveled a finger at Daisy, standing across the island from me wearing her fighting attire and a bored expression. She and Mordecai had not been invited with me to afternoon tea with Zander's wife, Juri. It was an exclusive invite (albeit a last-minute one), and Amber thought I should be doing backflips to celebrate. We'd already declined a handful of other invitations.

My kids couldn't come, my friends couldn't come,

my protection had to wait outside, but the cats had been invited to join me. I hadn't wanted to be the bloody cat lady in the first place, and now they were invited to exclusive, posh parties instead of my human companions. It felt like someone was playing a grand practical joke on me.

Worse, it felt like an awful time to leave the kids. Kieran was in meetings all day, so they'd have to go with the crew. To a Berserker fight.

Thane's challenge, delivered by courier, had arrived this morning, handwritten on elegant golden card stock. Five Berserkers—two women and three men, including Thane—wanted to battle it out to see who was king of the mountain. Or queen. Apparently they'd be fighting in a cage designed to contain highly dangerous magical beasts, something used for the magical beast fair held in the fall. Everyone was especially excited to see Thane's beast at play, given his rare ability to control it.

The thought made my body shake with the adrenaline.

"Just because you're getting the crew, doesn't mean you'll be protected, okay?" I told Daisy in a stern voice. "You will stay to the background, and if Thane gets through the electric wire, you will run and hide, you get me? You do not mess with Thane's caliber of danger."

She rolled her eyes. "I know. Thane isn't going to get out of the cage, though. None of them will. They have it rigged for Berserkers."

Which didn't exactly put my worries to rest, especially since another form of hate mail had been delivered sometime in the middle of the night. A splatter of red paint marred the stone pathway in the garden. A crude drawing of a Chester bow—the symbol of ignorant non-magical people everywhere—decorated the warm cement. It had been drawn in a different hand than the hate message a day before, but we'd gotten footage again, and the people scrawling the message had worn the same robes. According to Daisy, they'd also had on the same shoes.

"Stay with the crew. Do not, for any reason, go looking for your admirers." I leaned in. "Answering their challenge is not worth it. You are a teenager with no blood oath. You are not safe to try to kill your haters, do you get me?"

"Yes, I get you. Ew! It's not like Mordecai would let me slip away, anyway. He's been on me like a turd on a toilet."

I had to pause, my face crinkling at the wrongness of the image. I waved it away. "Whatever. Just stay safe. I should only be indisposed for a couple hours."

"Why aren't you giving this lecture to Mordecai?" she asked.

"Because Mordecai is sane. You are not." I grabbed my clutch off the island, gave her one last stern look, and headed for the door.

I was met at the door by Bertha, a bear of a woman, dressed in a crisp suit with a magenta tie and her hair chopped close. She was one of Kieran's second-string people, pulled off Kieran's detail with a couple of others to bring me to Juri's lodge. The council's approval of the mark meant I was a great deal safer, but Kieran still worried about me. So did I, truth be told.

Bertha's name was one she'd chosen after the "madwoman in the attic" in *Jane Eyre*. It spoke a lot to her personality. She had been overlooked for inner circles because of her appearance and all-around uncouth attitude. People didn't like that she dressed like a man and swore like a sailor. Kieran had snapped her up.

We didn't need a willow of a woman who fit stereotypes—we needed a battle-axe who'd cleave through danger.

As I exited, she turned to the side to let me pass, her hands clasped in front of her. Parker, a short, round man with a bulldog face, waited for me by a golf cart. He motioned for Chins, a stick figure of a woman with very little of her namesake. She stepped forward and held my dress as I climbed into the seat.

"Load up," Bertha bellowed.

I chanced a glance back at the lodge as we got underway, my guts a mess of nerves. I really didn't want to leave the kids. Magnus had called Daisy's hate mail a challenge. That clearly meant she was in danger, as we'd thought. I wanted to be there for backup.

Then there were Aaron's Necromancers who might be trying to call Harding. We'd talked to Kieran about it, and worry had crept through the soul link. If they could control Harding, they'd have a potent weapon on their hands. If they couldn't…I was terrified Harding might be pissed off that he'd been controlled. That had always been his rule when he'd worked with me—he had free will. If someone called him and tried to dominate him, I worried he'd retaliate, then maybe slip back into his old ways. No one would be safe, not even me. Maybe *especially* not me. If they could use Harding to get rid of me and even the playing field…

"You look lovely, Miss Alexis," Parker said, his voice rough, like rocks grinding beneath the sole of a boot.

"Thanks," I said, watching the pretty flowers as we lazily rolled by.

A spark of frustration came from Kieran, who'd been in the same location for the past hour. That guy would be mentally comatose by the time all this ended. The meetings were draining enough, but he also had to strategize about developing personal relationships with other leaders.

I knew the situation with Magnus was weighing on

him. The dutiful father act had seemed so legit, with the pictures and the history and his feelings for my mom…except it didn't add up when you considered all the things he'd done over the many long years he'd been in power. The guy was ruthless and brutal—everyone knew that. It was why he'd never experienced a decline like so many immortal leaders did. He was of Hades, too, and Lydia had opened Kieran's eyes to the trickery they could pull off. Guys like him had strategies within strategies. Kieran said he saw it in the meetings. Magnus had his fingers on the very pulse of magical politics.

I sighed. A huge part of me wanted to latch on to the idea that Magnus was conflicted. That was something I could understand, because I felt that way too. I had loved spending time with him last night. He'd known exactly how to win me over. It had almost made me forget he'd once dragged my kids into the thick of a battle. But if he'd been watching me, he'd known about Daisy and Mordecai for some time. They hadn't been strangers to him.

He'd done it anyway.

Yes, I wanted to believe he was conflicted, but logic said that it was likely an act. That he was Halloween dressed up like a Hallmark Christmas movie.

Maybe it wasn't Aaron or Lydia I needed to worry about. If the menacing presence that had appeared in spirit yesterday hadn't been one of them, logic suggested Magnus had summoned it. Maybe the person I needed to worry about had invited me to dinner in order to distract me from the real danger. Him.

The thought tore me in two.

"You okay, Miss Alexis?" Parker asked as we headed toward a large lodge, equal in size to Magnus's. Zander was one of the big dogs, so he'd have one of the largest living quarters, close to the summit building.

"Yup. Just tired of politics, is all. This stuff isn't for me."

Parker nodded and braced his hand on his hip as he drove. "Yeah. This shit's for the birds. I'd rather stab someone in the face than in the back. There ain't no joy in the latter, know what I mean? Ya can't see their face when they realize their number is up."

"Well...with the former, you wouldn't really see the person's face anyway, given there'd be a knife in it. The blood would obscure your view."

He barked out a laugh. "Right you are, Miss Alexis. I'll have to settle for stabbing someone in the heart."

I checked my phone and then made sure it wasn't on vibrate. We were supposed to leave our phones outside with our staff, but I wasn't going to. I wanted to be connected with my kids. Everyone knew to only call me in an emergency, and I didn't want to leave it to Juri's staff to decide if the situation was sufficiently urgent.

"A lot of these people just like to hear their own voices," Parker said as he took a left. Up ahead, another line of golf carts pulled into the round driveway in front, the entrance here much grander than the one to our lodge. "Sometimes it's best just to let them get on with it. They never even notice you're not contributing."

I nodded as a wave of frustration welled up in me—something was starting to really annoy Kieran.

"If you fall, blame someone else." Parker slowed, and I knew he was allowing time for the party in front of us to disembark. "If you spill something on yourself, also blame someone else, but then tell her staff to fix it. They'll know exactly what to do."

"It sounds like you're helping me prepare for making an ass of myself," I mumbled.

"You're not like the people in there, Miss Alexis. They're mostly full of hot air. You're good people. But even good people have their fair share of clumsiness. I figured I'd offer a few insights on what to do after."

"So...yes, then. You're helping me prepare for making an ass of myself."

"You don't mince words, I like it. Basically, Miss Alexis, I'm helping you prepare for what to do *after* you make an ass of yourself."

Chapter 19

Daisy

"AH CRAP, WHAT'S this?" Bria blew out a breath and slowed, leading the crew since Alexis had gone to that stupid afternoon tea with all the other hoity-toity plus-ones.

Daisy veered out a little to see around Thane's girth. If he was nervous about accidentally being killed by another nut-case Berserker, he didn't show it. He looked completely laid-back.

The Necromancers who'd had their asses handed to them by Bria the other day waited down the hall, one single body on the trailer behind them. A few of their crew waited behind them.

Bria didn't drop the handle of her trailer. She'd brought the cadavers and her backpack, not because she'd thought she would need them but because it was expected of her. "What do you guys want? We're on our way to a Berserker battle."

"This won't take but a minute," the man with the gray beard said, sounding smug.

Daisy glanced at their shoes, and those waiting behind them. Boots, all, black and finely polished. Not her secret admirers.

"We've done this song and dance, bub. Step aside. We've got stuff to do." Bria motioned him away.

"Don't think we will," the guy with the gray beard snapped. They brought forth their TV-tray-looking tables, the same style as last time, already all set up. They apparently walked the halls with those things. "Where's the Soul Stealer?"

"She's at Juri's tea party. I bet your mistress was left off the list this year, huh? Poor old Aaron is dragging her down. I wonder how long she'll stand for that." Bria checked her watch.

"Go ahead, Bria, we've got plenty of time," Thane said, crossing his arms and moving so he could lean against the wall.

It was true, they'd left early in case something like this happened. Thane had wanted to soak in some rage and battle energy before his big show-off. Daisy wondered if there would be a sweet release to it.

Bria eyed the one cadaver in the other Necromancers' cart, lying all by its lonesome on its wide trailer. Her knuckles turned white where they gripped the handle of her own trailer. She hesitated, something Daisy had rarely seen her do. Possibly going up against some like Lexi, though, would have anyone's nerves frayed.

"Your Soul Stealer wasn't on the list for Juri's party," the guy with the gray beard said. "She should be headed to the Berserker thing with you."

"Haven't you heard? Her mark was approved, and she's moved up in the world. What do you want with her?"

The two Necromancers down the way exchanged a few words, debating something. After a minute, the one with the gray beard shrugged and turned to his tray.

"Arm yourself," he yelled at Bria.

"Damn it," Bria said softly, unslinging her backpack. "Everyone get back. I don't know what they are about to unleash, but it's likely our worst nightmare. They were hoping to catch Lexi up in this. It's probably terrible news for us that they didn't."

Dylan fell in beside Daisy and gently wrapped his hand around her upper arm.

"Let's give them a little more space," he said, dragging her backward.

"When did you get so grabby?" Daisy asked as Zorn glanced back and nodded, agreeing with Dylan.

"You saw me cry for an hour. We're friends now," Dylan murmured, stopping well back from the action.

"I fail to see what that has to do with you getting grabby." Daisy frowned. "What are we expecting?"

"The other Soul Stealer. Bria is worried they won't

be able to hold him. I have better range, so falling back won't keep me from helping." He stepped partially in front of her.

She sighed and slouched against the wall as Mordecai joined them. This was all starting to get tedious. They treated her like she was breakable. And yes, okay, she was at a disadvantage, but good grief, this was a little much.

"Have you worked with that spirit before?" Bria called down, her hands moving quickly.

"We've taken him on a couple of trial runs, yes." That gray beard dude still sounded awfully smug.

"There is a nuance to Soul Stealer magic, you do know that, right?" Light flared, Bria using candles to prepare. "If you rip a soul out, it is not easy to put it back. The last Soul Stealer didn't know the ins and outs."

"What makes you think we've got the last Soul Stealer?" Gray Beard asked, and it was so obvious that was exactly who he had.

Daisy took another few steps back. She wasn't trying to mess with that. Not without Lexi on scene.

"Cut the crap. Are you hearing what I am telling you?" Bria demanded. "You have absolutely no idea what you are messing with. None. That is not a power to play with, dickface. Without Lexi here, we're all vulnerable. *All* of us, you included. If he gets out of your grip, you'll die first."

"If it *were* the last Soul Stealer"—Gray Beard paused for dramatic effect—"you wouldn't have to worry. He was ten times better trained than that naive girl you have."

Daisy noticed the other Necromancer, with the badly dyed hair, didn't share Gray Beard's delight. His face had closed down in an uncomfortable mask, his mouth a thin line and his bearing tense. He was nervous about what he was doing.

"He was ten times better at killing, yes," Bria said, and readied herself to call spirits. Daisy had seen her do it often enough to know. "But he wasn't trained in preserving life. It's easy to rip out a soul. It is *not* easy to put it back in."

"What do you know about it?" Gray Beard asked.

"Ten times more than you ever will if you let your hold on that Soul Stealer waver. You'll be first to see what spirit looks like, mark my words."

Across the hall, their single cadaver rose to standing on shaky legs. Bria had stuffed spirits into bodies in record time, so she had nearly a dozen ready to face him. Thane checked his watch.

"Watch yourself," Bria told the spirits. "If you get ripped out of that body, get the hell out of here. Don't stay and be a hero. They don't have a clue what they're messing with. Also, I'll remind you that I can't hear you.

So don't try to talk to me."

A strange feeling pressed in on Daisy, like intense hands pushing down on her shoulders. A black shape zipped out of the corner of her eye. She started and looked that way even as Dylan did, his brow furrowed. Nothing lurked in the hallway behind them. If someone had run by, they weren't visible, not even as a sparkly sheen.

"I take it back. I want to stay at the lodge," Daisy said.

"I might want to join you. Did you…see that?" Dylan whispered, looking around again. "Something feels off. It feels like something is pressing on my shoulders."

"Yeah. This feels like Lexi's shit. Things are about to get ugly."

A low growl rumbled in Mordecai's throat. He pushed in closer to her. For once, she wasn't annoyed by that.

The lone cadaver stepped forward once, then again, as though it were slogging through waist-high mud. Daisy could just see the faces of the two Necromancers turning crimson. The one with a really bad dye job and a tuft of hair implants rang a bell, and the cadaver took another step forward. There it halted, shaking all over.

"Get the incense," Gray Beard said, his voice strained.

"You shouldn't be having this much trouble controlling one spirit," Bria called, her hands working again. Hopefully she was setting up some sort of protections should that opposing spirit break loose. Or maybe it was just a matter of *when*. "He's more knowledgeable than you are. He's like a Necromancer on PCP. Your techniques are known to him, and he can work around them. Get him out of that body so he can't do any harm."

"This is standard…operating…procedure," Gray Beard ground out. "He'll…yield soon…enough."

"He feels…more powerful…now," Bad Dye Job said, and rang a bell. "This isn't…like when…we practiced."

The pressure increased, and the back of Daisy's neck and shoulder blades tingled as if someone were standing directly behind her, breathing down her shoulders. Something mighty and dangerous. Something different than that fae yesterday. Much different.

She glanced around again, ready for someone to sneak up on her.

Still nothing.

"Something isn't right," Dylan murmured, and rolled his shoulders.

Up the way, Thane was doing the same thing—looking around, rolling his shoulders. He felt whatever Daisy and Dylan did. Mordecai's hair was standing up along the center of his back, but he didn't react. It meant he didn't smell anything. He didn't sense anything tangible.

Bria's cadavers charged the opponent cadaver. When they were within ten feet, they fell. No pausing, no shuddering, just one step, then facedown on the carpet.

Just like when Lexi ripped out souls.

Gray Beard laughed. "So easy."

"Get the hell out of here," Bria yelled, and Daisy wasn't sure if she was yelling at the spirits or the crew.

"We've got it, Bria," Dye Job said, his hands curled around the handles of his bells. He rang one, then the other, then both at the same time. "We've…got him."

"Well, don't bring him over here," Bria said. "I yield. *I yield!*"

"Ah, but we were just starting to have fun." Gray Beard smirked.

One of Bria's cadavers wiggled, as though trying to find life again.

"What are you doing?" Dye Job asked his buddy, sounding pissed.

"Think what I could do with this sort of power at my disposal," Gray Beard said, a wide grin across his flat face. "My job would be so easy."

"Don't mess around with that magic, you nitwit. You don't know what it can do. *I yield!*" Bria yelled.

"She yields," Dye Job said. "Let's wrap this up."

"Wait. Just a moment," Gray Beard replied. "Can't you feel it? There are spirits hanging around. All I have to do is use him to—"

The cadaver wiggled again, started shaking, and then rolled over onto its back.

"Stand up, damn it," Gray Beard yelled.

"You are trying to control a spirit through another spirit—that takes twice the effort. Do you have twice the effort to give?" Bria asked, packing all her stuff away. She wasn't planning to watch these idiots play with their new toy. Daisy was one hundred percent behind her decision. Time to run.

The cadaver flopped over again, but it only got halfway before it stalled and started shaking. It didn't want to be manipulated. Lexi had strong spirits at her disposal—spirits who had been done wrong. They wouldn't go quietly.

The main cadaver was still struggling and had yet to take another step forward. Dye Job rang a bell to get it moving again, struggling with it.

"It's too powerful," he yelled. "Something has changed!"

"Nothing has changed. Hold it," Gray Beard yelled back.

Heat roared to life within Daisy. It melted through her middle and pooled really low, in a place she'd never felt before, but one she theoretically understood.

She looked around, knowing exactly what she'd find. Half afraid to find it.

A boy a few years older than her stood not far away, his body sparkling and shining within its glamour. Those green eyes from the beach, the most vivid shade she'd ever seen, with a flare of gold around the irises, sat below black, arching brows. His severe cheekbones would break a fist crashing against them, and the soft cleft in his chin gave a pleasing contrast to the strong jaw. His full lips were twisted to the side wickedly, as though he was thinking about an unsavory joke.

His gaze was like a brand upon her skin, awakening something she didn't want to set loose, sparking something primal and setting it ablaze. His rugged, almost cruel handsomeness was nothing compared to the sparkle of deviousness in his eyes.

Her heart beat too fast. She couldn't get enough air. She'd never felt this feverish, but she wasn't sick. Never felt this terrified, but she wasn't afraid.

He winked, and his wicked smile grew.

In a moment, he was gone, all hazy air and sparkling wind, rushing forward…toward the barely controlled Soul Stealer.

"No," she said, breathless, turning as he went.

It must be done, little dove. There is no better distraction on these grounds.

The haze dodged around Thane, slipped by Bria,

and stopped just before the cadaver. A spark appeared right before an earthy smell curled around Daisy's senses.

A bell rang out. Then another. Gray Beard was trying to goad his puppet.

Zorn started and stepped forward, his hand on Bria's shoulder. He'd clearly recognized the fae.

The fae darted so quickly that Daisy couldn't keep track of it. And then she could. It stopped next to Thane, and that strange, earthy smell flowered in her senses again.

"Shit—" Zorn lurched in that direction, but he was too late. The fae zipped away again, much faster than Zorn could ever move in his gas form.

Thane sucked in a startled breath, flexing his biceps as he did so.

"Fight the urge, Thane," Daisy called out as the cadaver in the hall cocked its head. It ignored the bells. If it had the ability to work its mouth, Daisy knew it would be smiling.

The cadaver turned slowly and looked back at its controllers. Their wide eyes, slack jaws, and bleach-white faces said it all.

Control had been ripped away from them. Their cadaver had been set loose.

In a heartbeat, the two Necromancers fell bonelessly to the floor. One minute they were panicking, starting to reach for their incense and candles, and the next they were on their faces, not moving.

"Fuck," Daisy said, taking a step back.

The cadaver took two more steps in that direction, avoiding a body at its feet, and two more people fell, those who had been helping the Necromancers.

The rest of Aaron's people shouted and stumbled backward. The one who stood closest to the cadaver fell. Its range appeared to be smaller than Lexi's, but not by much.

The cadaver turned toward Bria.

"Go!" Daisy yelled, her heart in her throat. Dylan stuck out a hand to stop her from running forward. "Get out of there!"

Lightning rained down, striking the cadaver. The cadaver shook and jolted, but it didn't go down. The body was already dead—it was just a shell. A little electricity wouldn't bother it much.

Donovan flung out his hands as Zorn yanked Bria to standing. The cadaver sailed backward and crashed against the little TV-tray desks the Necromancers had used.

"Go, go, go!" Boman shoved everyone in front of him, putting his back to the struggling cadaver.

Thane rolled his neck and then his shoulders. His eyes bled crimson. He was going to change.

"Make Thane chase us, or he's going to lose his soul

to that Soul Stealer," Bria yelled, jumping over her supplies and sprinting Daisy's way. "Go! Get the hell out of here. Only death awaits us here!"

Chapter 20

ALEXIS

A FAMILIAR CHIME echoed through the sitting room filled with paisley-upholstered antique furniture. It chimed again, and the heads of the powerful, rich, and influential people gathered around me slowly turned toward the source of the disturbance.

I didn't indulge in a new wave of embarrassment at my latest *faux pas.* I thrust my drink at Lady Marmalade, the name I'd come up with for the woman sitting next to me, whose name I'd instantly forgotten, ignored her squawk of protest, and dug into my clutch. My phone chimed for the third time, and Juri peeled away from her group of chatting socialites with an annoyed expression.

Bria's name flashed on the screen. With suddenly shaking hands, I dropped the clutch and answered the phone. The cats slunk out of the other room immediately, taking residence at my feet.

"What is it?" I asked, a wave of unease washing over me.

"Aaron's Necromancers called the last Soul Stealer, and he got loose," she said, out of breath. Screams and shouts echoed through the phone, as though Bria was caught in a stampede. "It took them out like they were nothing. It took them out like it was you! Dylan tried to take him down, but he didn't even feel the electricity. Then Thane went Berserk, of all things. We're currently leading Thane away from the Soul Stealer. After that… Fuck, Alexis, we need help."

Juri stopped in front of me, disappointment on her face. She waited expectantly for me to hang up.

I waved her away and showed her my back. "You mean Harding? Talk to him. He'll calm down. They probably just pissed him off."

"If it is Harding, Alexis, he is done being nice. He came after us. He nearly killed me."

I shook my head. "But that's impossible. He has a soft spot for you. He wouldn't—"

"He's out from under your thumb now, Alexis! He must have only played along because you could control him. They could not. Now he's completely free, and—Holy—*Look out!*"

Something crashed, drowning Bria out.

"What's happening?" I asked, clutching the phone.

"Fuck me, Thane has a knack for ruining a place. Turn right," she yelled, so loud I had to hold the phone away from my ear.

"Alexis, we have a strict—"

"*Shh*," I said to Juri, and hurried away, shoving the front door open and stepping into the bright sunlight. The cats padded after me.

"Right, damn it!" she hollered. "Lead him to that battle courtyard and try to lock him in. Then we can turn back and find the other Soul Stealer for Lexi. We can't have that thing running around, tearing out all the souls in this place."

"Miss Alexis?" Parker stepped away from the idle throng of magical people waiting on their bosses. Bertha pushed away from the wall down the way, apparently not into small talk or socializing.

"Get the cart," I yelled at him, hurrying toward the parking area. "Hurry! I've got to get to the summit building. Aaron's idiot Necromancers turned loose a Spirit Walker, and it set off Thane."

"Alexis, that's no longer your job." Juri stepped out of the lodge after me, her disapproval turning to a look of patience. "The…crews battle for status. That's what they do. You are no longer one of them—you must let them earn their place without interference."

Parker took off running and Bertha yelled at the rest of my party, getting them moving, then moving faster.

I took the phone away from my head for a moment in order to level Juri with a stare.

"You don't get it. A Soul Stealer, with my killing

ability, has somehow gotten away from *two* level-five, experienced Necromancers. He's loose. He knows how to siphon energy from others in order to keep going, and it sounds like he's pissed off enough to do it. With Thane set loose, the whole place will be in disarray. I have to help."

"That's what the Demigods are for. They have the power to fix this." She tilted her head a little to the side and then put her hand out, intending to lead me back into the lodge. "This all takes some getting used to, I know. I didn't expect to lead a territory either, and I wasn't trained for it. It came as a shock. With time, you will find your feet, don't worry."

Frustration ate away at me. "By the time the Demigods get around to noticing something other than their own mightiness, my kids, my people—*your* people—might be dead. *This* is leading. Showing up first when danger presents itself. I can help, and so I *will* help. Go back to your tea party and let me save the day, if you want. It makes no difference to me."

I flicked off my stupid high heels and ran for the golf cart that Parker had pulled out. Bertha was in the cart behind it, already loading up the cats. The others were waiting for us to get moving.

That was the great thing about a pack of misfits. They didn't care about the right protocol, only about doing what was necessary.

"Where to?" Parker asked, slamming his foot on the accelerator as soon as I was seated.

The cart lurched forward…and continued at a steady clip only slightly faster than I could run.

I leaned forward, my heart thumping. "Damn these things and their gutlessness. At least we're close."

"Reach in the back and grab that duffel. There's a change of clothes and a pair of runners in there. Your ward packed them for you in case your other ward got into trouble he couldn't get her out of."

I sighed with a smile and hurried to grab it. Bless Mordecai—his preparedness was a godsend.

The Summit building loomed, right up ahead. I grabbed out the shoes and didn't bother with the leather clothes that would have taken too long to yank on.

"Call Kieran," I said as I pulled on the socks. "I mean…" Demigods didn't get their phones in the meetings. "Call…whoever is with him. Interrupt Kieran's meeting. I might need help with that Spirit Walker. He's trained better than I'll probably ever be. He might be too much for me."

"Nonsense. He's a ghost. You are not. You have the advantage."

But if I'd learned anything about Harding, it was that he had a true mastery of all things spirit. I could hardly count the number of ways he'd surprised me over the last months, doing something I could barely wrap my head around, let alone duplicate.

Parker stopped the cart right in front of the entrance, turned it off, and jumped out. Bertha hadn't even completely stopped her cart before the cats leapt to the ground, running for me.

One of the staff raised his hand to tell us to move those carts, but I was already past him and through the door. The way was clear, the pandemonium not having reached this far. If it did, I realized, they probably would just assume one of the hallway battles had gone too far. They would likely get out of the way, assuming it would either die down on its own or the Demigods would handle it. By then, dozens of people would be dead.

I called Bria, and as soon as she picked up, I said, "I'm at the front entrance, which way?"

Several staff looked up from the front desk, appearing bored.

The cats stopped beside me and Parker behind. Bertha caught up and stuck out her hand, giving me view of her phone screen, where she'd pulled up a map of the building.

"We're just—*Duck!* We didn't make it to the outdoor battle arena, but we found a big hall that has been set for a meal. We're unleashing Thane there. The service staff should keep him busy."

She gave me the name of the hall where they'd left the Spirit Walker, and I repeated it for Bertha to find.

"I'm headed to Harding," I said into the phone. "It'll be fine. I can talk him through this." I couldn't believe Harding had lost himself so quickly. Sure, he'd been a hellion in life, but as a spirit he'd offered to help me of his own free will. He'd helped me trap himself, for pity's sake. He'd helped me heal people, something he had never done in life. Clearly he'd known how, but he hadn't had it in him. Without the pressures of the living, he was a better person. I truly believed that. Maybe this whole episode had messed with his head, but I had to believe I could talk him around.

"Alexis," Bria voice low and firm, "watch yourself. This isn't the Harding you know."

Bertha led the way, a large woman but fast on her feet. So fast that I was huffing just trying to keep up. The cats followed beside me, loping along like jungle creatures.

Near the battle halls, a man lay facedown in the middle of the hallway. His spirit stood just outside of his body, bent down as if in agony, withering away. A light trance showed me the violet cord attached to his chest, sucking his energy dry.

I snapped the cord and shoved the spirit into the afterlife. I could probably have reattached the spirit to the body, but it would have taken a lot of time and energy, and I needed to conserve both.

Around a corner, three people lay in a clump, their

positioning suggesting they'd been preparing for a battle they hadn't gotten the chance to fight. Their souls were in a similar state, tortured, even more so than the spirits in Lydia's house.

Had Harding done this? Why?

After I cut them loose and sent them on their way, we kept going, slower now. I pushed out my awareness and found a group of the living in a room off to the side. I knocked on the door, then opened it slowly. The souls were in the corner, barricaded behind a desk, still firmly lodged within their bodies. Another body lay broken in two, its soul nowhere in sight.

"What happened here?" I asked softly.

No one spoke.

"I'm Alexis Price, the Spirit Walker. I know you're there. Did a cadaver come this way?"

A middle-aged man with haunted eyes rose from behind the desk. He glanced around nervously before his gaze settled on me. He and the others were all low level fours, which meant they wouldn't have been in these halls on the first day. Maybe they shouldn't have been in them now.

"Not a…cadaver. A fae. A dark fae. There was a dark fae here! Beyond the borders!"

"Wait." I held up a hand, my mind reeling. "A dark fae? What would a dark—"

I cut myself off, remembering what Lydia had said

about her agreement with them. I'd thought their agreement would be null and void, but truthfully, I had no idea. I barely knew anything about the magical world—I knew even less about the fae lands and the people who resided there.

"What did he want with you?" I asked. I felt Kieran's confusion through the soul link, probably a reaction to the alarm and anxiety he felt from me and the rest of his people. He wouldn't be able to leave, though, not without just cause. It would ruin him.

Not leaving might ruin his family.

"What did he want with you?" I repeated, my voice an octave too high.

"To call Demigod Lydia out of her meeting, but we don't have that authority. We don't have her personal line. I tried to call—"

"Fine, fine, what about the cadaver? The other Spirit Wa—the cadaver with the Soul Stealer in it. Did you see him?"

The man blinked and pushed against his chest. "I thought that was you. We felt..."

I motioned for him to keep talking. "What? You felt it what?"

"It felt like fingers trying to tear out my...heart...or?"

"Your soul. It was trying to tear out your soul." He'd definitely gone off the deep end. The question was: was that because he was angry he'd been controlled, or because he saw an opportunity to get revenge on the Demigod who killed him? "Thanks. Stay in here until… Just give it a while."

I fled through the door and ran down the hall, finding the body of a staff member with the customary spirit standing beside it. Farther on, nothing.

"This way!" I looked back, and one of the second stringers whose name I couldn't remember—I'd never actually spoken to him, which now seemed shitty of me—stood at the opening of the hallway we'd just passed. He waved us toward him.

More bodies lay down the hall. More souls stooped, drained. We turned in that direction, following the string of dead. The Line pulsed as it followed me, happily accepting the wayward spirits I fed it.

Screaming cut through the quiet hallways. A pack of magical people rounded the corner and came into view, racing toward us. A distant crash sounded and the floor shook.

That must've been Thane.

Two people broke off from the group, turning my way. They waved their hands at me to turn back.

"There's a zombie," the woman yelled, trying to grab my arm as she raced past. "It's killing people. And a Berserker! It's out of control."

"Where's the zombie?" I yelled.

The woman tried to keep running. Bertha grabbed her by the shoulders, slapped her across the face, then turned her toward me as though she were a rag doll. "Answer her!" she shouted.

"Where's the zombie?" I repeated.

"Down… Down…" She pointed left, toward the crashing of Thane.

Was Harding actively seeking out my crew?

Fire sparked within me, kindling into rage. What game was he playing? He *knew* I would fight dirty when my loved ones were on the line.

Maybe this was his way of bringing me to him.

My legs had never moved so fast in my life. I didn't even register the anxious tightness in my chest as I flew around the corner, nearly tripping over a dead body, and slammed into a person running to get away from the danger behind them. I was on the right track.

I fought through a swell of people that came after, everyone fleeing without sense, panicked to the point of hysteria. Harding had been at their souls.

At least he wasn't killing everyone.

At the next intersection, the hallway was a mess. Magical people packed the space, all of them trying to get past me. Some sort of gathering or public battle must've been underway farther down the hall, before everything had gone to hell.

I fought through them as best I could, but the mass

of them continually pushed me back. I could barely see the point where people were shoving into the hallway, but I knew it had to be a door.

"Bertha!" I shouted.

"I gotcha." She pushed in front of me, forcing people out of the way like a linebacker. With the brute strength of ten men and the determination of someone who'd crack some heads to get her way, she created a hole and dragged me behind her. The cats stayed tight to my legs, working in with me.

The walls around me shuddered and the ground rumbled. Something enormous crashed away left. That was clearly Thane. Which meant he hadn't caused this mad dash.

We found the door—an entrance to a large hall with tiered seating—and squeezed through it. Once inside, I could just see a glowing exit sign across the way, above another door stuffed with people, no doubt. Tables lined with various types of technology stretched out along the sides of the room. One had been overturned, the electronics on it scattered and trampled. In the rear, a large stage held a podium and a large white screen, only a corner of it catching the image from the projector, which had been bumped off-kilter.

Souls I knew registered in the far corner of the stage, my group huddled together with Donovan, Zorn, and Amber out front, their faces a mask of cool efficiency. Red and Bria stood on the sides, blocking Jerry in the middle, who stood in front of Daisy and Mordecai in his wolf form. Boman was at the back of the stage, working at a door under another exit sign. Given he'd been reduced to battering it with his shoulder, he wasn't having much luck. Dylan and Henry were gone, and fear gripped me. I hoped to hell they were with Thane and not dead.

Unless Boman worked some serious magic, the crew was trapped, blocked off from the other exit by the cadaver pacing in front of them, walking with a smooth grace that shouldn't have been possible. From this distance I couldn't do much but a quick assessment of the situation.

He'd barricaded his spirit in the body with thick, beautiful prongs woven of spirit and power. I widened my eyes at the mastery, delicate yet extremely strong, something that would be a bitch to break through. His magical power pulsed in thick and heady waves, and my heart beat faster. Above a level five. Far above. Not quite the power of a Demigod, but damn near close.

How the hell was that possible?

His soul burned black and dense, malicious. I suspected it would take me a second to talk him around.

The thing was, I had been prepared to talk to Harding.

This was not Harding.

Chapter 21
Kieran

Kieran glanced away from the speaker in the large meeting hall as emotions poured into him from the soul link and his connections to the crew. Something had pulled Lexi and her portion of the second string away from the tea party. She had now reunited with most of the crew, and it felt like they were preparing for battle.

Something must have gone wrong. The tea party wouldn't have ended so early, and even if it had, there was no reason for anyone but Thane to be fighting. And while Kieran sensed Thane had changed and was busting heads, it felt like he was still in the building. The Berserker battle should be outside, on the grounds.

Kieran leaned forward and bent his head over his suddenly flexed arms. He would kill for his phone.

Thane wasn't a weak or inexperienced Berserker. It would take a Demigod or Lexi to back him down.

Lexi.

The dots connected, and some of his tension bled

away.

That was probably it. Thane had unexpectedly changed, and the crew had called in Lexi to back him down. They'd clearly thought disrupting Lexi was better than breaking up a Demigod meeting.

He turned his attention back to Demigod Lily droning on about the strained communication between her territory and the neighboring non-magical government. He debated taking notes, but none of this concerned him. Her arrogance and unwillingness to compromise was clearly the problem. Her situation would get worse before it got better.

"Have you tried..." Aaron put his hand in the air, waiting to be noticed so he could continue with his interruption. Yet again. This was the third time he'd interjected. He'd interrupted the two presenters before her, too, for no real reason. Clearly he just wanted to hear his own voice.

Kieran checked his watch, and he noticed Dara, next to him, doing the same. She caught his notice and rolled her eyes. At least Kieran wasn't the only one annoyed that Aaron was making them run late. They should be heading for a short break about now. Kieran could use his coffee and a phone call.

He hadn't expected the Summit to feel like he'd been locked up.

"If this suggestion is similar to the last two, Demigod Aaron," Lily said, amazingly calm, "I probably have. Now, if you will please let me finish..."

A blast of emotion rattled Kieran's nerves, fear pulsing through his links with the crew. Demigod Helga, on his right, frowned and glanced at him before putting a hand to her chest. A couple of other Demigods looked around, shifting in their seats, distracted.

Whatever was happening wasn't limited to his people.

A rumble shook his computer, perched on his desk. A muffled crash in Thane's direction made his heart beat faster. Thane was still a ways off, but he would not be easily contained. He'd stepped up a level with his magic since practicing with Lexi. When he let loose, it was as though the heavens were letting loose with him.

"I think your problem is that you put too much stock in communication with the non-magical people in the first place." Aaron glanced up at the clock. A smile spread across his face and he leaned back, half slouching. "But you probably see things differently. Go ahead and continue. We've wasted enough time today."

Aaron looked across the large hall to Kieran, the first time he'd met his eyes since the promenade. It felt like he was speaking directly to him when he said, "All will be beyond our reach, soon."

Prickles of uncertainty covered Kieran's skin. That had sounded like a threat.

"Yes, fine," Lily said dryly. "Very helpful, as always."

Kieran lost her next words as his mind spun.

Events connected quickly—Aaron making meaningless interruptions and suddenly losing interest in them, Kieran's team in turmoil, and now that not-so-subtle threat. Aaron had orchestrated something that affected Kieran, and it didn't take a genius to know what. Bria had been worried about Aaron's people summoning the last Spirit Walker. Lexi had been called away from the tea party.

Aaron was making his move.

Kieran let out his breath slowly and clasped his hands, trying to stay calm. Lexi had this covered. Summoning a spirit reduced its power level. Harding was more experienced, but Lexi would be more powerful. Harding also had a soft spot for Lexi. They'd become close over the past several months. If the experience of being summoned and controlled upset him, as Bria suspected it would, it would still only be a matter of time before Lexi talked him around. She had a gift for talking people down off ledges. Aaron was grasping at straws.

Except...why was Kieran's team spinning in fear?

"Do you feel like something is going on?" Helga whispered, her head bent a little.

He nodded, his mind still racing.

If Harding was in a temper and on the loose, he'd

kill more than a few people before Lexi could talk him down. The people in this room would be feeling the loss. They'd be feeling fear from their people as Thane ran through the halls. A big demonstration on technology was supposed to be going on, one Amber and Henry had planned to sit in on. If Harding or Thane got anywhere near that…

The door to the meeting hall burst open amid shouting. Lily paused in her talk as everyone in the room turned toward the door, some anxious, some annoyed.

Lightning flared and the staff standing in front of the newly opened door cowered, sinking in on themselves. The guards must've been using magic to keep Kieran's people out. Dylan strode past them, Henry behind him, fear and anger curling within them. A manic roar followed the clap of thunder, Thane's unmistakable sound of fury, some ways off but no less potent.

Kieran stood, as did many others.

"What is the meaning of—"

Dylan sent a peal of thunder rolling through the room, silencing Lily and the others. Zander and Flora both waved the sound away, and Zander stood, his power building, and pulled at the weather to bring a storm into the building.

Kieran shoved it away, helped by Demigod Daniela,

he had no doubt. She was of Poseidon's line, as old as the hills, and really crotchety about other people working the weather.

"Demigod Kieran, you must come now." Henry stepped up beside Dylan. He lifted his hands, and a shot of red veered off toward the ceiling. He'd assumed someone else's magic in order to deflect the halfhearted attack. He was good in a crowd like this, Demigod or no. "Demigod Aaron set loose a Spirit Walker, and he is killing people within the halls. He set Thane off, and—"

A chorus of complaints interrupted them. "What?" "Preposterous!" "Get out of here!" "This is a closed meeting!" "Leave them to sort it out!"

Zander, though, turned toward Aaron. His voice boomed, amplified by his magic. "Is this true? Your people called the last Soul Stealer?"

Aaron's smug smile said it all.

"How did you get the items to summon him?" Zander demanded, but from his tone, he already knew.

Aaron shrugged. "Finders, keepers."

"Get these fools out of here," Lydia said. "Get them out and let's proceed. The battles of the servants are nothing to us."

But Kieran sensed the fear riding her words. It seemed like she was desperate to stay in the meeting.

He didn't have time to wonder why, as Henry worked farther into the room. A zip of magic splattered where he'd just stood, his luck almost more potent than his magic.

"Besides, those items never belonged to you, they belonged to *my son*," Aaron told Zander. He puffed up as he stood. "He is mighty. Better trained than that girl. My Necromancers will help him steal the show."

"Oh, he stole the show all right," Dylan said. "He killed your Necromancers, set off our Berserker, killed anyone he came across, and caused a riot in the tech convention." Dylan turned to Kieran. "He looks like he has a grudge against our crew. He followed them and is moving to intercept. Lexi is en route, but she asked for you. She might need backup. And someone needs to handle Thane. He's ripping this place apart with no sign of slowing. *Hurry!*"

Raw fear and desperation rode that last word. It radiated through the soul link. It was clear that Dylan thought he was about to lose his new family—a thought he could not bear. The sentiment was clear on his face, in his pleading tone and the urgency in his eyes. In his willingness to silence other Demigods to deliver his message.

The decision was made before Kieran could think it through. He'd lose an incredible amount of status if he walked out these doors, he knew. Demigods typically left the battles alone. His team would seem weak if he intervened. Normally, he'd let them handle it.

This was not a regular battle. Perhaps the other Demigods were content to let their groups die, but he wouldn't leave his people to handle Aaron's screw-ups. Nor would he leave Lexi out to dry.

He'd always known he was a family man first and a leader second. It didn't even feel like a choice.

"I'm coming." Kieran tucked his laptop under his arm and strode from the room. He'd pass it off when he got outside, along with his jacket. There was a time for politics, and there was a time for fighting.

Chapter 22

ALEXIS

BERTHA PUSHED THE crowd away, and I strode down the aisle toward the zombie filled with not-Harding. Pressure pushed on my shoulders and black shapes darted at the edges of my vision. I was being watched again, and the next time I saw Harding, I was going to turn him inside out and shove him where he'd never see the world of the living again.

"Hey," I said, loud and clear, before flicking the other Spirit Walker's soul casing.

The Line pulsed in the room, and it struck me that I'd seen this soul before. He'd shown up at the mark hearing, looking out at us from spirit.

I let my touch linger on his soul casing as he turned around, keeping it gentle so as not to alarm him while I gauged the strength of his prongs. He deserved a chat, to air his grievances. He hadn't chosen to be pulled from beyond the Line and fastened inside this body—maybe he just wanted to go back.

"There you are," he said, though his lips didn't

move. "I've been looking for you. Remember me?"

"From the other day? Yeah. What were you doing spying?"

"Me spying? What were *you* doing spying? You came all the way to find me, *tap-tap-tapped* at my cage, and then walked away? Were you scared?"

I stopped just out of his range. He could slash at my middle, but he couldn't pry out my soul. Behind him, Zorn pushed everyone farther back, putting as much distance as possible between them and the zombie.

"What…" I let my very real confusion soak into my expression as I delicately analyzed the magic keeping his soul in that body. It was truly a work of art. One I could learn. But it had been done with more power than I possessed.

Could the two Necromancers have combined their power to achieve this?

A light trance allowed me to see the violet lines connected to him, feeding him with power. Most looked small and easy to break. One was thick and strong, however, larger than any I'd seen.

"What are you talking about?" I asked.

"You sought me out. Why? Is it because you wanted to know one of your kind?" He started walking toward me. I let him do it because he was distancing himself from my crew. If they had more room, hopefully they could run for it while still staying outside of his range.

Hopefully they'd be able to find Kieran. "I went looking for the Soul Stealer before me when I was still alive. I didn't have anything of his, but when I was strong enough, I searched for him anyway. Never could find him. I would've liked to talk about our craft. It's lonely at the top, as they say. And then you came along. I knew exactly what you were even though your presence was meager. You're just starting out, right? Just learning? You're old for a beginner. Do they train Spirit Walkers differently now?"

I continued tracing the prongs, trying to learn the construction, but his side of the conversation kept derailing me. What he was saying didn't make any sense, unless he was the Spirit Walker before Harding?

"I grew up outside of the magical world," I said. "I didn't have training until I summoned the last Spirit Walker...before me. The one right before me."

"There is another?" The zombie stopped walking.

"Harding. As far as I know, he was the last."

"Harding? Harding was..." His soul pulsed midnight black. "Ah, so that's why you backed off after feeling my cage. You felt what they had turned me into." He laughed. "Yes, all my goodness has dried up. The boy who was Harding was trained, tortured, and then hidden away, turned into a killer."

"Wait...no..." I felt dizzy, like I was falling. Things weren't making sense. I remembered the first time I'd sought out the last Spirit Walker. I'd felt a wall, and a presence pushing up against it. I remembered the seething anger from that presence. Anger that didn't feel a whole lot like Harding, I had to admit. "But…the guy who followed me said he was Harding. *His* name is Harding. The feeling of souls doesn't change—"

"I don't know who you found, love, but it wasn't Harding. It still isn't Harding. That kid died as soon as I went into training. They christened me Damion in the end, the left hand of the devil. They sent me out, in spirit or in body, to kill. And I did. I had no choice. I killed under their guidance. I killed under *their* orders. And still I was destroyed for my crimes, locked up in a cage beyond the veil where I could never properly rest. Locked up, and then that old Hades Demigod retired. He hasn't been to visit. No one has. Except for you."

"Damion…" I mumbled.

He stopped for a moment, analyzing me.

"Those disgusting Demigods in the trial room were interrogating you, weren't they?" he finally asked. "They were coming down on you for what you are, right? I saw them. Tell me, who has control of you? I can set you free and then punish them. I'm siphoning energy from a Demigod. The fool left my mother poor and alone, left *me*, and now he wants to make up for it when all is lost. He says he wants a son, but what he really wants is a weapon, like everyone else. His greed and his quest for power has made him desperate. What he'll get, though, is vengeance. They'll all get vengeance." If I could've seen his face through that body, I knew he'd be smiling. "With this spirit link, I will never wilt. With my power and my magic, I can create a semblance of a soul link between us. I can release you, my pretty pet. I can show you how to leave your body and its unwanted connections, and claim another. When that one rots away, we can simply take another, and another, until the end of time."

"Damion is the name of the reprogrammed Spirit Walker," Bria called out. "The last Spirit Walker. He was born as Harding."

"But..." I blinked, still utterly confused.

Jerry pushed to the outskirts of the group. He didn't like being inactive, I could tell. None of them did. But they couldn't help me here. If they got close, they'd get their spirits yanked out, no problem. I wouldn't have time to put them back in before it was too late.

Despite the danger the Spirit Walker posed, plus his extremely gross offer of living my days as a rotting corpse (Jerry would throw up every time he looked at me), one thought kept cycling through my mind: if this was the real Harding...who was the other guy?

In the end, though, it didn't really matter. This guy needed to be stopped. I could figure out the rest later.

"Do you know how to heal a soul, Damion?" I

asked, and magically launched into action, working at the prongs docking his soul into the cadaver.

The Line pumped power, throbbing around us.

He shoved my touch away forcefully. The power disparity between us was going to be a problem.

"We are Soul Stealers. Our job isn't to heal a soul," he spat. "Our job is to remove it."

I worked at that weave, frustrated by how much power had gone into creating it. He must've done it after the Necromancers had put him into that body, because the magic was definitely that of a highly experienced Spirit Walker. My efforts were clumsy in comparison, much like my attempts to weasel my way through his prongs.

"We are not just killers, Harding." A violet cord materialized before him, faster than Lydia had created one.

"Don't call me that," he said, rage lacing his words. The cord reached out toward me as a thick magical hand punched into my center.

I gasped, reeling. Primal terror welled up in me at the feeling of foreign fingers digging into my middle, scrabbling at the prongs keeping my spirit in my body, trying to destroy my life. This was how people felt when I used my magic. It wasn't pretty.

Remembering not-Harding's teachings, I pushed apart the spirit from Damion's attack and redirected the power. I forced his touch away, but the violet cord latched on. Energy sucked from me in heavy gulps.

Chaos roared and sprang into action, leaping for the zombie. A red lashing of spirit snaked out from the zombie and raked through Chaos's middle. Chaos cried out in midair, shaking. He landed on his side and twisted and turned in pain. Havoc roared next, flapping the spirit's soul within its casing. The zombie didn't even flinch. Havoc stalked around the Spirit Walker at a distance, probably looking for an *in* before engaging. She'd always been the smarter of the pair.

They weren't going to help me.

I peeled away the violet cord, freeing myself, and managed to slip past his prongs. But when I took hold of his soul, it was impossible to rip back out. He had too much power. It felt like fighting a Demigod.

"You have such amazing potential," he said, already attacking my soul box again. His technique was ten times better than mine. He'd had a lifetime of practice, whereas I was just starting. Lord, how it showed. "I can teach you. You can be mighty. Together we will bring Demigods to their knees."

"All you know how to do is kill!" I thwarted his prying magical fingers as I broke one of his prongs. He tried to rebuild it, but I quickly reconstructed it myself to block his attempt. My prong wouldn't do anything to keep his soul in place, but it would get in the way.

He grunted. "Clever lady. I wouldn't have thought

of that."

Thank God I'd become a fast learner under not-Harding's guidance.

"There is more to this magic than just killing." I didn't think there was much chance of talking him around, but I had to try. "You can save people with this magic."

"You become a puppet with this magic." His violet cord, never far away, attached to me again, draining me. He walked closer.

I backed up.

"You won't be a puppet if you find someone to protect and respect you." I ripped free of his violet cord again, tired now, and took out another of his prongs. I created a block to stop him from re-erecting it as he tore down the first block.

I nearly cried in frustration.

"Where is your protection now?" he asked. "Zander only took notice of me when I killed people he was using. When I killed his profit centers. He only took action when he, himself, was affected. But now, when it's just you trying to protect someone else's people, where is he? Where are any of them?"

"They are *my* people. We're a crew." I felt Kieran on the move. He was coming for me, but he was on the other side of the building with crowds of panicking people in his way. It would take him too long to get to me. Damion was too strong.

The violet cord sucked in another gulp of my energy. Damion's magical touch found purchase, seeping into my soul casing. In just a moment he'd have a choice—try to bind me in whatever spirit way he could devise, or rip out my spirit and end my life.

It was hard to breathe. Fear fogged my brain. I was outmatched and outgunned. Damion was more experienced and more powerful. My Spirit Walker magic wouldn't save me here.

Something Magnus had said in Lydia's house registered.

It is not easy to control someone with chaos blood.

Struggling to stay in this fight, ripping at his soul casing in desperation, I did the only thing I could think of. I sought my mother's help.

Chapter 23

ALEXIS

I THOUGHT OF my mother with everything I had. My energy drained a little more. I could feel Damion working, trying to build a link between us, and although it terrified me, it was the only thing keeping him from yanking out my life. I had precious few moments.

The Line pulsed as if trying to communicate with me, but I dared not slip into spirit, or Damion would have me. I called to my mother, pleading, begging her to forgive this interruption and come to me. The Line pulsed again, and then I felt a tug, like a rope had landed in my hands and someone on the other end was already tugging.

I pried off another of Damion's prongs, rebuilt it, and tore down the first, trying to work on multiple things at a time, like he was so adept at doing. I pushed away his violet cord and tried to attach my own cord to him. I could not banish him from my soul box, though. I could not stop him from touching the very essence of me, a place only Kieran had touched before.

Tears in my eyes, hands clenched in frustration, I wailed across all of spirit for my mother.

A shape appeared behind the veil, coming into crisper focus as it stepped into the plane of the Line. Another step brought her into my plane. Young and beautiful and vibrant, she was just as I remembered her from my youth. Her sleepy smile reminded me of Sunday mornings in the bright October sun, sitting in the backyard together as she indulged in her coffee and newspaper, remarking on what a fine life we had.

She blinked when she saw me, the confusion of the at-rest suddenly finding themselves awake again.

"Alexis?" She looked around in confusion. "Where are we?"

"Mom, help. *Please*. I'm in a fix. Kieran is on his way, but he won't make it in time. I don't have enough power to beat this guy. I don't have enough skill! But I have your magic. I know I do. If I can use it, maybe it'll at least help me stall until Kieran gets here."

It had never taken my mother very long to get into the flow of things.

Her next blink cleared the haze in an instant. She looked down at my chest, where the spirit connection was forming, and slanted a glance at Damion down the way. He was still fighting my efforts to get him out of the cadaver, but it hadn't hindered what he was doing.

Despite the obvious danger, her smile was as blasé

as I remembered. My heart swelled. She might look younger now, but this was my mom. This was the woman who'd always faced the craziness around us, which she'd apparently had a hand in creating, with unparalleled confidence and effortless efficiency. This was the woman who'd saved kids off the street, and built a loving home from nothing. If ever there was a role model for survival skills, it was this woman.

"Of course you have my magic, my darling. But let's not wait for a man to save us." She winked. "They have a way of stealing the glory. Now, remember when I was talking you through how to get that really nice steak for Christmas each year? Yum, I miss steak. You used my magic then. Just like in the MGB. Remember?"

MGB was what she'd called the Magical Government building so non-magical people wouldn't catch on. I used to sit in that testing room chair, scared out of my mind, and focus on what she'd told me.

Think of that little red dial going haywire. Isn't that a funny joke? It's supposed to be very scientific, and it just spins and spins, out of control. When you have that in your mind, then believe.

That had always been key. Believing. *Believing* we'd get that steak and have a marvelous Christmas dinner. *Believing* we'd find a way to pay that tax bill so we could keep our house. *Believing* I could fool the testing machines so we could stay in the dual-society zone.

I got to it immediately. The little red dial in my mind's eye spun and spun. It spun so fast it turned into a red blur. A tickle formed in my belly, and then nervous butterflies. The dial kept spinning until the butterflies flew in every direction. The feeling reminded me of standing in that crowded grocery store, waiting for the right moment to grab that steak. Of sitting in the testing room in the MGB, hoping for the best. Truth be told, it reminded me of a great many incidents that had started normal and escalated to crazy. I'd been using the magic all along without knowing it.

Right now, with my mother present, it also brought back memories of laughter. Of running and playing. Of jumping on the bed and singing songs at the top of my lungs.

It reminded me of our fine life together.

Choked up, tears in my eyes, I dove into that feeling. I poured my energy into it, dwindling my remaining supply nearly all the way to zero. I ballooned it out and prepared to cast it around me, like I might do with my Spirit Walker magic.

"Yes!" She clapped in delight, a large smile on her face, as though this wasn't the direst of situations. "Look at you! Someone has taught you a thing or two. Now send it out into the world."

"Whatever you are doing won't help you," Damion said, his connection to me strengthening even as he blocked my attempts to tear down another of his prongs. "That is the only reason why I am allowing your mother to stay. I am not a monster. Not always."

My mother laughed, as though his words were a grand joke. And I pushed her magic into the world, filling up the large room and letting it spill out beyond. Letting it flower and spin. It felt like sparklers going off all round me, fizzing and zipping and dancing from the room. I wanted to laugh right along with my mom. I wanted to shrug off Damion's touch and take control of the situation.

I wanted to at least be on equal footing.

"What do I do now?" I asked, my fingers clenching and releasing. My friends hadn't attempted to leave, and I could tell they were getting restless. Red had pushed forward to the farthest edge of the stage, knives in hand, not far from trying to help regardless of what it might mean for her.

"You prepare to take the opportunities presented to you," my mom said. "Who is this Kieran? Is he your beau?" Her eyes crinkled. "Yes, I can see that he is. You have the glimmer of a woman in love." A soft smile crossed her lips. "Does he treat you well? Does he show you how much he loves you?"

Damion broke one of the prongs holding my soul, his touch hard and brutal, meant to pull back my attention. I gasped but did not look away from my mom. I didn't need sight to work at his soul. To thwart his attempts to suck my energy. To claw at his efforts to connect us. I soaked in the look of her face and the brightness of her eyes. God, I'd missed her. I'd missed our walks and our talks. I'd even missed our struggles, working together to provide for our misfit family. I'd been tempted a million times to call her back, but I'd honored her wishes until now.

"I created a misfit family of my own," I told her through gritted teeth, forcing his magical touch away from another of my prongs. He was amazing with all things spirit, but he wasn't a god. There were limits to what he could do. "I'm really happy, Mom. Usually, I mean. This isn't exactly a shining example, but other than this, I'm happy."

She glanced behind her, at the door. When she turned back, her image wavered, and the Line pulsed, calling her back.

"I'm glad, my heart," she said, and her voice echoed.

"I'm sorry for what you sacrificed for me," I blurted, needing to tell her. Screams and shouts and noise filled the room. The ground shook and a bronze statue of someone's head rolled in through the doors and crashed into a line of tables. "I'm sorry you had to leave the magical world because of me. I'm sorry you had to be poor."

"Anyone who is blessed enough to know love will

never be poor." She tilted her head to the side. "The happiest years of my life were with you. None of it mattered. I never looked back. We had a fine life, you and I. It fulfilled me in every way. Now, it is time for you to save the day. Go with the flow, just like I taught you, and seize your opportunity to shine. I have faith in you, my heart, and I love you."

The Line sucked her back, faster than a breath. It closed down on itself and vanished, stealing all the ultraviolet coloring with it as it went.

It must have appeared in the same position for Damion, because he watched it fade away. His head swiveled as a roar shook my bones. He stared at me for another silent moment.

"You dare keep me from spirit?" he asked in a low voice.

I lifted my eyebrows in a silent question. I hadn't known that was possible, and I certainly didn't know how to do it. I was pretty sure the Line was acting of its own volition on this one.

Another roar, closer this time. Something large and heavy hit the wall outside the room, probably the other half of that statue.

The Chaos magic had called Thane to the room. Which made sense, since nothing was more unpredictable than a Berserker set loose, but I wouldn't be able to fight him. Not tied up like I was.

Go with the flow, just like I taught you, and seize your opportunity to shine.

This wasn't any different than any of the other times I'd given chaos magic the reins. If I hadn't used it at the magical government building, I would've been exposed, pushed into training, and either taken or killed by Magnus. If I hadn't gotten that steak, we would've gone hungry. If I didn't flow with it now, this Spirit Walker on Demigod steroids would tether us together, rip me out of my body, and make my life hell for all of eternity.

Okay, so it was a little different, but we didn't get to choose what we survived, just *how* we survived.

"Get ready," I yelled out, staying loose with my hands at my sides.

I left his soul alone and just worked on his grip on my soul. All my energy, all my focus, went into detaching him. If Thane came in here and battered one or both of us, I didn't want the act of flying across the room to rip my soul out.

"What's the plan?" Bria yelled.

"React when the time comes, and don't die!" My limbs shaking, my energy faltering, I worked as fast as I could—ripping at his grip, rebuilding my soul prong, and clipping off that violet cord.

"Great plan," Bria said, and she wasn't kidding. It was usually the one she used, after all.

Someone screamed and ran into the room a moment before Thane burst in, huge and muscular, his whips flying around him. He caught sight of Damion and me, paused for a moment, and then lifted his head and roared.

Damion flinched, his head jerking to the side. He might've been able to shrug off my attempts to mess with his soul, but he clearly hadn't had practice with a Berserker of Thane's magnitude. There was more than one form of death incarnate.

Havoc darted toward Damion, finally seeing an opportunity. She growled and latched on to one of his legs, tearing through it with her claws before clamping it with her teeth. Bone cracked. Damion couldn't feel it to scream.

Mordecai jumped down off the stage.

"No!" I yelled at him, but he dodged in Thane's direction and ran with the speed of a large wolf.

I pried most of Damion's hold off my soul. He only had a toehold left, but he was now prodding my soul instead of stroking.

"What are you doing?" Damion howled, trying to kick the cat off with his other leg. The broken leg buckled at the thigh and the body fell. Havoc went after his good leg, trying to keep him immobile. "I am your only hope if you want to live free!" It occurred to me that he was talking to me and not the cat. "I'm your only hope. Without me, you will become their puppet.

They will always be stronger than you. They will always rule you."

"I'd rather trust Kieran than a guy who thinks my magic is only good for killing." Sweating, hardly able to stand, I kept on, nearly there. His touch weakened further, but still he clung on.

Mordecai ran in our direction, silently urging me to come with him. He didn't seem to realize Damion still had a grip on me.

"No, no, no," I said, waving him away and shutting my eyes to focus.

His hold on me was an intricate mix of spirit and power, but I could feel the cracks. I forced my way into those cracks and injected my own magic. I felt it start to give. His energy sucker attached again, but I ignored it. I couldn't waste time on that.

Thane's heavy footsteps pounded the ground. Tables flew out of the way as he followed Mordecai. Jerry yelled for me to get out of the way. Rocks underneath shook and vibrated the earth.

A little bit more. I just had to push Damion a little more.

My head swam with dizziness, my energy almost depleted. A *swoosh* made me open my eyes right before Thane's huge hand smacked into my upper body.

Pain lit up my world. My feet lifted off the ground. The connection on my soul was yanked taut, clattering my soul against its casing. I clutched at my chest as I popped off the last shred of Damion's presence. My soul flopped back into my casing where it belonged as I flew through the air, ass over end.

Bright white lightning filled the room—Dylan! He'd returned! Kieran was running in, too!

I turned my head and squinted even as I crashed into a table and something hard and heavy fell on top of me. I shoved it to the side just as the lightning subsided. Thane stood over Damion and howled, a sound I recognized. Damion was going for his soul.

"No, please." I struggled to my feet, fighting a wave of dizziness, utterly spent. I pushed on, staggering, trying to throw the exhaustion off magically and get to Thane. To help fight Damion, even if it killed me.

Something pure and vibrant pumped into my middle, and it took me a second to realize what it was.

Energy! Kieran had somehow figured out how to feed me energy through the soul link.

I saw him at the door, his hand coming out to brace himself. He struggled up straight, ready to head in after me.

"No," I yelled at him, flinging out a hand. "He's got more power than me. If you are giving me your energy, you won't have a solid defense against him. Stay back!"

Red ignored what I'd told Kieran and ran at the zombie, throwing knives. When she got closer, she pulled out a gun, stood over the body, and shot down into his chest, quick-fire. It wouldn't kill him, given his body was already dead, but it would give him some serious motivation to find a new suit.

"Get out of there—"

I let out a strangled cry when her body fell to the ground and her soul popped out. A violet link latched on to her spirit immediately, sucking at her energy.

Gritting my teeth, I ripped away the siphon and shoved her spirit across the room. I'd put it back in her body after I got rid of Damion.

I didn't waste the time her distraction had given me. As strength poured into me from Kieran, more than he should have given, I attacked Damion's soul prongs with ferocity. I cracked one, crumbled another, and pried a third clean off. It was so much easier now, and it occurred to me that his attack had been so successful because he'd drained my strength in the beginning. I'd have to remember that.

Jack popped up beside me. His eyes widened as he noticed Thane howling. "Jesus, Lexi, what's going on? What do you need? How can I help?"

"Try to help me wrestle this spirit out of its body."

"On it!" He dove forward, his hands passing through the cadaver. I honestly didn't know what he could actually do, but the distraction was what I was going for.

Damion's magical touch clutched at me again, but I deflected and continued to attack those damn prongs, so much stronger than in any living body. He'd fortified them to withstand me.

Thane stomped on the Spirit Walker's body, crushing his head and neck. Jerry ran forward to join the fray. They were all helping, my crew. The fear of death wasn't stopping them.

Power swelled, filling the room, and Kieran pushed Jerry out of the way with air. He also shoved Bria, who'd dashed in, trying to grab Thane's attention and get him out of the Spirit Walker's reach.

Thane was resisting all on his own. I'd created a monster, and I was so thankful for it.

Thane whipped down at the half-flattened body, which still somehow housed the spirit. He pummeled the ruined cadaver, his howls agonized, his face screwed up in torture. I took one step closer, then another, dodging Thane's fists. The decreased distance made my magic stronger. With a strong grip on Damion's soul, I magically smacked the last prong like a hammer.

Thane kicked the body. It flew at Jerry, who was pushing himself to his feet.

The final prong snapped and the soul popped out, into my grasp. With his bald head, bushy eyebrows, and broad face, his expression held hatred and rage.

The body hit Jerry and knocked him back. He staggered in place and then flung the body away before retching.

"Take Thane down," Kieran yelled, jogging into the room.

To my great surprise, Zander and the regal woman from my hearing ran into the room after him, magic ballooning with them, focused on poor Thane. Thane turned toward them and let out a great roar. Zander flinched, and the regal woman took the lead, her head turning down a little and her eyebrows lowering, a warrior entering the battlefield. I wondered if her magic came from Ares.

Thane cracked his whip at her. She didn't alter her course. She stuck out an arm, and the whip slashed through her light sweater and opened a deep red gash. She didn't even flinch, and I wondered if that arrow shooter who hadn't balked from my magic was on her team. She kept running, but my attention shifted to someone else.

Magnus had just entered the room.

He saw Damion caught in my grip and quickly skirted the scuffle with Thane, heading toward me.

"No!" I jogged backward and threw out my hand to slow him. "This spirit is not going into another spirit cage—which I really wish someone would've told me about. This spirit—"

"Will be handled by me." The words rang through

the room. The pressure I'd grown accustomed to—the feeling of invisible eyes watching—lifted from my shoulders. The little black shadows that had been plaguing me, darting to the sides and out of my vision, now came toward me, enlarging as they did. They coalesced into one shadowy being who stepped out of the spirit realm…and into the world of the living.

The shadows slowly peeled away into the face of Harding—the spirit I'd known as Harding, anyway, with his bedroom eyes, tousled hair, and lazy smile. His level of power lit up my world, off the charts and nothing like I'd ever felt from him in the past.

Magnus lost his breath and staggered backward, against the wall, his eyes as big as saucers. Kieran froze solid, his eyes fixed on Harding. But we weren't the only ones who saw him this time. Zander and the regal woman, who'd been focused on dodging Thane, jogged backward in obvious shock. Only Bria didn't jolt in surprise.

Thane, still going, spun and roared. Harding flicked his hand, and Thane jerked back and reduced into his human form. He was left breathing heavily and staring at his hands in confusion.

"Hi, Alexis," Harding said with his little smirk. Someone at the door gasped.

"Who the fuck are you?" I demanded, and then pointed at Damion. "This guy says he is Harding—well,

Damion now, but Harding once. I believe him—he's as cracked as I would expect for someone with his history. You aren't the last Spirit Walker, but you know the same stuff. Who are you?"

Harding put out his hands. "April Fool's?" He laughed. "I fooled you, I'm sorry. You have to understand, I'm not *technically* supposed to interfere in the lives of humans. That's the agreement I made not long ago with my brothers. Well…not long ago by my standards. A few of your lifetimes, at least."

I put my hand to my head, dizzy again. Disbelief rolled through the soul link.

Harding put out his hand to me, and I flinched away.

"We don't have time to walk through spirit right now, Alexis, but I'm going to give you energy so you and your Demigod don't pass out on me."

I furrowed my brow but let him touch my shoulder, a real hand, not spirit. Then again, he'd always felt real to me—more so than any spirit should.

Energy flooded me.

"What the hell is going on?" I whispered.

He took his hand back, and I sucked in a breath, feeling better than new. Kieran straightened a little more, and I could sense the energy had transferred to him through the link.

"Here's what the hell is going on. We are related."

He grinned at me. "I am"—he pointed at Magnus—"that guy's dad, many, *many* moons ago. His mother was very pretty. I couldn't resist." He gestured between us. "Makes our interactions a little gross by your standards, I grant you, but just remember that by my standards"—he shrugged—"it's just another day."

"Wait…" My mind went blank, the enormity of what he was saying starting to sink in. "You're not… You can't be…"

"Yeah." He spread his arms wide. "I'm Hades."

Chapter 24

ALEXIS

EVERYONE IN THE room except for Bria and me dropped down to a knee, their heads bowed, paying their respects to one of the three most powerful gods. I realized my mouth was open, but I didn't know what to say. I honestly hadn't even really believed the gods existed. Theoretically, sure, but they'd been away for so long (lifetimes and lifetimes) that part of me had wondered if someone had invented fake people to go with the magic that had existed as long as humanity. It was easier to understand the magic when you had a myth to go with it.

To have one of them standing in front of me, claiming he'd sired my biological father… Saying he'd been training me!

There were no words.

"First, I just need to…" Harding—*Hades!*—turned and spied Red's spirit up against the wall. He put up his hand and beckoned her closer with his finger. She came as if pulled. "Time to say goodbye, love. You've had a good run, but you should've died in Lydia's mansion. You felt that, right?"

Her eyes were tight and her mouth had reduced down to a thin, tense line. She nodded.

"Wait a minute," I said, finally finding my words. "No, she shouldn't have. She was fine. She's not too far gone. I can still save her!"

Hades shook his head slowly. "Not this time. No, her time came and went. I didn't have the heart to take her when you were dealing with your daddy issues. She knew she was on borrowed time. Why do you think she sacrificed herself?" Comfort and the feeling of protection washed over me, and I knew it was his magic. "I'll watch out for her, Alexis, don't worry. And when you're skilled enough at your craft, you can come visit. How does that sound?"

I knew I didn't have a choice, so with tears stinging my eyes, I nodded.

"You were excellent," I said to her. "You did a really excellent job. You'll be missed." Tears slid down my face. "I'm sorry to—"

She held up her hand. "Don't say you're sorry. Most magical people would give their left tit to have been in my place, even if they had to die for it. We were trained for battle, and that's exactly what you gave us. I felt alive when guarding you. Thank *you*. And now, look"—she hooked a thumb at Hades—"I have an *in*. Can't beat that."

"Warm fuzzies all around," Hades said sarcastically. A moment later, she was gone.

My body shook with suppressed sobs, but I held strong. I couldn't go to pieces yet over losing another of our people. I couldn't let guilt surge up and steal my focus.

"Okay, what's next?" Hades looked around the crowded room, all eyes on him, no one speaking. "It's been a while since I've been in this kind of scene. I've missed it, I'll be honest with you. A golden throne and someone to feed me grapes would be just the thing."

I opened and closed my mouth like a fish, wiping my renewed tears. I still couldn't find words, not for any of this.

He laughed. "You had no idea who I was, I know. I thought maybe your Demigod would catch on, but he's so young, and I've changed my image recently. What do you think? Like it?" He framed his face with his hands. "Only that clever little Necromancer figured me out. It was the whole 'spirit in a cat' shtick—Possessors inhabiting a body wouldn't be able to get through your magic, even in a cat, and neither would they be able to communicate with you through the animal. Animals can't talk, you know. It was a little far-fetched, but you lot are so ignorant when it comes to my magical type. I figured I'd take a chance."

I looked around until I found Bria, leaning against the stage next to a kneeling Jerry. "You knew?"

She shrugged. "I suspected based on legends I'd heard, so I did some research. He appeared to me when I was about to take the info to you."

My body had gone numb with shock. "And you never said anything?"

"You needed training, and he's the only one that understands the full gamut of your magic. He said he'd stay if I kept silent. I figured it was a good trade, though it made it tough to convey the seriousness of the Damion issue."

"Yes. I'm rather amazed you didn't spill the beans on that one." He winked at her. "That's why I like you best."

I could not believe her ability to keep a secret. She'd gotten drunk since then—several times, in fact—and still she hadn't uttered a word. The woman was a vault.

"But…why me?" I asked, not knowing what else to say, half wondering if I'd gotten knocked out and was dreaming.

"Yours is my favorite kind of magic." He snapped, and a recliner appeared behind him. He lowered to sitting and then gestured for me to do the same. A wooden chair had poofed into being beside him.

I narrowed my eyes at him. "Really? A wooden chair and you get that? If you're holding a grudge because of the cat thing, I'll remind you that you *chose* to be a cat. That wasn't my fault."

He laughed. The wooden chair turned into another recliner. "I do so love working with you. You're so accommodating…until you're not. It tickles me to find out what annoys you. I chose the cat because I thought you liked cats. How was I supposed to know you hadn't decorated that office? Speaking of, have my gifts grown on you?" He gestured at the cats. Chaos still lay curled up, not moving. Havoc sat by his side, licking his head. "Oops." He waved his hand, and Chaos roused, mewing. "Don't worry about them; they're undead. I can teach you how to rouse them when they suffer a mortal wound. They're hellcats. Cool, right? I know I usually do hellhounds, but…well, it's our little inside joke. It suits you and your pajamas."

My frown deepened. No one around the room even swayed or shifted their weight, still on their knees with their heads bowed. It was like he'd frozen time for a moment. Or maybe he'd just frozen them.

"As I was saying," he went on, "yours is my favorite kind of magic. It is light and dark, death and rebirth, healing and killing. It has so many facets, but it has been misused for so long, those wielding it being mistreated."

"But why me? Why not Harding—Damion?" I gestured to his spirit, frozen like everyone else.

"I haven't shown much of an interest in the human

lands of late. I didn't know about him until they caged him in my domain. His mind had been altered at that point. They'd tortured him, turned him into the worst embodiment of your magic. It was a shame, really. But then I learned of you. You can thank dear old Dad for that. He kept making treks through spirit to peek at you, and finally my curiosity won out and I followed. There you were, a little budding Spirit Walker. He didn't know that at first, of course, and when he did..." Hades gave Magnus a sly look, my father still frozen in place. Could he see or hear what was going on? "He tried to grab your spirit at one point so he could hold it hostage until he could grab your body, but oops, you were protected. I've always been good at cock-blocking." He bit his lip, tamping a delighted smile. "He's been wondering why he could get so close in spirit but not close enough. Now he'll know. Riddle solved."

So he could hear, then.

My heart sank. Riddle solved indeed. The inaccessibility of my spirit was the only thing that had kept Magnus from grabbing me physically. He'd hesitated because of Valens. But once Valens was out of the picture...

I blew out a breath and leaned back, tears crowding my vision. "Thank you," I said, "for protecting me. He didn't kill me before he knew my magic, and he has saved me a couple times... Right? That was him and not you?"

"He helped and saved you of his own free will, yes. There are layers to that onion."

I nodded, not sure how to feel, but this behavior was in character for my father. I understood it. In some ways, I felt more comfortable than I had after that confusing dinner.

Hades's expression grew serious and he leaned forward. "There is goodness and badness in us all. You are mostly good, however. You are a shining light in this muddy magical world. I know how close you came to joining my kingdom just now, but I couldn't interfere until I knew, without a doubt, that you were the defender I had hoped you would be. I allowed Damion the added power. I made him more powerful than you because I wanted to put you to the test. I wanted to see what you would do when faced with the absolute worst situation. And you didn't give up. You turned to your guiding light. You turned to goodness.

"You relish the magic that can heal people, and you use it when most magical people wouldn't bother. You stop from killing whenever possible, and you defend the wholeness of the magic I love so dearly. You defend those in spirit who cannot defend themselves. It is your goodness, with a splash of sin, that does your magic justice. You are the first *true* Spirit Walker in many a long age. For that, I will reward you—"

"Wait."

The voice came from everywhere and nowhere at once.

"Ah, fuck," Hades said, and leaned back again, put out.

A bright light blinded me for a moment, and electricity made my hair stand on end. When the haze cleared, a man stood before me in a crisp red velvet robe with a golden belt and a golden wreath around his large shoulders. His incredibly handsome face was all planes and angles, like it had been chiseled from stone. His power trumped Hades, a touch more robust, just like the man.

One name flashed through my mind: Zeus.

"I'm dreaming," I said softly, not able to stand or bow or do any of the things I should've done given freaking Zeus had touched down before me. "I must be dreaming. This isn't real."

"What are you doing here, Zeus?" Hades asked. "Can't you see I'm busy?"

"The question is, what are *you* doing here?" Zeus replied, and Hades snapped another seat into existence, which Zeus didn't take. "You've been leaving the underworld often of late. Is this why? Have you been dabbling with the humans?"

"Brother, really, what are you wearing? A velvet robe? Hello, glory days." To Zeus's prolonged stare,

Hades pushed out of his chair. "I'm just making sure the best kind of magic isn't sullied by humans. What's it to you?"

Thankfully, Zeus ignored the dig about the "best" kind of magic. I didn't want to be dragged into a family matter between ethereal beings.

"We agreed to leave the humans to their own affairs for a while and see what happened," Zeus said.

"Yeah, we did, except Poseidon went and turned someone into a Demigod. I'm just taking my turn, that's all. Fair is fair, isn't that what you preach?"

Hades snapped his fingers and Kieran shuddered, animated again. He bowed his head in reverence, emotions rolling through him so fast I couldn't catch them all. The theme I caught just fine, though—heart-stopping shock and joy.

Hades pointed at him, and Kieran's eyes widened.

"His mom gave birth to a healthy baby boy, level-five magic. I looked it up," Hades said. "Does that feel like level-five magic to you?"

"Poseidon," Zeus called, and his voice was like thunder, rolling through the room, rattling my bones.

The air chilled just a little. The scent of salt water drifted in, and a man followed in its wake, stalking through the doors, his long, wet hair draped over his muscular shoulders. Water dripped down his perfectly cut chest and onto the wide golden belt around his waist. A sort of skirt flowed around his legs, green and blue, almost like seaweed turned into fabric. His built thighs peeked out of it when he walked, and a rush of heat ran through me. Apparently I had a type, and that type was of the sea.

"What in Hades's flamethrower are *you* wearing?" Hades asked, his handsome face contorting into mocking disbelief.

"Using your own name in vain?" Poseidon asked in a deep voice. "How simple of you."

"Says the guy who couldn't be bothered to buy a whole dress and instead chose half a skirt to save a few bucks." Hades huffed out a laugh. "That's probably not even real gold on your belt."

"What do you want?" Poseidon asked Zeus, sparing a glance for Kieran as he walked by. He did a double take, and guilt and then indignation crossed his face. He'd done something naughty, that was clear.

"Well?" Zeus asked, gesturing at Kieran. "Did you do that?"

Poseidon's shoulders sagged just a little. "I couldn't ignore the situation. His mother was a great favorite among my people. Everyone lamented her ill treatment. Given your…rules, I was forbidden to interfere. What was I supposed to do? There was unrest. It had to be resolved. I merely gave a gift to her son, like a birthday present."

"It was our mutual agreement, and you don't think giving her son the *gift* of Demigod magic was interfering?" Zeus boomed.

Poseidon straightened, his expression hard. "It calmed my waters, and no, it was not interfering. I did not alter his mother's future—she had made certain choices, and I left her to her path. The child's future was yet undecided. I gave a kid a present, that's all."

My heart beat faster. My gaze settled on Kieran. I wouldn't have agreed to see him again had he not given a present to *my* sick child. A blanket. Maybe Poseidon had done something greater than padding Kieran's power—maybe he'd turned him off the path Valens had set for him.

If I hadn't already been shell-shocked into paralysis, I would've fainted from the sheer enormity of all this.

"It's not like he can say *boo*," Hades said, hooking a thumb at Zeus. "He freed one of *his* favorites. That was definitely interfering. My people were all set to welcome the guy in, teach him how good sex could actually be, and lo and behold, he was ripped away by the god of thunder himself. Imagine…" Hades *tsked*. "Guess how many times he's been laid since? Guess. Zero, that's how many. I don't think you did the guy a favor."

Dylan unfroze, and his eyes widened immediately. He braced both hands on the floor and bent over them, his forehead nearly meeting the hard wood. "Your

Almighty. I am humbled and honored to be in your presence. Please accept my gratitude."

Zeus nodded at him before turning back to his brothers. "See how he greets me? Proper respect. You should do something about your line." He nodded at me.

"My line is good. Much more fun." Hades crossed his arms over his chest. "If you insist on stalking me and lurking like a creep, Zeus, you'll have your secrets exposed. You saved one, cheapskate over there elevated one, and I'll have my turn. I choose her." Hades pointed at me.

"Yes, but I didn't meddle, I just saved one of my own. Someone else poisoned them," Zeus said.

"That's what meddling—" Hades threw up his hands. "Whatever, I don't care. This is happening. I'm taking my turn."

"There are a lot of sassy women in this age. I wouldn't mind…meddling a little," Poseidon murmured, looking me over. "I bet they're good in bed. My line is weakening in the human world. It's time for some new blood."

"Hands off, fancy dresser," Hades said, shooing Poseidon away from me. "This is your grandson's betrothed. They frown upon grandpa fucking in this age. Find someone else."

"You should talk," I said, wanting for all the world

to leave this room before it got any more awkward.

My face heated further when Hades winked at me and said, “I know, right? I won’t tell if you don’t…”

“Fine, yes.” Zeus nodded slowly, looking over the room. “Yes, okay, maybe a little…meddling is warranted, but in the future we mustn’t do it as gods. We must assume human appearances and hide our true nature, as much as it grieves me to say. I hate going incognito. There is no glory in it.”

Poseidon gave Zeus a dead stare, and I knew that was his version of rolling his eyes. He nodded at Hades before turning and strutting for the door. As he passed Kieran, though, he paused.

“Human, what is the name she finally settled on for you?” he asked, his voice gruff, as though he hated that he cared.

“Kieran. Against my father’s wishes, she named me Kieran.”

Poseidon nodded. “Good. Make sure you are worthy of her. Songs are sung about her still. She is sorely missed.”

“Yes, sir,” Kieran said, and then bowed low, like Dylan had done.

Zeus looked at Hades. “Just the one. Do not get carried away or I’ll be back.”

A wide smile crossed Hades’s face. “You need to catch up on modern media, brother. You have no idea how ridiculous you sounded just then. Though it matches your ridiculous look, so…"

Distant thunder rolled through the sky. Lightning flashed within Zeus's turbulent stare, and then he was gone, electricity and light pulling him from the room.

A breath rushed out of me and my whole body shook. My expression must've matched Kieran's and Dylan's wide-eyed stares. Even Bria seemed to have gone more rigid, as if in utter disbelief that we had been allowed to witness all of that. None of that seemed like it was for human ears.

"Well. That was annoying." Hades dusted himself off like he'd just wrestled in the yard with his brothers. He turned back to me, his eyes sparkling with glee. "I've always hated rules. So. Let's see how much I can meddle before Zeus sticks his big nose in again, shall we? You need training, and I am the only one who can do it. So that's still on the list. And then there is this…"

He shoved his hand toward me, and a rush of power infused my every muscle. It pushed at my skin and sparkled through my muscle and bone. My heart leapt and I felt like laughing. Or like exploding my magic out in all directions.

Our chairs disappeared and I fell on my butt, not having expected it.

After I stood, the rest of the room roused.

"Listen to me," he said to everyone, his voice filling

all the available space, full of power and authority, nothing like how he'd been with his brothers. "You will squabble over Alexis Price no longer. From now on, with my power and my blessing, she is Demigod Alexis. Have a care with her—she does not like being bullied."

He waved his hand over me, and something heavy touched down on my head. It felt like a crown.

For a great many reasons, I was too stunned to speak.

He looked into my eyes and grasped my upper arms. "I will supply you with gold and jewels and whatever you need to get started. You will truly be your own woman. Your little gremlin should be pleased. Maybe now she'll accept a blood offering and get a little protection. She's fun to watch—I'd hate for her to join my kingdom too early." My heart glowed. "Your fortune will be up to you to maintain, however. You will be on your own after this." He cocked his head. "With money, I mean. I'll be hanging around. If you need help with money, ask your Demigod. People of Poseidon are *very* good with conserving money. But by the dark places of the world, buy a piece of property worthy of Hades, would you? It pains me to see you in that tiny hovel. Now, to honor the facet of your magic that you, and only you, have embraced…" He paused for a moment. "I have a gift for you."

Jack was yanked across the room until he was standing beside us. Hades snapped, and what was once spirit became flesh and bone. His bronze skin was dull in the harsh light, not shimmering or translucent like it would be in the ultraviolet light of the Line. Real skin, existing in the world of the living. He lifted his hands, eyes wide with awe, and wiggled his fingers.

My breath caught in my throat and my eyes teared up.

"I'd ask if this was a dream, but…I don't have those anymore," Jack said. "I don't sleep." He looked around the room. "But seriously, is this really happening?"

Donovan stepped forward, disbelief and longing written across his face. The rest of the guys exclaimed their shock, and Bria's face lit up.

"What's happening?" Jack asked. "*What's happening?*"

"It's beyond rare for a spirit who's been released from a blood oath to stick around to help his Demigod," Hades said. "You had nothing tying you to this world but your love and your loyalty. I've felt your struggles, and I've seen your sacrifice. You earned your place in this world. Welcome back. I trust this time your mistress won't allow someone to take over your body with their spirit."

I made sure to hide my shock and confusion. Apparently I could give my people some sort of spirit protection. That would've been nice to know *before* Jack had been possessed...

"Alexis, I give you leave to...well, leave," Hades said, his hand still on my arm, the crown still on my head. "You have no more dealings at the summit this year. Demigod Kieran, Demigod Alexis, you have shown your true characters, and those characters are shining examples of what Demigods should aspire to rather than all this petty infighting and one-upmanship. Go home and plan that wedding. Don't invite me—unless a certain Necromancer plans to get drunk and let down her guard. In which case, definitely invite me. Oh, and Zander—where's Zander?"

"Here, my lord." Zander stepped forward with a pale face. He bowed so low that I wondered how he didn't fall over.

"Zeus types are so obnoxious with the bowing," Hades muttered. "I'm sure you realize that Dylan will be staying where he is, and that Zeus himself will take it as a personal insult if you continue to dabble in his business?"

"Of course, my lord, yes. I'd come to that conclusion, yes." Zander bowed again.

Hades slid his hand across my back, pulling me in for a sideways hug. Before he left, he leaned in and said, "You never tried to control me, not once. You never stepped over the boundaries I'd set, even when I knew you wanted more training. You're a helluva woman,

Alexis Price, and I will personally make sure your mother is invited into my kingdom's elite. You, however, have been given immortality. I hope you will stay topside and change this ridiculous Demigod culture, one century at a time. If you offer your blood magic to your Demigod, he will also be blessed with immorality. See what I did? I one-upped Poseidon, that cheap bastard. He'll give an inch, but he won't give a pound, or whatever that saying is." Damion flew to his side like a rag doll. "Don't worry about him. I'll take him down with me. Maybe he can have a better life as a spirit than he had as a man."

He summoned the Line, and it became clear to me that he was the one who'd given it a life of its own earlier, and probably also in Lydia's mansion.

"Wait," I said before he stepped into it. He turned back with raised eyebrows. "Why did you set Thane off? Was it so he could help if I needed it?"

He laughed, holding his belly. "You should ask Lydia about what set Thane off." He covered his mouth for a moment. "Oops. You can't. She's dead." He laughed again. "There are certain magical creatures with flair, I'll say that. Be thankful for them; they helped you in the end. This worked out exactly as it should have. She was of my line, but she strayed a bit too far. I'll need a little heart-to-heart with that one."

With that, he and Damion were gone.

I let the breath gush out of me, deflated, exhausted, confused. Red's body lay at my feet, her soul in the hands of Hades now. I knew he'd treat her well. Jack was at my side, and the Six would be reunited again. I couldn't ask for more than that.

"Alexis—"

It was my father who'd spoken, but Kieran strode toward me, his eyes on fire as he held his hand out to cut off Magnus. "*Demigod* Alexis, you mean, Demigod Magnus. Hades himself has boosted her magic to Demigod status. She is one of us now." He wrapped his arms around me and hugged me tightly. "My heavens, did that all really just happen?" he murmured.

"Well, I'll tell you what, sir." Jack clapped his hands, not worried about his lack of clothing. "I'm standing here, in my own flesh, back from the dead. Yeah, that just fucking happened."

Chapter 25

KIERAN

KIERAN WALKED THROUGH the gardens with Alexis's hand in his and all of his people at his back. He hadn't wanted to take the golf carts directly back to the lodge. He needed time to process the revelations of the day. They *all* needed it.

He hadn't been born a Demigod?

He hadn't been born a Demigod?

He might need a few months to process that, actually. A walk through the garden wasn't going to do it.

He'd thought one thing all his life, only to find out…he was god-touched. His mother had been a favorite, and her people had loved her so much that their righteous indignation on her behalf had drawn the attention of a god.

Kieran was god-touched.

On second thought, maybe it would take longer than a few months for him to accept the truth. All he knew was that his gifts felt more special to him now. They felt precious.

He wandered along the path, ignoring everyone he saw. He didn't care about status right now. He didn't care about politics. He cared only about the woman sharing this lovely walk with him, and the misfit family behind them.

Alexis had been silent since they'd left the destroyed meeting hall. She'd allowed him to lead her down the hallway, past the flocks of staring people, and out the closest door into the sunshine. All of their people had followed at a respectful distance, stunned out of their fucking minds.

Hades had given Alexis Demigod magic and therefore Demigod status.

Hades had been training her!

Hades!

After Hades left, Magnus had fallen all over himself reminding Kieran that he was the one who'd guided Kieran through feeding Lexi energy via the soul link. The power boost had allowed Alexis to handle the Soul Stealer situation on her own.

But wow, to see a guy like Magnus yapping at Kieran's heels…that was surreal. All of this was surreal.

Souls lingered in the trees. Kieran could feel them now. Alexis's magical boost had bled through the soul link, giving him more of her magic. Which likely meant she'd be able to access more of his abilities, too.

She waved her hand and her magic rolled through

the trees. People groaned and someone screamed.

"Crap," she whispered, curling her fingers. "I need to get used to the heightened power."

She stopped dead, staring at nothing for a moment.

"What's the matter?" he asked.

"Kieran...am I a Demigod?" She paused for a moment. "Was that really Hades? It wasn't Harding, I know that now, but...was it... It couldn't have been..."

She continued to stare at nothing, and he couldn't help chuckling. None of their team said one peep, not even Daisy. He took a deep breath and pulled her into his arms.

"It was really Hades, yes. And yes, love, you're now a Demigod. I can't imagine there is a story like this in all of the history books—a woman born to nothing, discovered on the streets in a forgotten place, and then crowned by Hades himself as the best Demigod the world had ever known."

She pushed away from him and delicately touched the golden crown sitting atop her head before she started walking again. "The biggest clusterfuck Demigod the world has ever known, you mean."

"Yes. That's probably better." He laughed, feeling so light, like a huge weight and been lifted. They wouldn't need to be so vigilant about her protection now. If anyone *did* attack her, she would be equipped to handle it by herself.

She would need some help with money matters, though, and political maneuvering, and all the things he'd been learning since he was a boy. But they had time for that. Being god-touched would grant her at least a few decades of high status. The vultures would forgive her almost anything in those first years. It would give her time to prepare, and Kieran had every confidence that he was right. She *would* be the best Demigod the world had ever known.

He glanced back, finding Jack in the middle of the pack, his face turned up, his eyes closed, and a serene smile on his face. Daisy walked next to him, her arm looped within his, and Mordecai had taken the other side, contentment plain in his movements.

"Is this real life?" Lexi said softly, and she must've plucked those words right out of Kieran's head.

"That's my line," Dylan said, directly behind them. "I just saw the almighty Zeus, lord of the gods. He said I was a better subject than the Demigod I was sworn to. He chose to save me and not her."

His voice held all kinds of awe, like a boy who'd shaken hands with his hero.

Kieran shook his head, looking over the clearing at the wide-open ocean. Poseidon resided in there, somewhere.

His chest constricted with emotion.

How many guys could say their mother was a favorite of the gods?

He looked at beautiful Lexi.

If they had a son, there would be one more.

"Give us a minute," Kieran said over his shoulder. "Actually, head to the lodge. We'll meet you there."

Kieran pulled Lexi into the trees and then beyond them to an empty bench hidden within a beautiful array of flowers. When he was sure the others had moved on and they were alone, he took her into his arms and kissed her.

"I need to teach you how to mark me," he murmured against her lips. "To make it fair."

He flitted his tongue into her mouth, and she yanked at his belt, her movements hurried and desperate.

"I can probably figure it out," she said, panting, the air between their mouths heated. "You need to teach me the blood magic thing. I don't want to live forever by myself."

A swell of passion and emotion raged through him. He bunched her dress over her hips and ripped off her panties. She moaned as she pushed down his pants, allowing his hard length to spring free.

"Take me," she begged, wrapping her arms around him.

He held her tightly against him and thrust, plunging into her. Her fevered lips were on his, their tongues swirling together.

She swung her hips into him. He clutched her tightly, plunging as deep as he could go.

"I love you," he said, their bodies retreating and coming together in a delicious dance of lust and power. Their connection spiraled and blossomed, deep and solid. "Be mine for the rest of time. Together we'll never go wrong."

"Yes!" She swung and retreated, passion and love drenching their soul link. She groaned, and then fire sizzled across his skin in the most sensuous of ways. Her mark. "I'll always say yes."

He let go, reveling in the feel of her soft skin and the sharp bite of her magic. His magic seared across her as he soaked hers in, boosting the effectiveness and pushing them higher.

"Oh, Kieran," she said, wild now, moving against him, he within her. "Yes, Kieran!"

Their combined power joined and then sizzled, the marks becoming one and encompassing them both, binding them together. Skin and soul, internally and externally, they merged as only two Demigods could. As only two equals could.

He soaked into the sensation, frenzied and wild, so damn in love. He buried himself in her one last time and called her name, exalting in his release. She shuddered against him, groaning in pleasure.

Breathing hard but not ready to be separated, he let her push off his jacket and throw it down on the bench.

He sat with her on his lap, still within her, needing a quick reprieve and then fully intending to go for round two. With their combined magic, he had no fear of their safety. No one would sneak up on them. No one would get close.

"I might like a garden like this," she murmured, her lips still close to his. "It's a pretty spot to make love in."

"You should buy a place out in the country."

"It'll have to be enormous or Harding will just make fun of me."

"Harding?"

She shrugged and leaned closer, trailing the tip of her tongue along his bottom lip. He was already stirring within her. "It is too crazy to say the other name. I figure…I was introduced to him as Harding. Might as well stick with that. It's a reminder of what the last guy could've been if he'd been in charge of his own destiny."

He curled his hands around the swell of her hips and lifted before pulling her back down, the slick slide revving him up again. "Hmm" was all he could manage.

"A place in the country sounds nice, with huge gardens. We could go there to get away."

"I'm in." He kissed her slowly, sensually, moving within her again. "If it's anything like today, it'll be a crazy eternity."

Warmth and love bled through the soul link. "Yes, it will, and we'll spend it together."

Epilogue

DAISY

"YOU READY?" MORDECAI asked Daisy the next day as she entered the kitchen of the lodge. Most of the Six crowded the space, with Jerry and Dylan lingering on the outskirts.

"Nearly. Where's Zorn?" She grabbed a bottle of water out of the fridge before peering around Jack to see what he was cooking at the stove.

His big arm flared out, pushing her away. "It's a surprise. Go away."

"Is that any way to talk to the favorite gremlin of the almighty god Hades?" Donovan asked, standing beside Jack, working a different pan.

"The almighty is Zeus, Dylan says so," Boman said, leaning against the sink.

Jack turned from the stove, spatula in hand. "Well, Hades brought me back, so he gets my vote."

"Yes, and Zeus would've left you dead, so he gets my vote," Donovan said.

Thane stroked his beard. "The way I see it, Zeus

brought Dylan back, and Hades brought Jack back—Poseidon is the turd in that threesome."

"But Poseidon turned our fearless Demigod into a fearless Demigod. Without him, there would be no us." Boman shrugged. "Tie."

"Yeah, like you guys wouldn't piss yourselves if they all appeared again." Daisy drained half of the water.

"We weren't the only ones starstruck," Jerry told Daisy. "We may have been frozen in place, but I saw your expression. I've never seen you so befuddled."

"Don't pick on the cherished gremlin, *Jerry*," Donovan said.

"Yeah, *Jerry*, or the gremlin might kill you in your sleep," Thane added.

"I cannot believe you kept that secret, though," Boman said to Bria as she mixed a drink. "How in the… What in the…"

Bria shrugged. "My girl needed training. Besides, who would have believed me?"

The guys nodded. It was probably true.

Zorn stepped into the room and jerked his head at Daisy. "Let's go."

A flurry of butterflies took flight in her stomach. Before she could put her water down, though, Henry stepped in behind Zorn, his folded-up laptop in hand. "I've got news."

Kieran entered the kitchen, followed by Lexi. Both

of them practically glowed—the aura from their Demigod marks was like a radiant light, making them both even easier on the eyes. It would take some getting used to.

Lexi wore jeans and a plain shirt, having chosen to stay in and pack this morning, but Kieran hadn't been idle. Even though they were all leaving in the afternoon, he was in his customary high-dollar suit and had already been out and about, shaking hands and hearing proposed alliances, soaking in the heightened status. He did not plan to let this situation go to waste. He had a chance to get ahead, and he was taking it, for himself, his family, and his territory.

Now that Alexis had the power to get herself out of a jam if Kieran ever went crazy, Daisy felt comfortable enough to let down her guard and say that he was one helluva guy. He was Mr. Political when the situation called for it, but yesterday, despite what it might've meant for him personally, he'd walked out of his important meeting to help Alexis. When it came down to it, his family meant more to him. That meant something. It was what kept the crew together. Red had given her life—twice, apparently—to fight beside them. Jack had earned his way back because of his loyalty. Kieran had created those bonds of loyalty, and Lexi had strengthened them. Together they would be incredible leaders. Daisy sincerely hoped Kieran could keep it together so they really could live out eternity together. Lexi deserved to be this happy forever.

"I would turn around and give you my full attention, Henry, but I don't want to burn anything," Jack said.

"Ditto." Donovan raised a spoon coated in brown sauce.

Henry pressed on as though he hadn't heard. "Through my…friend, I was able to get full access to the Summit surveillance. I've been downloading the info onto our cloud. We've got a lot of excellent information, sir." Henry nodded at Kieran. "A *lot* of excellent information. Secret meetings were going on all over the place, as you'd expect. But some of the Demigods seemed to have an awareness of the cameras. They only spoke freely in places where the surveillance lacked audio. Less-established leaders, even those known for being more tech-savvy, didn't show that same pattern. The pattern should help us glean a lot more information than what was said on tape."

Kieran leaned against the wall and pulled Alexis against him. "I agree. You're recording it on our servers, you said?"

"Yes," Henry said, adjusting his computer under his arm. "We're downloading it to our cloud in increments, picking times when the surveillance team isn't watching things quite so closely. Their team is pretty good."

"Did you find out what the story was with Aaron?" Dylan asked. "Did he get in any trouble for what went on with the…with Damion?"

Kieran slipped a hand into his pocket. "He lost a lot of status."

"That's it?" Daisy asked, not bothering to hide her disgust and outrage. "How many people did that guy get killed?"

"Losing status isn't as mundane as it sounds," Kieran said. "His lesser status means fewer allies. Less people to stick up for him. To help him. He's vulnerable, and I suspect he has an enemy in Zander. Zander hasn't come out publicly, but a few of the things he said… Trust me, Aaron's loss of status today will be his ruin unless he can figure out a way to right this wrong. Given Alexis and I plan to cock-block his every attempt to climb out of the muck, well…"

"He's done," Lexi said. "He's messed with me one too many times. His demise won't be fast, either. We're going to make sure he hangs himself nice and slow. Make him feel it until he's so weak that his wife eventually kills him. Magnus will help, I know he will. He'll do it to help himself as much as suck up to me, but he'll do it."

Dylan nodded, and Daisy's outrage started to ease. She'd been saved and pulled out of the stink, but Dylan had only escaped his situation by dying. He had a vendetta against Demigods behaving badly that Daisy fully supported. If he was satisfied with the punishment, she was too.

"What's the story with that?" Mordecai asked, picking at his nail. "How are you going to leave things with Magnus?"

Alexis sighed and leaned her head against Kieran's chest. "He's been shaped by the life of an immortal Demigod. I need to accept that. There is a lot of terribleness in him. A lot of things to dislike. He did let me live, though, even when he could've let me fumble my way to death. He's been helpful at times. I won't give up on him, though I will never actually trust him. Not completely. I guess that's just how life has to be."

"I have faith that eventually you'll be allies," Kieran said, squeezing her. "That's a better relationship than Demigods have with most people. It's about as much trust as they are willing to give."

"I know," she said softly.

"It's all right, Lexi, I'll be your daddy," Jack said, flipping something.

"Death really killed your sense of humor, dude," Donovan said. "That joke was not on point. She might kill you again for that one."

"Nah, not when she sees that I am making her Christmas steak," Jack replied.

Alexis stared at the back of his head for a moment,

and her lips tweaked up into a smile. "How did you know?"

"I *may* have heard you calling your mom and then I *might* have listened in. You were loud as hell. The whole spirit world heard you, I think. That was probably Hades's work." He turned back, and his bright white smile lit up his face. "Who's your daddy now?"

"No." Donovan shoved Jack. "Still no, dude. Let it go."

Alexis laughed. "It's so wrong it might just be right."

"It's not right, Alexis." Thane shook his head with a pained expression. "It is weird, but it is not right."

"Speaking of other things that aren't right..." Henry said.

"Good segue," Boman said, laughing.

Henry grinned. "Zorn was right—a dark fae had business on the premises."

Daisy couldn't help the flash of heat that burned through her body at the memory of those vivid green eyes above that wicked grin. She hadn't told a soul about it—she was too afraid to—and she'd put the fear of God into Mordecai so he wouldn't either. Although she didn't know what he was capable of, he'd made two bodies disappear. That meant he was incredibly powerful.

A sizzling chill made her shiver. She hadn't even known it was possible to feel so hot and so cold at the same moment. It was like her body was being operated by someone else.

"Demigod Lydia was slain in her golf cart yesterday when everyone else was trying to subdue Damion or Thane." Henry tapped his computer with his thumb. "I haven't seen the footage yet, though I was invited to later if we're still here…" Daisy imagined he'd been invited for more than just that. "Word is her throat was cut and the wound didn't heal before she bled out. All of her people were left alive, but they were in a magically induced sleep. None of them saw anything. They don't know who did it."

Kieran nodded slowly. "She hired the fae to ransack my memories. She must've signed a contract by that point, and since she didn't live up to her end of the bargain, she paid the price."

"Yeah, but if they didn't do the work, then why would they expect to collect money or whatever?" Alexis asked.

"They wouldn't just be expecting money," Zorn said. "When pulling memories from Kieran, they'd learn his secrets. They'd learn about him and all he knew. They would've had his knowledge. She denied them that when she failed to deliver him. They took hers instead, and then made her pay the ultimate price. Only a fool makes a bargain with the fae."

"So the fae set Damion and Thane loose so he could

create a distraction?" Jerry said, his hands braced on his hips.

"I didn't have a hope of hanging on to control." Thane shook his head. "Not a chance. I can't even tell you why. One minute I was good to go, and the next I was looking at a young dude and seeing red. I don't even know what made me snap, just that I did."

"I don't know that he was royalty, but whatever he was, he was incredibly powerful. They wanted the job done right," Zorn said. "And it looks like they got what they wanted. Lydia's debt has been paid."

"Did they want a rematch with you?" Mordecai asked Thane. "Since you missed the Berserker thing?"

"It is believed that the Berserker cage, as they call it for the Summit, isn't strong enough to hold Thane," Kieran said, the pride in his voice ringing loud and clear. A few of the guys started to laugh.

Jack turned around and nudged Thane with his fist. "I'd like to see if that's true. Certainly your ability to withstand Damion makes you the most dangerous, and therefore best, Berserker in the world."

"Ah now." Thane slipped his hands into his jeans pockets. "If Lexi and her cats hadn't already dropped that guy down a peg, I wouldn't have gotten through it. I was fighting for my life."

"We done patting each other on the back?" Zorn asked, shifting his weight.

Another wave of butterflies rolled through Daisy's middle. She pushed forward.

"Wait a minute." Lexi pushed off Kieran, stepping in Daisy's way, and leveled a finger at her. "My blood magic might help you heal fast, but you can still die, do you understand?"

"Yes," Daisy said, seeing Amber out of the corner of her eye, dressed in black leather and strapped with weapons. The swarm of butterflies kicked it up a notch. She'd refused to accept Kieran's blood magic, for obvious reasons, but when Lexi had offered last night, Daisy had been one hundred percent game. Kieran had walked them through it. Daisy had gotten a shot of awesome, plus an amazing side gift of feeling people or souls or presences or whatever from a distance of thirty feet. Game changer.

"Do not take any unnecessary risks," Lexi said, her voice as hard as nails. It was the voice Daisy didn't dare defy.

"Fine."

"Do what they say." She pointed first at Zorn, then Amber, who would accompany them in the hunt.

"I know, I know."

"Do not get seen or caught."

"I'll help with that," Henry said, tapping his computer. "I got a…meetup on standby if necessary."

"Whore," Daisy murmured.

"It's not a job when it's a good time." Henry blinked, and Daisy got the impression it was supposed to be a wink.

She wrestled with a smile. "I'll remember that when—"

"Oh no, you will not," Lexi said, her finger still leveled at Daisy but her scowl on Henry. "Don't encourage her." Scowl back on Daisy now. "Do not kill them. Maybe one, but no more. We don't need their Demigod on our asses. Find them, and send a message."

"We'll definitely send a message," Zorn said with a growl, adjusting his machete.

"Crap on a cracker, I want to go so bad," Bria said, practically bouncing up and down. "It isn't fair that only Zorn and Amber can go."

"The bonus of training a kid." Amber shrugged, waiting patiently for them. "This will be child's play, Lexi, don't worry. This kid is good. Won't take but a minute to track them all down and slice them up."

The color bled from Lexi's face. "Oh God, why am I letting her do this? This isn't right—"

"She's kidding, Lexi, she's kidding." Bria rolled her eyes. But she shot Daisy an excited thumbs-up on the sly.

Boman clapped. "The gremlin goes on her first ride. Dang it, I want to go too."

"Join the club," Dylan said. "Are you sure you don't

need me? I can lurk in the background in case—"

"She doesn't even need us." Zorn motioned for Daisy to get going. "We're just there to keep things quiet."

Daisy walked out the door with Zorn and Amber, into the bright sunlight. Something about this moment felt so completely right, as if her life up until this point had been preparation for what was to come.

Not looking back, she sank into the frame of mind Zorn had taught her. She lightened her step, like Amber had coached. They didn't take the golf carts. Instead, they slipped from green patch to green patch. The blood power had given her strength and speed, and running felt effortless now.

They had a good idea of who'd made the threats. Daisy had seen a few of them clustered together when leaving the Summit building yesterday, the shoes familiar. One of them had even worn the ring she'd noticed in the surveillance video. She'd quietly pointed them out to Amber, who was confident one of them was on Demigod Rufus's team. If one was, they all probably were.

At Demigod Rufus's lodge, though, most of the golf carts had been taken. They were probably at the Summit building, gossiping and schmoozing, or else just drinking. It was only late morning, but the whole event had been thrown off the rails.

Still not winded, they slunk around corners, entered

the Summit building, where interior bars and restaurants were positioned on the west side, and blended in with the crowd. Daisy had been trained by Zorn for over a year now, and Amber for six months—not a lot of time. Even still, this felt perfectly natural to her. Effortless, almost. If someone happened to glance her way, she simply slipped behind someone else, playing it off as though she'd been moving that way all along. Her short and slender frame was a benefit, allowing her to hide behind women as well as men.

Near the doorway of one of the interior bars, a pair of scuffed boots caught her eyes' attention. Next to those walked the runners she'd memorized. And she saw the tarnished silver ring on a swinging hand.

Zorn turned into gas, the easiest cover and one that allowed him to stay close, as she slipped behind a doorway. Amber paused in walking, looking down at her phone, her hair obscuring her face and her body language distracted. It was the look of a million people, and despite her leather and weapons, the eye cataloged her as a known quantity and slid right by. So easy.

The scuffed boots belonged to a man of medium height with messy brown hair, stubble, and a belching problem. He led the tall guy with the runners away from the bar. They met up with a woman whose combat boots Daisy didn't know, plus another group of boots she did.

Ta-da.

"Time for bait," she said for Zorn, and slipped out of the doorway. The group was headed to the far exit, smelling faintly of beer and bourbon. They were starting to let their hair down as the week droned on. She would've been happier if they'd been stone sober, but whatever. She didn't have time to wait.

Amber cut across her path and then slunk through a group of people chatting about the gods' visit. They didn't give her any notice. Zorn increased his distance, so when she eventually waltzed in front of her target group, making Scuffed Boots stutter-step so as not to trip over her, he'd be behind them.

"Hey, ain't that that Chester?" one of them said.

She started, glanced back with a frightful expression, and then hunched, playing the scared little rabbit. She headed toward the nearest exit, hurrying her steps.

"Why yes, it is," another said, his voice low.

"I feel like a little fun, how about you all?" one asked.

"Should we? That's that new Demigod's kid," one of them answered.

"That new Demigod ain't gonna know who roughed up her kid if her kid can't talk. She doesn't have the blood bond. Not our fault if she accidentally dies because she can't withstand a little beating."

"Nah. I'm out."

Daisy, nearly to the exit, hurried to the side and into a hall, not seeing who took off. It would be the smartest thing they ever did.

"Coward," the leader said, and they turned after her, following her around the corner instead of heading out the door, too stupid to know it was a trap. Zorn followed behind, and Amber would go around back and cut through the building to make sure there was nowhere for them to run.

Daisy stopped at a dead end, turned, and put up her hands. A group of five, two less than the crew that had delivered her hate mail, crowded in front of her, excited expressions on their faces, and a couple with alcohol-hazed eyes. The one in the back would go free, she decided, the woman whose shoes she didn't recognize. She nodded slightly to Zorn to convey the message.

"Looky, looky," the leader, Mr. Scuffed Boots himself, said.

"You have no pride in your footwear," she said, straightening up and then loosening, dropping her Little Miss Rabbit act.

Scuffed Boots frowned, his confusion probably from her change in demeanor. "Huh?"

She pointed first to his boots, and then to the footwear around him. "I know you're the ones who left me the love notes in pig blood. Well, pig blood and paint, but whatever. Cute messages. Unoriginal, though."

Scuffed Boots puffed up in pride. "Your kind doesn't belong here. Consider this your exit pass."

"What's amazing is, by being a close-minded, intolerant turd, you've shown that you are no better than a Chester. And now you'll be killed by one. Oh the irony."

Without wasting another second or allowing them to activate their magic, she attacked, sprinting forward while throwing her knives. The first landed in the base of Scuffed Boots's throat, a little low, but the second stuck him right in the eye. One-in-a-million shot. He went down before he could fire off one of his useless magical flares. Clearly that would be the token dead guy.

Another shocked her with a blast of static electricity, painful but not fatal. She pushed through the pain and raked her blade across his throat, not deep enough to kill. She jabbed him in a couple more places, just so he hurt real good, was hit by another blast, used him for a shield, and threw a throwing star at the guy in the back before Zorn could slice him with the machete.

She unslung the dagger from her side, and Amber covered the opening of the hallway. Daisy kicked the groaning human shield out of her way and felt a horrible wave of sadness wash over her, an emotive magic. Growing up like she had, she'd never had time for sadness, depression—any of it. Logic saved your ass. Logic got you through. The rest could be ignored. It had to be.

With both hands, she jammed the blade of her dagger into the soft spot between the shoulder and the chest of Mr. Sadness, his expression of rage doing nothing to sell the magic he was trying to cast on her. She yanked the blade out, dodged a fist filled with a knife, just missed a kick, and turned. Dagger in her left hand, she swept her right hand across her upper thigh and pulled out a small throwing knife she'd taken from Red to remember her by. Daisy had her own knives, but it felt better to hold on to Red's memory. Besides, Red had always liked being a part of the action—she would've wanted her knives to keep working.

Daisy slammed Red's blade into the upper thigh of the fourth guy, yanked it out, and slammed it in his stomach. He reached for her. She swung her forearm across her chest, blocking his attempt, stepped to the side, and rammed her knife into his side, right next to his kidney. That would freak him out.

Stepping back, she turned, knowing that all these wounds wouldn't kill them before they could heal. Zorn had schooled her from the beginning on how to fight someone with the healing magic, and how to terrify someone you didn't plan to kill.

He held the woman of the group at bay, his machete at her throat and her eyes as big as saucers.

Daisy stepped up to her, having to look up to reach her eyes.

"I'm that filthy Chester these guys undoubtedly

talked about. I don't recognize your boots. Maybe you weren't in on that whole hate note thing, I don't know. Doesn't really matter—you're still keeping with the wrong crowd. I mean…you're here, right, trying to take out a teenager without magic?"

Daisy glanced at Zorn, who stepped away, giving Daisy space. The woman lunged forward, but Daisy was already moving. She jabbed her knife in the woman's side, yanked it out, and stuck her twice more. The woman tried to twist away, crying out. Daisy punched her in the nose. *Crack.* Blood immediately gushed down the woman's lips. Daisy kicked her ankles, sweeping them out from under her and taking her to the ground. A stomp of the boot and lights out.

"Too bad I don't have a Chester ribbon," she murmured, putting her hands on her hips and looking around.

"I gotchu." Zorn put his machete away and then dug into a pocket. "Boman brought it. He's been carrying it around in one of his pockets. He gave it to me when he heard Lexi gave you permission to look for your haters. He figured…" Zorn shrugged. "I have no idea what put the thought in his head. I didn't think of it. Anyway."

The green ribbon had a simple name in white cursive. *Chester.* Daisy had no idea where the term had come from, or who had started it, but some non-magical people wore it like a badge of pride, just like these clowns wore their hate for Chesters like a cape. They were all idiots.

She replaced one of Scuffed Boot's laces with the ribbon. That oughta leave a message.

"We have a couple left, don't we?" Zorn asked in a lazy tone, walking toward Amber.

Daisy smiled. "Yes, we do. Where is my friend with the ring? We probably have time to go find them, too."

"We certainly do."

The three of them kept up their hunt, the act turning into a training exercise, and Daisy felt the reassurance of this in her bones. She was meant to be in this life. Zorn, Amber, Bria, the guys—they were all part of her family now. She was growing to trust them like she trusted Mordecai and Lexi. Hell, even the cats, which were currently stalking them to make sure she didn't come to any harm. She might not be magical, but she knew in her soul that she belonged with these magical people.

Lexi had gotten her happily ever after, and with her, Daisy had gotten hers. She'd found purpose. She'd found a life. And one day, when she was old enough to manage it, she'd find that wicked fae who turned her hot and cold, and she'd teach him a lesson for endangering her family.

THE END.

About the Author

K.F. Breene is a Wall Street Journal, USA Today, Washington Post, Amazon Most Sold Charts, and #1 Kindle Store bestselling author of paranormal romance, urban fantasy, and fantasy novels. With over three million books sold, when she's not penning stories about magic and what goes bump in the night, she's sipping wine and planning shenanigans. She lives in Northern California with her husband, two children, and out of work treadmill.

Sign up for her newsletter to hear about the latest news and receive free bonus content.

www.kfbreene.com

www.ingramcontent.com/pod-product-compliance
Lightning Source LLC
Chambersburg PA
CBHW031036090325
23209CB00021B/148

* 9 7 8 1 7 3 4 6 2 4 6 3 2 *